'3

Away

MOON

SHINE

by Sylvie Grayson

GREAT WESTERN PUBLISHING c/o
sylviegraysonauthor@gmail.com

For information contact

sylviegraysonauthor@gmail.com

www.sylviegrayson.com

ISBN: 978-0-9947345-6-3

Great Western Publishing is a registered trademark of Sylvie Grayson.

Cover art by Steven Novak   novakillustration@gmail.com

Other books by Sylvie Grayson

contemporary romantic suspense

Suspended Animation

The Lies He Told Me

Legal Obstruction

My Best Mistake

sci-fi/fantasy

Khandarken Rising,
The Last War: Book One

Son of the Emperor,
The Last War: Book Two

Truth and Treachery,
The Last War: Book Three

https://www.amazon.com/author/sylviegrayson

facebook.com/sylvie.grayson

www.sylviegrayson.com

SYLVIE GRAYSON

Praise for Sylvie Grayson's books

I've been reading Sylvie Grayson - can't seem to put them down. How do you come up with these exciting mysteries? Very fun reading!!

Suspended Animation

Wow! This book is amazing, its very well written and the characters are very well developed. This is my first book by Sylvie Grayson and it won't be my last. I was hooked from the first page and this book was very hard to put down.

Interesting characters, family conflicts and divided loyalties make this a book that kept me up half the night

Legal Obstruction

I loved this book! I've found my new favorite author. Emily is a fiercely professional woman who is on her own and determined to protect her little family. Joe is a solitary guy who often doesn't deal with problems until they are front and center. But boy does Emily wake him up and does he take notice. Add in a wildcard assistant and a few unsavory characters and I was up all night finishing the book to find out what happens.

The Lies He Told Me

If you are a fan of the heartwarming craftiness and domesticity of a Debbie McComber romance, and the intense intrigues of Danielle Steele, you'll enjoy the writing style of Sylvie Grayson; where the bad guys are not heartless, and the good guys are virtually flawless.

Just a quick note to let you know how much I enjoyed your book. You drew on your vast experience as a result of being a female, a wife, lover, mother, business woman, lawyer, friend, gardener, homeowner, compassionate and caring individual. It was an intriguing read which kept me guessing and very interested. Well done, Sylvie.

The Last War: Book One, Khandarken Rising

The General of Khandarken sends his son, Dante, to investigate the situation. When Dante meets the lovely Beth she eyes him with suspicion. But he won't stop until he solves the tangle of motives, fueled by greed, which threaten Beth and her family. I enjoyed this book very much. The well-developed characters and sensuous love scenes make this a page turner. I look forward to reading Book Two and Book Three

... this story is one of a kind in its own and couldn't be truly compared to anything but itself. It has so many unique characteristics to it. The personal relationships are intriguing and different from many other fictional relationships. The names are cool, the plot gets thicker with each page, and I loved the author's style. It became evident that I was addicted to reading the book once I was sad to be finished. I'm going to give this a strong recommendation. It's my kind of book.

The Last War: Book Two, Son of the Emperor

I am a big fan of The Last War series. I loved Book One, the story of Major Dante Regiment and Beth Farmer. The dystopian world Grayson has created, where women are scarce and Clones are used to replace them, where the Emperor has finally been defeated but his son takes up the fight, just gets better in this second book. ...Thrills abound on the race to freedom and home. I really enjoyed this book and can't wait for Book Three. Grayson has great imagination, the fantasy series is awesome.

DEDICATION

I am blessed with wonderful support that has enabled me to write. To my husband, who is always ready to listen, read and lend a hand with difficult passages. To my children who had faith in me and helped with their interest, support and practical suggestions.

To my critique group who supported me to polish the words for publication, my many thanks.

Any errors or omissions are mine alone.

Sylvie Grayson
www.sylviegrayson.com

MOON

SHINE

Part One - Strangers

CHAPTER ONE

O
h, Wagsy, please stop!" Julia stripped off her canvas gloves as she walked up the grassy path from the garden. The collie studiously ignored her, continuing to bark as he pawed at the entrance to the root cellar. He stopped and growled low in his throat, then threw himself at the door, attacking it ferociously with his claws.

"What is it? What's got you so excited?" She paused to push her hair off her hot forehead. The animal wasn't usually this excitable. "Is your ball in there?"

"I don't think so, Mummy," seven-year old Maggie contributed from the side yard. "He did that this morning, too, but his ball is over by the porch, I was throwing it for him before."

As Julia drew near, Wagsy turned to swish his tail at her, but immediately went back to growling and digging at the ground in front of the root cellar door.

It was a beautiful clear sunny afternoon, in a string of beautiful days. End of summer weather with clear skies and less intense heat seemed to stretch ahead of them. The garden was producing well, and a lot of it was already at the stage to be gathered in, for storage or canning.

Julia had just finished digging the onions, piling them in baskets and dragging them into the shade to be braided and hung in the root cellar to air dry. Maggie liked to help with the braiding. She carefully pleated the onion tops and tied the ends with string, her tongue pushed to the side of her mouth in concentration. Years ago, when he'd first dug the cellar, Julia's husband Stephen installed a rope that ran along the roof like a clothesline to hang them from.

Julia swallowed a lump in her throat at the thought of how she missed him, and pushed her hat up with the back of her hand. She looked at the dog, and sighed. "Well, there must be something in there, if he was barking this morning. Maybe we had better open it up and take a look."

Dropping a basket of onions on the ground, she put her hands on her hips. "We should be airing it out anyway, before we have to start stocking it up for fall. And we have to clear whatever is left rotting in the bins. It's probably a rat or something. It's best to get it out or it'll eat our winter food."

Then she hesitated. "Oh, I see, the bar has been taken from across the door." That certainly put a different light on things. It meant *someone,* not something, had meddled with the door. There could be someone in there even as she stood here in indecision. She turned to her young daughter. "Maggie, I want you to go in the house. Where is Jims?"

Maggie squinted at her against the glare of the sun. "He's on the porch, right there." She pointed to her brother who was on his knees dragging his wooden fire engine with its two red-painted cars across the boards of the verandah.

"Then get Jims and go in the house. Take him with you. Tell him this is our Plan, our Special Plan." She gave Maggie a pointed look, and watched her young mouth fall open. Her fearful gaze darted to the door of the root cellar, and Julia put her finger to her lips. "Remember our Plan?"

Maggie nodded her head exaggeratedly.

"Well, tell Jims it's our Special Plan and he's to go into the house with you. Go now."

Her daughter darted away, looking nervously back over her shoulder as she ran.

After Stephen died, Julia knew things had changed forever. No longer could she rely on the strength of her husband to handle events as they occurred. Now everything was up to her, whether it was decisions or actions.

One of the things she worried most about was their isolation, especially after so many men became unemployed and began wandering the roads looking for work or food.

By the end of 1930, she'd decided more vigilance was needed. The house was only a couple of miles from town, but a young woman and her two small children were pretty isolated by those miles. The few houses they passed on their way into Creston were set far apart along the North Road.

Old Jerome Hoskiss lived across from them, his house set well back amongst a stand of alders. Julia could just make it out from the verandah. He was a bachelor who spent a lot of time out in his fields or working with his herd of cattle. And if he was at home, he was a bit of a hermit and didn't always answer the door when people called.

None of the houses had telephones. Their next nearest neighbours, the Morrises, were a mile past Hoskiss on the other side of the road. There was no way to get word quickly to anyone in case of an emergency.

Since Stephen's death, she'd come up with the Special Plan. She trained the kids in the Plan often, reminding herself to go over it regularly to enforce it in their minds.

It became a game, but she knew that the more they played, the more likely her children would remember the important details. It had been as much for her own peace of mind as any thought of needing to protect them. But now, suddenly, it wasn't a game any longer.

The first step of the Plan was for the children to go into the house and lock the door. Julia had hidden a couple of sharpened sticks outside in case they were needed, in places where she hoped they would be close at hand if she was caught unprepared.

There was the pitchfork in the barn, and a few other tools that she'd identified, items that could be used in self defense, or just to make her feel more empowered while confronting an intruder.

Most of her worries concerned the homeless wanderers. Ever since the economy crashed, lean, hard-looking men had begun to wander the byways, their skin a deep nut-brown on hands and face.

As the years went on, they were thinner, browner, their clothing more threadbare. They didn't often come right into her yard, usually just walking by in an effort to get to the next town. But when they did stop at her gate, she fed them and sent them on their way. They were, as a group, generally very respectful and especially careful around the children. They were often fascinated by them, liking to sit and watch them play.

This both touched Julia's heart, and scared her in equal measure. They were likely just lonely for their own families, but she didn't want anyone to get too attached to her children.

There had been a few times when one would stay on at her invitation, working for food for a few days or even a week. She'd been glad of the help since Stephen died because there were plenty of jobs that she couldn't manage on her own. She'd been equally glad when they moved off to carry on down the road, just because she was never sure.

Now they would use the Plan. She checked to make sure the kids were in the house, hopefully with the door locked. Then she found the sharpened stick that lay in the grass at the side of the root cellar, and heaved the first flat door up and open. Wagsy leaped past her and into the gloom, growling.

Julia pulled up the other door to let in more light and stood uncertainly on the top step, the staff in her hand pointed down into the dark. The dog barked louder, bouncing on his back legs. Julia could hear a voice, it sounded small and frightened.

"Who's there?" she called. "Wagsy, hush. Who's there?"

"It's just us," a little voice called. "Please don't let the dog bite us."

"Wagsy, here boy! Here, now!" The collie stopped barking, but held his ground, growling deep in his throat.

Julia slowly descended the stairs and peered into the gloom, the stick held carefully out in front of her. She saw a shape in the dark of the cellar, something that looked like a small bundle of clothing lying in the turnip bin. It was covered with a burlap bag.

As she got closer the bundle moved and two eyes appeared, glinting out of a bush of thick black hair. Then the bundle slowly stood.

It was a young boy, not more than eight or nine. His clothes hung in rags, and he must have been using the burlap sack as a blanket. The turnips in the bin were mostly withered, in the height of late summer, but she could see a few nibbled turnip tops scattered around. Food for the waif, no doubt.

"Wagsy," she ordered. "Come here." The dog backed up till he was by her side, still growling softly at the intruder. "Quiet, I say." Wagsy calmed but didn't sit, the hair stiff along the ruff on the back of his neck.

The waif motioned behind him, and a second face appeared over the low wall of the turnip bin. This one was just as dirty but surrounded by limp brown hair, and its appearance prompted more barking from Wagsy. She shushed the dog, gripping him by his collar to keep him by her side in order not to frighten the children any more than they already were.

"What's your name?" She addressed the first child with the bush of dirty black hair.

He regarded her solemnly for many moments, then finally answered, "Ben."

She huffed out a breath. "Well, Ben, how many of you are there? I see two, are there more?"

"No," he said after a long moment.

This was a child slow of speech. She glanced at the other child. "And what is your name?"

The eyes blinked in the gloom. "Ollie," it said.

"Stand up, Ollie."

Ben stirred, and gripped Ollie's arm. "He can't." The second boy struggled and flayed about but only succeeded in getting to his knees and leaning on the bin wall.

"How did you get down here, if Ollie can't stand?"

Ben looked at her and then at Ollie. Finally he said, "He could walk when we come but he got sicker after we was here a while. I thought he'd get better if he ate, but the parsnips ain't helped much." He gazed unmoving down at the turnip tops scattered at his feet.

Julia looked around the root cellar. There didn't seem to be any damage. It was a pretty small space, just room enough for bins for the root vegetables - potatoes, turnips, beets and carrots, ropes to hang the herbs and onions, and shelves for other things she wanted to hold over through the winter.

Right now it was almost empty, a thin layer of old and wizened potatoes hidden in the sawdust. In the house they were eating the new crop already.

She stared at the boys as a shiver of alarm eased down her spine. They stared back with vacant expressions. "Is there anyone else with you, your father perhaps, waiting for you outside?"

Ben looked at her for a long time, then shook his head.

"So there's no one else in here and no one outside waiting for you. No one who might come to get you?"

Ben looked at Ollie and the boy gazed back at him. They seemed to share their thoughts without speech. Ben finally glanced up and shook his head again.

Julia sighed. "I think you had better come up into the yard so I can talk to you," she said. "If I get on one side of Ollie and you get on the other, perhaps we can help him up the stairs. After all, he walked down here." As she stepped toward them, the boys cowered in the bin.

"Come on, Ben," she encouraged. "Grab Ollie's arm and let's get him up." She softened her voice as she drew closer. "I won't hurt him, and between us we can help him up the steps. It's much better in the sunlight."

Ben straightened slowly from his crouch, watching her every move.

"I'm not going to hurt you," she said again. "Let's try, now."

After a minute, Ben turned to Ollie and gently shook his arm. "Come on, Ollie," he murmured. "Let's go." There was a touch of resignation in his voice.

With one of them on each side, Ollie moved his legs and managed to climb over the side of the bin and stumble up the stairs into the sunlight. He stood unsteadily at the top of the steps, supported on each side, then moved forward out of the doorway of the root cellar onto a patch of grass and gazed fearfully around.

~~~**~~~

CHAPTER TWO

Julia's children peered anxiously out the side window. When she waved to reassure them, that was all the encouragement they needed. They came tumbling out the door and across the porch, then both slowed to a halt when they caught a glimpse of the two grubby figures standing on the top step of the root cellar.

Julia seated the boys on the grass. No wonder the sight of them halted Maggie and Jims in their tracks. They were a sorry sight, grimy from head to toe, with ragged and filthy clothes clinging to their thin frames. Their hair was long, matted in clumps around their heads. They wore no shoes, but she hadn't noticed that at first. Their feet were the same colour as the dirt where they stood. Ben had a piece of twine keeping his pants up and Ollie's seemed to be held closed with a length of wire. They were both still panting from the effort of climbing the steps, and Ollie looked pale under the filth. She could smell them, not an unpleasant smell but musty, sweaty and stale.

Julia squatted down in front of them. "Ben, are you the oldest?"

He nodded slowly.

"How old are you?"

He studied her a moment. "About ten," he said. He didn't

take his eyes from hers.

He certainly didn't look ten. He was lean and stooped, his chest thin, the cords of his neck standing out sharply. "And is Ollie related to you? Or are you friends?"

He nodded again, his head bobbing on the little stick of a neck. "Yup, and brothers too," he said.

"I see." She looked at Ollie a moment. "How old is Ollie?"

"About eight," Ben said.

"About eight," she repeated.

Julia glanced behind her at Maggie and Jims standing stock still on the porch, holding hands and staring at the two boys. What was she going to do with these waifs? They looked so hopeless standing there, their skinny bodies too small for their age. Their eyes too old.

She glanced back at Ben. "Would you like something to eat right now? I think I will get you some food, to start."

Neither boy said anything. Ollie was reclining against his brother's arm listlessly. Julia took his shoulders in her hands and gently pressed him down onto the grass. "Sit here, both of you, just rest for a few minutes."

She stood and carefully examined her yard, scrutinizing the foundations of the house, then across to the chicken coop and over toward the barn. She squinted down the garden and beyond to the trees, searching for any sign that someone else was here, watching or waiting.

She didn't see anything out of place. The goat was staked out in the back yard, grazing, and where she'd been working in the field her pony was still tied to the small plow, resting in the shade.

Wagsy would almost certainly have alerted her if there'd been anyone else on the property. She gazed up at her children on the porch. "Maggie, you and Jims stay there and keep an eye on these boys, make sure they're okay until I come back. I'm just going to get them something to eat."

Maggie nodded. Jims stood beside his sister holding onto her dress, his thumb in his mouth, not saying a word.

"Wagsy, you stay right beside Maggie and keep an eye out as well."

By the time Julia returned, Maggie, with Jims trailing, had progressed down the porch steps and halfway across the yard. She was talking but the boys were silent. Maggie could talk the ear off a mule. If anyone could get these boys to say something, it might be her daughter.

She set a tray down in the grass and studied the small figures. They were listless, seeming to droop further the longer they sat there. Probably been a long time since they'd had anything much to eat other than wizened turnips.

She presented each with a glass of water. They sipped it and eyed the bowls of porridge, milk floating on the surface. Finally she took back the glasses, set them on the tray and handed a bowl to Ben.

He considered it carefully before taking it, as if she were going to poison him and he was doomed anyway, so might as well get it over with. She smiled inwardly, and waited while he picked up the spoon. It took him a moment, but he finally put a small spoonful into his mouth and rolled it around on his tongue. He swallowed, then carefully took a second bite.

Julia picked up the other bowl. Ollie showed little sign of life where he leaned against his brother. She dipped the spoon and held it to his lips. "Come on, Ollie. Time to eat something. No one ever gets feeling better when they're hungry. Open your mouth, now."

Ben watched guardedly, and then nodded at Ollie. So Ollie obediently opened his mouth. In this way, very slowly, all of the porridge was eaten and the empty bowls returned to the tray.

She sat back and regarded these two intruders who were staring miserably at the ground. *Now what?* These weren't local children, she knew all the kids at the school at least by sight. They seemed to be alone. Getting information out of them was a bit daunting. Ben was so careful, his answers were non-answers, and Ollie was past being able to talk.

By this time, Maggie had wound down and fallen silent as she watched the small meal being consumed. But she quickly got her second wind. "Who are they, and where did they come from, and aren't their mom and dad looking for them, and how come they were in the root cellar?"

Ben looked startled at this new stream of comments, so Julia made the introductions. "Maggie, Jims, this is Ben and his brother Ollie. And I think they were in the root cellar because they were hungry. They were looking for something to eat and a place to rest. They found the turnips."

The children regarded each other. "Maybe they want a bath," said Jims around his thumb. Julia laughed out loud.

"Not right yet," she said. "We need to find out what's wrong with Ollie. Has he been sick a long time?"

Ben shook his head, his gaze guarded. "It's his back," he said finally.

'He hurt his back? Is that why he's in pain?' she asked.

Ben nodded.

She really didn't know how to handle this. If Ollie had hurt his back, he probably needed to rest until it felt better. Maybe he even needed to see a doctor if he had wrenched it badly.

And they desperately needed a wash, as well as some clean clothes. She didn't have anything that would fit, they were too big for the children's clothes and too small for hers. And she was hesitant to touch them. There was a strong odour pouring off their little bodies, dirt and grime covered them from head to toe, literally. Well, there was nothing for it.

"Ollie, can you stand now?"

He moved slowly to his hands and knees. Ben leaned to grab his arm and heaved with what little strength he possessed. Ollie wavered unsteadily to his feet and Julia grabbed his other arm as he swayed.

Then she seized the hem of his sleeveless vest and lifted it carefully over his head. He made a belated grab for it, but she was too quick. Dropping it on the ground, she walked around the boy to take a look at his back. She gave a quick gasp at the sight.

Ollie hung his head. Ben held his brother's arm and stared straight ahead in silence.

~~~**~~~

CHAPTER THREE

Ollie's back was a mass of dark red marks, criss-crossing his skinny frame. There were scabs, with dried blood flaking off in drifts. Festering wounds showed in a dozen places where the skin was gone and pink inflammation showed through. The dirty shirt had obviously been stuck to the mess, because fresh blood oozed from those spots. The wreckage continued on down past the waist of the wired-together pants. She slowly eased him back to the ground, and he crouched there in pain and humiliation.

"Ben, do you know how this happened?" Julia's voice was low with repressed emotion as she struggled to control her anger.

Ben hesitated before he nodded.

"How? How did this happen?"

Ben looked at her in stony silence.

She eased Ollie to a sitting position in the grass and squinted against the sun's rays. "Tell me, Ben. What happened to Ollie?"

Ben climbed to his feet and stood looking at her uncertainly. He moved his mouth but no sound came out. Finally he said, "They hit him." He blinked rapidly, staring at her like a deer in the headlights.

"Who, Ben? Who hit him?"

"They did. They hit him."

He hung his head and stared at the ground.

Julia stood there for a moment in indecision. Then she knelt beside the smaller boy. "Listen, Ollie. I want you to lie down like this." She motioned for him to move and shifted his legs for him. "Lay on your tummy, and I'll get some medicine that will help make you feel better. Just lay down." She turned to Ben, understanding in her eyes at his uncertain stance and obvious discomfort. "Sit by your brother, Ben. He'll feel better with you close by."

The compassion in her eyes seemed to touch the boy and he blushed a dull red under the layer of dirt on his skin. He knelt by Ollie and put his hand on his brother's leg.

"That's good," Julia said. "I'll be right back." She hurried up to the house, her own children trailing in her wake.

As she lit the gas ring on the stove and put the kettle on to boil, she fielded questions from them both. "I don't know, Maggie. His back looks terrible. Someone hurt him badly. But I think we can help him feel better. Go and get my bandage sack by the sewing machine upstairs on the landing. You know, the cloth bag that I put scraps of fabric in, it's hanging on the nail by the window."

She turned to her son. "Jims, you sit here where I can keep an eye on you." Her four-year old climbed onto the bench by the kitchen table, and Julia grabbed her mixing bowl and spooned salt into it. Then she darted into the bathroom and came back with a bar of soap, the jar of salve and a couple of clean towels.

The kettle had boiled and she poured it over the salt in the bowl. Grabbing the wash basin from the kitchen sink, she cleaned it out carefully, added lukewarm water and headed back outside.

"Okay," she said briskly.

Ben and Ollie both startled.

She knelt in front of them. "I'm ready to get started. Ben, you sit up near Ollie's head so he can see that you're there. It'll make him more comfortable to know you're near him. Jims, give Ben the cookie, and one for Ollie. I'm going to begin by washing all around the area."

She caught sight of Maggie running down the steps with the cloth bag. "Thank you, Maggie. Lay it right there. I'll need it in a minute."

Ollie said not a word as she gently washed his back. She reached around and undid the wire holding his pants together, and lowered them down his buttocks. The vicious marks continued down his back and right across his bottom. As she washed, she held her breath in case it was too tender, but he didn't move. The cookie was clutched in his hand in a death grip. *This boy is used to pain*, she thought. *My children would be crying pretty hard by now.*

She got most of the dirt and dried blood off, then went back in the house for the bowl of salt water that had cooled slightly. She dug out cloths from the bag Maggie handed her, and began to lay warm salt compresses across Ollie's back. She heard him take a deep breath each time the cloth hit his skin. When they cooled she returned them to the warm water and laid them across his back again.

"Ollie, you're a very good boy," she encouraged as she worked. "I can't believe how you have just lain there and let me look after you. Jims," she said, turning to her son, "I need the medical tape. It's in the medicine cabinet in the bathroom, do you think you can get it for me?"

He nodded importantly and ran with his short chubby legs back into the house.

"Maggie, you go with him and bring my scissors, I'll need them for the tape."

"Now," she said, "I'm almost finished. I'm sorry it hurt, Ollie, but it couldn't be helped. It had to be cleaned. How does it feel now?"

"Okay," Ollie mumbled sleepily.

"Well, it's going to feel even better when I'm finished. You won't be completely healed, but you'll feel a lot better than you did."

She peeled the last cloths off his lacerated back, and let the sun dry his skin. It already looked better, the swelling down in some spots and the raw flesh looking healthier.

Huffing and puffing, Jims arrived with the tape and Maggie with the scissors. She opened her salve jar and slathered it all over, making sure she covered every open wound. She didn't want the scabs coming off with the bandage next time.

Then she laid a fresh piece of cloth over the entire area, and taped it in place. Ollie was sleeping by the time she finished, his cookie crushed in his hand. The sun had moved and their grassy spot was in shade.

Julia sat back and sighed. "You're a good brother, Ben. You stuck right by him. I know he trusts you, and you deserve that trust, for sure." She flexed her shoulders and stood to dump the water into the grass by the side of the house.

She turned back to the older boy. "Now let's see your back."

Ben stared back at her in alarm for a moment, then his shoulders slumped and he gingerly peeled off his filthy shirt. He stared at the ground.

"I can't see anything that way, Ben. You have to turn around." But she *could* see and what she saw made her ill. Old scars, burn marks all over his torso. Scars in stripes, like a prisoner might have after a lashing with ropes or whip. Ben turned and she saw the same injuries as Ollie, fresh scourging, raw chunks taken out of the swarthy skin. She gently laid her hand on his shoulder, and he flinched.

"Lay down, Ben, let me care for you."

He sighed and slid to the ground, stretching out on his stomach.

Julia picked up her basins and cloths and headed back into the house for more supplies.

~~~**~~~

CHAPTER FOUR

The boys lay in the grass and slept most of the afternoon, covered with blankets from the house. Julia fed her children their lunch. They sat at the table on the verandah overlooking the yard, chewing sandwiches and sliced carrots and talking softly.

They watched the two sleeping figures in the side yard. Wagsy lay at Julia's feet, thumping his tail occasionally. But as soon as she rose to clear the dishes, he bounded down the steps and sniffed cautiously around the sleeping boys.

Maggie and Jims stayed on the porch playing quietly with Cat sleeping contentedly against Maggie's knee, while Julia went into the shed and checked the tick mattresses she kept there for the men passing on the road who sometimes spent the night. She'd discovered she didn't have the heart to turn them away if they asked for work in exchange for a meal. So she set up the end of the shed as a place for the travelers to spend the night in some comfort, sheltered from the elements.

Untying the sacks of ticking, she took them into the chicken run to empty out the old straw. She and Maggie stuffed them with fresh straw, tied the tops shut and put them back in place on the floor of the shed. She pushed straw into a couple of flour sacks for pillows.

When supper was ready, Julia set the small table on the porch for the two boys, who were just beginning to stir. She gave them Stephen's old shirts to put on over their bandages and they staggered unsteadily up the porch steps. She fed them small bowls of tomato soup. When that was finished and the bowls nearly licked clean, she served scrambled eggs with toast, afraid that anything heavier might come right back up from such untended little stomachs.

It certainly didn't look like they were used to eating on a regular basis, given that she'd been able to count their ribs almost through their shirts.

She was also afraid of who might be coming down that road looking for them. For the moment they'd stay outside, for the safety of herself and her children.

There was no talk at the table. The boys sat where she pointed. They ate when she told them. When they were finished dinner, she showed them where the outhouse was across the yard behind the barn, and then escorted them to their beds in the shed and tucked them in, covering them over with the blankets they had slept under all afternoon.

Ben looked up at her dully from the makeshift mattress as she finished arranging his blanket. "You stay for the night, Ben," she said. "We'll talk tomorrow about what we need to do. But don't think about leaving yet. I want to give you breakfast and see how you are. Now have a good sleep, and I'll see you in the morning."

He blinked but didn't make a sound. Ollie was already asleep.

~~*~~

The next day was Sunday, and Julia would normally have bundled her family into the wagon and headed to town for church. But she didn't feel she could leave the boys alone, and she certainly couldn't take them to church in the condition they were in. Nor could they see the doctor.

Their backs looked somewhat better under the cloths. She

fired up the stove, placing pots of water on the burners, and set out the laundry washtub on the porch.

While the water heated, she took Ben into the yard and told him she was going to cut his hair. He didn't say a word, but by now she didn't expect him to.

She'd come to realize that Ben was a very wary child, and only talked when he was absolutely pressed. So she sat him on a stool, tied a tablecloth around his shoulders and assaulted his head with her sewing scissors. His hair was kinky and ink black. She'd never cut hair like it before, and given how dirty it was, she just did her best, trimming it short. When she was finished she couldn't believe the difference.

Ben looked like a handsome young man, no matter the dirt. His eyebrows slanted across his forehead, and his eyes were large and dark, dominating the thin face. She showed him his image in the hand mirror, and he grabbed it to stare for the longest time. Julia wondered if he had ever even seen himself before.

Next came Ollie. His hair was different, straight and fine in texture, a dirty brown. She was more used to this type of hair and gave him a decent cut that allowed them to see his mischievous gray eyes and bold nose.

She put her scissors and comb aside to be sterilized. Lord knew what pests or infestations they had.

Then came the bath. Ben fought bravely. Julia had set out the washtub on the verandah and filled it with buckets of water from the stove. She added enough cold water to make it bearable and commanded Ben to climb in. His modesty was offended. She gave him a wash cloth to cover himself and ordered him into the tub. Then she went in the house. When she returned he was in the water, with his knees to his chest, looking totally miserable.

She came back with a jug, dipped some water and wet his hair. He squealed. She told him to close his eyes and vigorously soaped his head. He squealed louder. "Ben, this isn't going to hurt, unless you get soap in your eyes. Or in your mouth. So keep your eyes closed and let me get you clean!"

After a great deal of activity, Julia had him washed from the top of his head to his waist, and his legs and feet were passably clean. Given how long he'd probably gone without shoes, it would take a while to completely scrub the soles of his feet. She was pretty wet herself.

Leaving him with the soap, and under threat that she'd wash the rest of him if he didn't, she hung a towel on the railing and went into the house. When next she saw him, he was wrapped in the towel, seated on the bench by the washing machine, warming in the sun. Jims sat beside him, chatting about the dog and Ben was listening.

He smiled when he saw her.

"Not so bad, eh?" she laughed.

"No, not so bad," he agreed.

Ben dressed in another of Stephen's long shirts and a pair of makeshift shorts that Julia had run up on the sewing machine. He helped her dump the tub of water, and lift the buckets to fill it again for Ollie.

She prepared herself for the next battle. But there was no battle with Ollie. He climbed into the washtub without a qualm. He was careful of his back, which was still very tender, but he cooperated while Julia washed his hair and he let her scrub him down, lifting his arms, poking his feet out of the tub. When the boys were both dry, Julia inspected their heads again, and discovered to her relief that neither of them had lice. In fact, Ollie's hair was a lovely red-blond colour, and she saw freckles on his cheeks.

She brought out a pair of nail scissors and showed Ben how to cut his fingernails. "Don't forget the toes," she said. "And make sure Ollie does his."

By the time they were finished with the scissors, Maggie had helped Julia bring lunch outside onto a blanket on the grass in the shade of the house. They sat down to ham sandwiches, sliced vegetables and cups of goat's milk. The boys especially seemed taken with the milk, drinking three and four glasses each with the meal, until she stopped them from having any more.

"You'll get sick if you have too much," she said. "It's good for you, but you aren't used to so much food, I think." When they finished, the boys sat around with full stomachs, little burps and belches arising.

Julia took a deep breath, knowing she was going to be treading on delicate territory. "Ollie, Ben, I need to ask you some questions."

Ben immediately straightened and looked wary, the unguarded expression fading from his face.

"I'm not threatening you. But we need to know where you came from. Who are your parents? Where do you live? Is your home nearby?"

The boys stared at the ground.

"Do you know what town was near your home?" No answer, but the boys were looking at each other now instead of at the grass, engaged in their own form of silent communication.

"Do you know the name of the towns you came through on your way here from your home?"

Ben looked wary, but then said, "Donegal. Yahk. We didn't come through them, but we walked around."

Okay, this was a start. Good Lord, Donegal was a good fifty miles away, she wasn't sure about Yahk. What a long way they had come. They must have been walking for days, poor little tikes.

"How many nights have you slept out since you left home?"

Ben and Ollie looked at each other, almost as if they could communicate without words. Finally Ben spoke for them both, "We think six nights."

Julia nodded. That supported what she'd seen in the wounds on their backs, these weren't recently inflicted, but had been festering and scabbing for some time.

"Where did you sleep each night?" Might was well get as much information as she could.

The boys regarded each other again. "In a haystack one night, and once in a ditch that was dry," said Ben.

"And in that old shed," said Ollie.

Ben nodded. "Yeah, in the shed."

"What shed?" she asked.

They looked at each other. Finally Ollie said, "Just an old shed, it was empty."

Then she asked what she most wanted to know. "Who did the beatings? Who put the marks on you? Was it your Dad?"

Both boys shook their heads, and avoided her eyes. Ollie looked at Ben, Ben looked down at the blanket.

"Who then? Was it an older brother?"

Ben shook his head vehemently. "Not our older brother. He wouldn't." He glared at her.

Ollie whispered, "Our Ma."

That shut her up. A mother who could beat her own children like that—it was totally out of her ability to comprehend. If their mother beat them like this, then she had probably inflicted the old scars as well.

"Where was your father? Did he know that she was beating you or was he away when she did it?" The father had probably left the boys in her care while he went to work.

Again they looked at each other. "He was drunk," said Ben finally. It was just a statement, said in a matter of fact way as if that explained everything.

Julia was silent, her stomach in a knot. The whole situation sounded awful. The fact that they'd run away was not only not surprising, it was admirable. Until she remembered the sad shape they were in.

"Just one more question," she said. "Did your older brother see what happened?"

"No," shouted Ben. He stood. "He wasn't there, else he never would have let her!" He turned and ran down the garden. Wagsy galloped after him and stood leaning against the boy's leg. Julia could see Ben's shoulders heaving.

"Ollie," she said gently, "what's your older brother's name?"

"Charlie."

24

"And where is he now?"

"I don't know," he whispered and subsided into sobs on the blanket.

~~~**~~~

CHAPTER FIVE

*N**ow you've done it, Julia*, she thought, as she rubbed his soft furry head. *You've got them both crying.* That has to be enough poking into their lives for one day.

She glanced at her own kids and realized they were regarding her as if she were the wicked witch of the west. *Yeah, you're right*, she thought, *I was way too heavy handed. These little guys don't deserve to be beaten up with words after being beaten up with... what?*

She wasn't sure, and certainly couldn't ask. But the marks on their little bodies looked like they were made with a whip, not that she knew what a whipping would look like.

It was definitely time to carry them off to the doctor. Old Doc Farley, who had been the town's doctor for as long as Julia could remember, finally retired after he became too ill to continue with his practice. That had left the town of Creston without a doctor, a precarious position for any village. But she'd recently heard rumours someone else had come to take Doc Farley's place.

Her own children needed a medical exam. School would start in a few weeks, and it was best to be on top of things. No point in waiting until the whole community was lined up to see him. Maybe luck would be with her, and they could get in and out without attracting too much attention. Maybe they'd catch him on a slow day.

She grinned to herself. Now she was thinking like a detective.

Early the next morning, she had everyone dressed and Prince backed in between the shafts of the town cart. The boys were still wearing the makeshift shorts she'd stitched for them, and Stephen's oversized shirts, but that couldn't be helped.

As Julia escorted the children out the front door, closing it behind them, a vagrant walked down the road and stopped at the gate. He looked hopefully up at the house. She paused, then tied Prince's reins to the verandah railing and went down the path to the gate to talk with him.

He was a decent-looking man, tanned dark brown by the sun, but fairly clean. He said he was headed to Cranbrook, hoping for work cutting timber. He'd heard there might be jobs there.

When she came back up the path, she seated the children on the step. "Wait here, I need to get some food for this man."

The children sat and watched him, taking in his faded clothing, the mends in the pants, the knotted laces in the beat-up boots on his feet. Julia arrived back with a sandwich, a handful of cut up carrot and a jar of water. She asked Ben to take it out to the vagrant, who thanked him and headed on north.

Then she loaded the children into the cart, stopped at the gate for Ben to climb aboard, and sent Prince trotting along the road that led south to town. Dust flew up under the pony's hooves. There had been no rain in so long that it hung like a haze over the gravel and dirt track.

Thankfully, Doc's shingle was still hanging where it always had, attached to the gatepost of the first house on the north edge of town. Julia only hesitated a moment, sure she had heard that a new doctor had arrived.

She tied the reins to the gatepost and hustled the children down the walk. Banging on the door, she looked carefully around. No other vehicles, that was good. Maybe she'd beaten the rush. She giggled. Not that there was usually a rush to see the doctor. She knocked again, just as the door opened.

"Oh," she gasped in surprise. The largest man she'd ever seen filled the doorway.

He had one hand on the doorknob and the other held a small towel as if he'd been drying his hands. He looked at the group and raised his brows at Julia. "Are you all here to see the doctor?" he asked.

Julia straightened her shoulders in determination. "Yes, we are," she said, and made to step inside. He backed up as they crowded into the waiting room. She looked around. Nothing much had changed. The same faded magazines on the side table, maybe with a few newer issues. The same slightly sagging couch against one wall.

Julia looked back at the man. "Are you the doctor?" she asked.

He nodded, looking over each child. "Yes. Okay, is there an emergency? Which one of you wants to go first?"

"I will," she said immediately, settling the children in a row on the faded couch and turning back to face him.

"Very well, this way please." He reached for a white jacket hanging on the coat rack by the desk and pulled it on before leading her into the same examining room that old Doc had used.

Here things had really changed. Julia had been in this examining room many times, bringing each of the children in for various needs, accompanying Stephen when he slashed his hand so badly. Doc Farley had scolded him roundly about that, puffing on his pipe as he stitched the flesh back together.

Now there was a new examining table, and large array of medical instruments lined the bureau. Julia looked around for a minute, then sat on the only chair.

"Usually I sit there," the doctor said, "And you would lie on the table." There was amusement in his voice.

Julia chuckled. "I know. But this is different. I don't need you to examine me. It's the children I want to talk about."

"Okay.'" He folded his arms across his massive chest and leaned against the counter behind him. "I'm Dr. Stoffard. And who are you?"

"Oh, I'm sorry. I'm Mrs. Butler. I live just a couple of miles up the North Road, on the way out of town." She pointed vaguely in the general direction. "The two youngest out there are my children. And the other two are living with me right now. So what I need is to have you look at Maggie and Jims, they're seven and four, or four and a half as Jims would tell you, just for their yearly check up, before school starts. You'll find a file on them from old Doc, I'm sure. They haven't been in for quite a while."

She took a breath as the doctor nodded, his eyes keen on her face. "And then the other boys, their names are Ben and Ollie. I think Ollie is short for Oliver. Anyway, they just arrived three days ago, and I've been working on them, but they're not in great condition. I hoped that you would give them a thorough check up."

"Okay." Dr Stofford straightened away from the counter and reached for the door. "Let's start with Maggie, shall we?"

The doctor did a careful exam of Maggie and Jims, pronouncing them both healthy. Then he called Ben in. After a few minutes, he came back out and asked Julia to follow him, he had a few questions.

She handed Jims the comic she'd been reading him, and rose from her seat. Stofford took her through a short corridor and into what looked like his own parlour. When he turned to face her, she was driven a step back by the rage on his face.

"Please tell me what has happened to that boy?"

~~~**~~~

Part Two – The Doctor

CHAPTER SIX

J ulia slapped her hand over her heart as she stared at the doctor. "You don't think I beat them? Don't be ridiculous! I've never beaten a dog, let alone a child." She glared back at him. "Those boys turned up at my house three days ago, and I've been trying to figure out what to do with them. Their backs looked a lot worse when they arrived, believe me."

He snorted, and she took a half step forward. "I found them in my root cellar! In the root cellar! They were eating last year's wizened turnips, poor bumpkins. Ollie could hardly walk, they couldn't travel any farther. I don't know where they came from, but they'd been walking for days, maybe five or six, judging from the wounds on their backs, but…"

She took a deep breath, and half turned away to glare out the window, then quickly recoiled. "Oh, no, here comes Mrs. Shandy!" Her face paled. "She's such a gossip. You have to hide the boys, really you must. I don't know who they are and they may be in danger. They need protection. Please! I need to keep them private, at least for a while longer."

The doctor glanced out the window at the older woman walking at speed toward his office door. She moved with a limp, but was still coming at a pretty fast clip. She had a weather-beaten hat on her head and a determined look on her face.

"I'll look after her," he said, ducking under the door frame as he left.

Julia could hear bits of the conversation as she waited out of sight behind the curtain for the doctor to return.

"I just wanted to make sure Mrs. Butler is okay," Mrs. Shandy was saying, standing on the walk leading to the doctor's surgery. "I saw her pony and cart and she's so healthy. I says to myself, poor soul, her all alone with those two babies. She must need some help. So I says to myself, I'll just stop in and see if she's okay." Mrs. Shandy was still muttering as Dr. Stofford ushered her back down the walk and away from the front door with his hand under her arm.

"She's fine. Just a routine exam for the children, Mrs. Shandy, and I'm not open for general drop in this morning. You can make an appointment in the afternoon when Sheila is here. She'll help you out with that."

"No, no," protested Mrs. Shandy. "I'm not sick, I just wanted to see if poor Mrs. Butler is alright, poor little lamb. I see her coming and going with her pony and cart, doesn't even have a car to get around in. Course she doesn't have anyone to drive it for her, either, does she?" She hesitated a long moment, staring at the door to the surgery, then hustled off down the walk, still muttering.

Dr. Stofford re-entered the surgery, locking the door behind him. Julia came out of the parlour but he shooed her back in with his hand. He talked to Maggie briefly, patted Jims and Ollie on the shoulder as they sat on the couch reading the comics. Then he poked his head into the examining room to converse with Ben. Presently he was back in the parlour and closed the door behind him.

"Have a chair, Mrs. Butler," he commanded.

'You mean, poor Mrs. Butler, don't you?' she commented dryly as she sat down.

The doctor gave a short guffaw and took a seat. "Apparently so. Now, tell me again how you came across these boys."

Julia told the whole story, ending with the news that according to the boys it was the mother who beat them, at least this time, and the father who was too drunk to protest, if in fact he would have. Also there was an older brother but no one knew where he was.

"That's all I've been able to discover. Ben thinks he's ten and Ollie is eight. They certainly don't look it, they're so skinny. They don't know when their birthdays are. They thought they passed the town of Donegal. They also mentioned Yahk. At any rate, I can hardly believe they walked that far in the condition they were in. I'm afraid I don't know the whole story. And they are not talkative. I pried so much yesterday I had them both in tears."

She'd been talking too fast and gasped for breath as she wiped at the tear on her cheek. "I'm not sure what to do, but the first thing was to make sure they're healthy."

She gave the doctor a searching look. "I bathed their backs with hot salt compresses, then used a comfrey salve to soothe the wounds, and then covered it all with a bandage. They don't really need the bandage any more, but they take such comfort from it that I did it again this morning, just because it seems to reassure them. If there's anything more that needs to be done, then we should do it. Perhaps they have parasites, worms or scabies. I just need them checked out. You understand."

The doctor nodded encouragingly, so she continued. "They need clothes. They're wearing my husband's old shirts, and the pants I just whipped up on the machine the other day. What do I do about school? They need to go, neither of them can read, although Ben is already picking up a bit from Maggie."

Dr. Stoffard held up his hand and she ground to a halt.

~~*~~

Mrs. Butler sat there, gaze fixed to his face. He'd never seen such eyes, large and gray with the longest lashes. Her little girl had those same eyes, big, gray, and very solemn. The woman's hair was chestnut coloured, and curly, pinned under her hat but coming down in ringlets on the back of her neck and around her ears. And those must be freckles, just a few, across the bridge of her short nose.

He shifted on the chair. "Well, let's do one thing at a time, shall we, Mrs. Butler? Let me finish examining them. You wait with Ollie while I have a look at Ben."

He paused on his way out of the room. "And I'm sorry for jumping down your throat like that. I was taken aback at the mess on their skin. I've never seen anything like it since I started practicing medicine." He gave her a piercing look.

She nodded, her face pale, then put her hand on his arm to detain him. "I've been trying to figure out what would make marks like that, Doctor. Does it look like a whip? That doesn't make any sense, using a whip. They wouldn't just stand there and let that happen, would they? But I can't think of anything else." Tears gathered in her eyes again. "Why would you do that to your own children?"

He looked down at her hand on his arm, and she hastily withdrew it. But he reached and took her fingers in his. "No, it's okay. I don't know either. I don't think I've ever seen a case quite like this before. But I'd imagine a switch, maybe a willow branch peeled down, or something like that."

She nodded, and slowly turned to leave the room.

~~*~~

When the boys finally emerged from their examinations, the doctor reported there were a few spots on their backs that were tender but would heal. In general, they were in good health, if underweight, and perhaps under height. "But nothing that a few square meals won't fix," he said, and Julia smiled.

Yes, there had certainly been a few square meals eaten in the last days. The boys had become like vacuum cleaners, consuming anything that was placed on the table. They never complained, or even asked for more. They just ate whatever was put in front of them.

"What I recommend, Mrs. Butler, is this. I'll give you a couple of powders to give them tonight, and again in three days. That should take care of any common parasites that might be present."

He turned to the cabinet, pulled out a box of medicine and handed it to her. "Now, if you were to take them home at once, no one will be the wiser about this trip. I'll come out to your place tomorrow or the next day to check on them.

"It'll give us space to come up with a plan," he said, offering a smile. "That's what we need here. School isn't for a couple of weeks, and that gives us lots of time to figure out what we should do."

Julia nodded as the tension eased from her shoulders. She rose and picked up her purse. "What do I owe you for our visit? Or should I call in and see Sheila? Does she still handle the accounts? When Doc Farley…"

Stofford held his hand up to stop the flow of words. "We'll talk about that when I come out to check on the boys," he said.

Gathering the children around her, Julia nodded and peered out the front window, but there was no one in sight. She ushered the children toward the door. "Okay, let's go, be quick. We'll get Prince moving and hurry on home."

The Doctor followed them out and handed her up into the wagon, and then Jims, as the other children scrambled in. "Let me," he said as he handed her the reins with an encouraging smile. "Head on home, and take it easy for the next few days. Not just the boys, all of you. It's been a stressful time, eh? Go on home now."

~~~**~~~

CHAPTER SEVEN

Doctor Stoffard stood at his gate and watched the little town cart receding from view up the North Road. He'd never seen such a mess as the marks on the backs of those two boys. It was astonishing how quickly his rage had risen, and he'd nearly taken it out on Mrs. Butler.

What a beautiful woman, and such passion. He thought if she weren't married, he might have a great deal of interest in her, even with two children, or possibly four. He shifted his shoulders, grinned to himself, and went back into his surgery.

~~*~~

Heddie came on Monday, as usual. She lived farther up North Road past the Morris' farm, and with her husband worked a piece of land with some cattle and pigs. She had no children at home, all having grown and gone. She helped in the garden during the summer, did laundry or canning, whatever Julia was involved with. This Monday it was laundry.

Julia had burned the boys' clothing, both because they were beyond redemption, and because she didn't want anyone to see those awful rags, or to know what those little boys had been

35

wearing. She let them take any items out of the pockets, but there wasn't much. A polished pebble, a bent spoon, some string. Ben had a knife that had been sharpened down to a small blade, the handle cushioned with binder twine wrapped tightly around it.

She wanted to bring the boys into the house, and yet she hadn't done it. If they stayed in the shed on the pallets, it felt like she didn't care about them, letting them sleep outside like any vagrants that spent the night on their way by. If she brought them into the house, it felt like she was making a permanent addition to her family, and panic arose every time she considered that step.

What to do? She bided her time, sewed up a set of pants for each of them and cut down two shirts to give them something to wear that didn't look like a tent on their skinny frames. At least, if it came down to it, she could take them to church, and not be embarrassed by how they looked.

The boys were thrilled with the new clothes, such as they were. Ollie preened as he walked around the yard, straightening his collar and smoothing the lapels of his shirt.

Heddie was a hard worker and not given to gossip, something that Julia had always admired. But she looked the boys over for most of the morning, chatting with them if they were near as she stood on the porch pushing the clothes through the wringer and hanging them on the line. "Fine young fellas," she finally said. "Are they come to stay?"

It was a common question, times being what they were. Family members sometimes got spread around to wherever they could be looked after in the hopes that better times would arrive and they could go home.

"For a while anyway," said Julia, nodding. "I'm not sure how long."

Heddie nodded back. "Lots of families in distress, these times," she said, and cranked the handle to start the washer agitating. "Want me to shell peas while I'm waiting for this load?"

"Yes, please. I'll go and pick some more. And this afternoon if we could dig potatoes for a while, maybe just an hour. I don't have too much energy today."

"No worry," said Heddie. "I'll do it. Look, you shell the peas, that way you can sit for a spell, and I'll go pick more. You call me when the load is finished washing."

Julia gazed after the woman with deep appreciation. She did love Heddie, she was the best and most accommodating woman.

Dr. Stoffard came by late that afternoon, just after Heddie had gone. He drove into the yard in a black Model A that Julia guessed was at least ten years old, chugging and belching a little smoke. It looked like old Doc Farley's car, maybe he got it as part of the package when he took over the medical practice. He turned it off and it sputtered and coughed a bit before it subsided.

The boys approached cautiously, like dogs on a scent. Ben reached out to open the door, and the doctor grinned at him, climbing out with his long legs. "Thank you, sir, would you care to try it? You sit in there, Ben, see what you think."

Ben looked at him in disbelief, and then leaped at the chance before the doctor could change his mind. The look of wonder on his face was something to behold.

"You get in too, Ollie, and you Maggie. Just don't touch the gears, those things." He leaned in to tug on the handbrake. The kids clambered into the car, talking excitedly.

The doctor took the steps two at a time, stopping where Julia paused on the top step with a handful of clothes pins and a bundle of dry clothes under her arm.

"Hello, Mrs. Butler. How are you today?"

"Fine, thank you, Doctor. And you?"

"Couldn't be better. Thought I'd check in and see how it's going with the boys."

Julia looked past him toward the car where a great deal of talk and activity was taking place. "It's going," she said, "definitely going. They certainly like your car."

The doctor smiled slightly. "All boys like a car. I think it's in the male makeup. Are they settling in alright?"

She gazed into his eyes and wondered what to tell him. This

was a very interesting man. He seemed to care about the little boys, and he was offering something. *Friendship perhaps?* She liked the idea. "I'm not sure, but I'd like to talk to you about it."

"By all means," he said. "Do you mind if I sit down?"

She laughed. "Sit here, on the porch, Dr Stoffard. Its cooler, and I'll get some lemonade."

"Call me Will," he said and removed his hat, laying it on the porch railing. Julia entered the house and tossed the dry clothes on the dining table. Then she grabbed some lemons from the basket in the kitchen and sliced them in half. She looked up to see he had followed her in.

As she worked, she talked. "I think the boys are here to stay, at least for a while. I haven't even brought them into the house to sleep yet." Julia stopped working, the juice press still in her hand. "I feel bad about it. They're sleeping outside in the shed, that's where the transients sleep when they stop for a night or two."

She frowned down at her hands. "I've been afraid to make the move. It feels like a commitment to bring them inside. But I know it's time." She finished the lemonade and placed the jug and glasses on a tray. "Come sit on the porch where it's cooler."

He took the chair beside her as she poured lemonade into a glass and handed it to him.

"What are you most afraid of?" he asked.

She cleared her throat and took a sip. "I don't know if anyone is looking for them, for one thing. These must be pretty violent people, the folks in their family. I mean, look at their backs. It's not just the new marks. There are so many old scars, it takes my breath away. Especially on Ben. I don't know if you noticed but some look like burns."

Will nodded, his mouth tight. "Believe me, I noticed."

Her breath caught in her throat. "You'd have to hold him down to do that, wouldn't you? I have nightmares at the thought. And they're so skinny you can count their ribs. No schooling, they can't read a lick."

She paused, and looked earnestly into his face. "I'm afraid of their family." She glanced at the car, where the children were playing. "But I'm also afraid of the obligation. You can't just take kids in for a little while, then tell them you're tired of it. It's a big commitment, probably a permanent one, to bring them into the house. I've been delaying." Her smile was rueful. "But I'm okay with that now, I think. It's definitely time. I guess I've talked it around and I've come to that point in my decision. I have a room behind the kitchen that will make a nice bedroom. I just need to clean it out and find a couple of beds."

The doctor nodded, watching her face as she talked her way through the knotty problem. He smiled and his gaze switched to the children in the car. Jims had climbed onto Ben's lap and was turning the steering wheel, making engine noises with his mouth. Maggie hung out the window on the passenger side, and Ollie was squeezed in the rear, with his head thrown back gazing up at the clouds.

"There are a couple of single beds at my house," he said, turning back to her, "from when Doc Farley had it. He just left everything the way it was when he lived there, which is both a blessing and a curse."

Julia burst out laughing and he grinned.

"I could bring them by tomorrow. There are mattresses on them, they look in fair shape."

"That would be perfect," she exclaimed."I've managed to make them both an extra pair of pants, so that will get them started in school. But they don't have shoes. I'll see what I can find in the drop box at Church. Shoes are especially hard to come by. They're simply too expensive to replace until you absolutely have to. I know lots of the farm boys don't have shoes at the beginning of school, but when it gets cold, they'll need them."

The doctor drained his glass. "Do you know anything about your neighbour across the way?"

"You mean Jerome Hoskiss?" she asked in surprise. "Yes, what do you need to know?" Julie frowned in the direction of the old cabin almost hidden in the grove of trees.

"Well, for instance, is he a danger to you?"

Julia burst out laughing. "Jerome?" she choked. "No, not Jerome. He's totally harmless. Why do you ask?"

Stofford frowned and his mouth hardened. "I heard something in town, and when I stopped in to see him, he wouldn't come to the door. Just shouted that he wasn't home today."

Julia laughed softly, and placed her hand on his arm. "He's just an eccentric, maybe a bit of a hermit. I've known him for years, and we get along fine. He's certainly getting older, and I don't think he takes very good care of himself. I've invited him here many times, but he doesn't always come, he doesn't like company much. He used to come for dinner sometimes, and once for Christmas but since…."

She trailed off, thinking of how it had been when Stephen was alive. "He's harmless. Maybe I should get over more often to see him. I'll try to do that."

The doctor took her hand and pressed it between his. "I didn't mean to imply that there were more people you should rescue right now. You have your hands full as it is."

There was humour in his eyes. "I think you're doing enough. Well," he stood and picked up his fedora hat. "I'll bring those beds by tomorrow after I finish my rounds. I don't think it will hurt the boys to sleep outside one more night. It's certainly warm enough."

As he stood, Julia realized again how big he was. Stephen had been tall and whip thin, his muscles lean and ropy. This man was massive, with a big head and wide shoulders. His arms were as suited to a lumberjack, as a doctor. He leaned down to her, one wide hand resting on the table. "Thank you for the lemonade. I'll see you tomorrow."

Julia smiled back. "Would you care to stay for dinner tomorrow?"

His gaze warmed. "That would be very nice. I'd like that."

She watched him lope down the steps and across to his car. The kids jabbered excitedly as they clambered over the back of the seats and out the doors. They watched as he lifted the hood on the engine, and inserted the crank. Ben leaped back when the Doctor gave a heave and noisily cranked the engine. Stoffard tried to lay a hand on Ben's shoulder in reassurance, but he was gone, running for the stairs to the verandah.

Julia got to him just as he gained the top step, and pulled him against her side. "Look, Ben, he's just starting the car. See? It's ready to go now. You can wave goodbye."

Ben's trembling slowed and he raised a tentative hand to Dr Stoffard as he drove out of the yard and down the North Road.

~~~**~~~

CHAPTER EIGHT

The next afternoon, Julia put the finishing touches to a pie and placed it in the oven. Rhubarb apple, their favourite. She wasn't sure about Ben and Ollie, but the other two had no ambivalence about it. Of course, Stephen had been vocal in his liking for it, and they simply followed along, mimicking everything he said and did. She'd gotten a laugh out of that. It had made cooking for the family pretty easy, all things considered. Maggie copied her dad, and although Stephen was gone now, Jims copied Maggie.

She had spent the day clearing out the spare room. She couldn't believe the amount of stuff that had accumulated—a lot of winter clothing, old coats and boots full of dead spiders, plus a few pieces of travel luggage. There were extra kitchen items that they had taken out of Stephen's folk's house when they cleared it out. Julia was pleased to see some of the clothing, already turning over in her mind what she could use for the boys.

The spare room finally had a purpose. Ben and Ollie were very excited. Not that Ben was jumping about, or even extra loud. But there was a curious tension about him, and the colour had been high in his cheeks all day. They knew the doctor was bringing beds tonight, and they were moving into the spare room. Ollie didn't know what to make of it.

She heard the sound of a car outside, and the kids went running to the door, Jims last in line, pushing through the sea of legs to get a look. Then they stopped short. Julia stepped closer to peek over their heads. Sure enough, Dr. Stoffard had two beds and mattresses balanced precariously on the back of his car, anchored with cord.

"Well, go and help," Julia urged. "The Doctor could use a hand to get those beds in here." They didn't need more than that, and had arrived at the side of the car by the time it stuttered to a halt.

With much pushing and hauling, the bed frames were dragged into the spare room and re-assembled. The metal headboards could use a coat of paint, and she'd tend to that when she had the time. The mattresses were heaved into place, and Ollie leaped onto one and lay down.

"This one's mine," he said.

Ben grinned and dragged him off. "Nope, it's mine." There followed a tussle that ended when Julia threw a blanket over them to cool things off.

The doctor had sheets and some blankets, and the beds were quickly made. Ben already had his spare shirt and pants hanging on the hook against the wall.

Julia remembered an old dresser in her sewing room that she could manage without. She transferred everything onto the bookcase up there and cleared off the top. With the help of the doctor, they wrestled it down the stairs and into place. The mirror was foggy but still useful, and the boys could share the three drawers.

By this time dinner was ready, and Julia just managed to save the pie from burning. She served the meal in the dining room tonight. The doctor was their guest and this was an important occasion. Maggie insisted on getting out a tablecloth and setting the table with the good china, cups and saucers for everyone but Jims. The good silverware was set out by each plate, with cloth napkins arranged to the side. There were even candles in the candleholders in the middle of the table.

Ben was very quiet during dinner. Julia wondered what he was thinking, but every now and then he would look at her and grin. She grinned back.

Dessert was a success. Ollie said he'd never had pie. Ben said he had so, once at a neighbour's house, but he apparently didn't remember.

Julia had made whipped cream, and the entire pie was devoured. Ollie surreptitiously used his fingers to get the last bits of rhubarb from the bottom of the pie plate as he helped to clear the table.

Julia made tea and every one had some. She had to make two pots. The milk and sugar was used extensively. It was like attending a very big tea party for kids, with a couple of adults in attendance.

By the time tea was finished, the children were yawning. Jims was the first to be sent off to wash up, while the doctor organized everyone else into showing him where the soap and dishcloth were to be found. He talked them into drying for him and putting the dishes away as they were cleaned.

Maggie was happy to show everyone where the good china was stored. Ollie was especially interested in restoring the silverware to the right slots in the flatware chest.

As Julia tucked Jims into bed, he hugged her tight. "Lots of boys," he said, his face anxious.

"Yes, sweetheart, but none as precious as you." She kissed his forehead and pulled the cover up.

Back downstairs, she managed to drag her daughter off to bed, with promises from Ben that he and Ollie would get washed and into their pajamas.

When she came back down, they were both in bed, sheets pulled to their chins. She paused in the doorway to gaze at them. They looked so satisfied. Ollie was smoothing his sheet, and arranging the blanket just right. Ben watched her as she stood at the door, that little smile on his mouth.

"Oh, look at you both," she said. "I can see you belong right here. Can't you?" She straightened pillows, and smoothed brows, planted a kiss on each forehead, and patted their chests. "You look perfect. I'm so glad you came to stay with us. I feel like you're part of the family now."

Julia felt tears gather in her throat. She glanced up to see the doctor peering around the door frame. "Don't they look at home?" she asked. "Now go to sleep, both of you, and I'll see you in the morning."

~~~**~~~

CHAPTER NINE

Doctor Stoffard had placed a bottle of brandy on the table in the parlour along with two small glasses. "Shall we have a toast? I thought I'd bring this along for the celebration," he said.

She settled on the brocade couch, watching him seat himself at the other end. She was exhausted from the emotional day.

When she took a sip of the liquor, it burned all the way to her stomach. "Whew! I'm pretty tired. It's been a very busy day. I think I'll have to call it an early night, Doctor."

"Call me Will,' he said once more. His smile quirked.

"Will," she replied. "I might have to go to bed, I'm beat."

"Don't worry, I won't stay long." He arranged himself comfortably on the couch, then angled to look at her. "Now that the boys are settled with a room and beds, what's next? They obviously need clothes, what about school? Will they have to be registered soon?"

They talked it over, small sips of brandy taking the edge off the tension, until Julia was relaxed against the cushions.

Will took her hand in his and pressed her fingers. "I'm not trying to give you more work," he commented. "I'm just trying to let you know what I can do to help. I've written to my sister-in-law in Winnipeg to see what she can do about clothes. My brother,

Ray, has four boys and the youngest is about Ben's age but he's bigger in size. Polly thinks she can send some things that will be useful, so that's a start."

He gave her a keen glance. "I'd be surprised if anyone is looking for them. I know that's a concern, and a legitimate one. I took the liberty of talking to the police in Nelson. Their constable comes through here once a week on patrol, and he promised to stop in this time on his way by. I'll bring him out, with your permission, and we can talk about the situation. How does that sound?"

Julia nodded, looking at her hand in his.

He moved his fingers to link their clasp. "I want to help all I can. You have enough to keep you busy with your own two children. Economically this whole area has been in a deep slump for years. How will you manage?"

At her surprised look, he hastened to add, "I don't mean to pry, but two more mouths to feed is one thing. I can see you have a big garden, and a milk goat, chickens and all, but it'll be nearly twice as much work. And you don't just have to feed these little fellows, you have to clothe them and see to their needs. It's a huge increase in the size of the household." There was a frown on his forehead, and his gaze was steady on her face.

Julia heaved a sigh, and sat up. "I'm in pretty good shape, relatively speaking." She smiled. Her mother would have rolled her eyes at hearing that. "Julia," she used to say, "Can't you just say a straight forward sentence? You always sound like you're reading a novel."

She cleared her throat self-consciously. The doctor didn't need to hear a novel, just a few facts. "That is, I have a small income that keeps us going. There's no guarantee that it will continue forever, but so far we've been fortunate. It pays the taxes on the property and a few little extras in the way of clothes and necessities. It keeps the pony fed." She grinned at that. If that wasn't a straight forward sentence, she didn't know what was.

Will nodded and grinned back. "That's excellent. You'll still

47

need help though, and I'll do everything I can to aid you. How do the children get to school? It's almost two miles and certainly Maggie didn't walk that last year, did she? The snow can get pretty heavy here in the winter, I hear."

Julia shook her head. "No, Mr. Morris picked her up, it was her first year. He lives a mile farther up North Road. He gets her in the morning when he takes his own two children in to school, which lets me stay at home to look after Jims, and I pick them up in the afternoon, Maggie and the Morris boys. It works out well for me. I'll have to talk to him to make sure he can pick up three of them, instead of just one."

She'd already thought about that. Prince was a good little horse, and he could certainly pull all of them in the small wagon. They wouldn't have any trouble for trips to town, they'd managed fine on the way to Will's office. Adding the two Morris kids would work, they were little guys about Ben's age.

But that would probably be the limit, especially up that last hill before the Morris house. But she'd make it work. She'd walk, if she had to, lighten the load for the pony however she could.

Will must have seen the look of determination on her face. "What are you trying to work out? I can help. I could pick the kids up after school and bring them home some days," he offered.

Julia looked at him doubtfully. *What was he offering?* He'd just arrived in town and probably didn't know what his time demands were going to be. And his car certainly wouldn't hold that many kids, would it?

She shook her head. "That's a kind offer, but I can't imagine what your schedule will look like once you get more involved in the medical practice. Old Doc Farley used to say, there was drought sometimes, but then it would pour, you just never knew. You'll probably find the same thing."

She paused to glance her apology at him. "It works with Prince. And Mr. Morris can do it in both directions if I really can't manage. We have a kind of system between us. Wait and see how busy you get, then if you still have time we could talk about that."

She softened her words with a smile.

Will bowed his head to her wishes, thanked her for dinner, and rose to take his leave. Julia walked him to the front door. "Thank you for talking to the police about this. It eases my mind. Is there a complaint about missing children?"

At the negative shake of his head, she shrugged. "I thought not. I wonder where they really came from. Or what their last name is. It's all such a mystery. You'd think the family would be looking for them, you can't not notice when your children disappear."

She stood on the porch and waved as he backed the car onto the road and drove away. The evening was calm and warm. The light was dim in the yard, and she could hear the frogs saying good night down at the creek. The chickens made feeble noises in the henhouse and Wagsy stood beside her, his tail banging leisurely against her leg. Prince thumped once in his stall, then was silent.

She went back into the house and closed the door. Four children under her roof. She felt a little tense, and yet much more comfortable than before.

It hadn't seemed right that those little boys were stuck in limbo, sleeping in the shed in the yard. She peeked into their room. Ollie had thrown all his covers to the floor. She picked up the sheet and tucked it around his warm body. Ben was lying still, but his eyes opened as she moved around the room. "Sshh, it's alright, go to sleep," she whispered.

She slowly climbed the stairs, turning off the light in the hall. She peeked in on Maggie and Jims. They lay entwined, the blanket at the bottom of the bed. She straightened it and moved on to her own room. When she lay down, she sank quickly into oblivion.

~~~**~~~

CHAPTER TEN

Sunday was church, and Julia felt the boys were finally ready to go. It would be better if they could be introduced to some of the local children before they met them all on their first day of school. It might be less overwhelming.

She explained what it would be like. They'd sit in long pews, like benches, with all the other people. They'd kneel to pray. Did they know about God? They seemed not able to decide whether to nod or shake their heads at this question.

Julia thought God was a big topic and they should approach it simply, so she was happy to let Maggie explain. God lived in heaven, her daughter said, and loved everyone, and when you prayed to him with your problems, sometimes he changed your problems for you, and sometimes he changed you so you could handle the problems better.

She stared at Maggie in amazement. She couldn't have explained it half as well or as simply. She brushed her hand over Maggie's dark auburn curls and hugged her close to her side.

So they set off for church, Prince trotting in the traces of the town cart. Sometimes Jerome Hoskiss had been to church with them, but not today. Maggie had run over to ask but he declined.

They arrived in a long line of horses and carts, cars and trucks, and people walking. Prince was tethered securely to the railing at the street, and the whole crew trouped into the churchyard, amid calls of greeting and children running. Julia took them straight in and they sat halfway back.

The minister was a local farmer who did a good job of sermons, his wife played the organ. Other locals led the prayers of the people. Julia had asked for special prayers for the two boys with her, for their ability to settle into their new home, and not be too homesick for the family they were missing. She thought that was the best wording, as it was possible they were just missing their brother Charlie and not their parents at all.

There was no Sunday school today, it would start up again at the same time that school started in the fall. So the children wiggled and squirmed their way through the service, standing when Julia stood, kneeling when she knelt.

Ollie peered through his fingers at the people around him as the prayers droned on, then twisted around and waved excitedly. Julia leaned over and grabbed his arm. "Hush."

"But Doctor Spofford is here!" Ollie whispered.

Julia looked over to see the doctor winking at the boys from across the aisle. She frowned and he grinned unrepentantly back at her. When they stood to sing the last hymn, the children had reached their limit of patience, and a small tussle ensued. She held them in check just long enough to finish the service and led them at a trot toward the exit. Doc Stoffard was right behind her.

They became caught in the traffic jam outside the church door and Julia caught sight of Betsy Whittaker and her husband Brent, with their four-year-old daughter Nellie. Jims tugged on Nellie's hand and they ran off to the wagon to examine Prince. Betsy chatted with Maggie and was introduced to Ben and Ollie, who stood speechless by Julia's side.

Will interposed himself into the group, introducing himself and chatting with Brent, while watching Ben and Ollie. Finally, he reached down to shake their hands. "Good to see you, boys. How have things been?" He pulled them aside and squatted on his haunches to chat eye-to-eye.

Julia was grateful. They needed to be social, but it was difficult with so many strange faces. She watched Will out of the corner of her eye as she talked with her friend. He really was a thoughtful man, aware of and attentive to other people's needs.

Mrs. Chin approached, her two children trailing behind. "Hello, Kinko, and Lu." Julia shook the husband's hand. "It's good to see you. How is the restaurant doing?"

The Chins ran a Chinese restaurant in town and Julia had been there once with Luke Harrison for dinner. The food was quite different from anything she'd ever had, yet she loved the spices and tastes. "Are the boys working in the restaurant with you?" She smiled down at the two youngsters. The eldest was certainly old enough to help out in the business, he looked about fourteen. The younger was ten and he eyed Ben curiously, who eyed him back.

"Boys lots of help,'" said Lu Chin. "'Chop vegetables, wash dishes, they work good."

Julia nodded, that made sense. "I'd love to come in again and taste your food. I really enjoyed it that once I was there. As you can see, I have too many children to afford to eat in a restaurant right now."

Kinko nodded. "Lots children, new boys I see. Look good and strong, too." Her eyes crinkled as she laughed. "Maybe they come work in restaurant, chop vegetables."

As Julia laughed, Kinko continued, "You come, bring children, we feed you not too much money. We look after you that way."

"This one," Kinko pointed at Ben, "maybe he come play with Fin sometime. They same age, I think." Ben looked at Fin and back at Julia and didn't say a word, but she detected a hint of a smile in his eyes.

~~*~~

They hustled themselves home, and Julia fed them a quick lunch, then launched into her Sunday routine. Today was bath day, and she lit the gas oven and slid the chicken in for a slow roast.

Stephen had set up their water system, and she didn't know of another like it. Once electricity reached their house, he bought an electric pump for the well. He buried the water line underground to keep it from freezing in the winter, and put a water tank upstairs in the attic. "That will give us some water pressure," he explained, "with the tank up high like that. Not a whole lot, but some." The tank was filled from the well and thus they had cold running water into the kitchen and the bathroom.

Then he began planning a system for hot water. Julia had thought it was too much, there was no real need. She'd never had hot running water and managed fine with the reservoir on the stove, and buckets on top to heat water.

But Stephen wasn't satisfied with that, he was a systems man. So he found a second water tank and ran pipe from the bottom of the tank through the gas stove and back to the top of the tank. "Hot water rises," he explained. The water in the pipe heated, rose and filled the top of the water tank, pushing the water down and drawing cold water from the bottom back into the pipe to be heated.

It worked like a charm. And Julia had hot water in the tank an hour after she lit the gas stove. As a consequence, she used cooking Sunday dinner as the perfect time to count on hot water. The water was piped into the bathroom and direct to the kitchen sink.

She turned on the tap in the big claw-footed bathtub and began filling it. Then she called Maggie and Jims. They both ran to get their night shirts and disappeared into the bathroom. Julia adjusted the water temperature and threw in the bath toys.

Ben and Ollie were very interested and Julia assured them they'd have their turn. A great deal of splashing and shrieking later, she went back in to wash hair and make sure all body parts were clean, then pulled the children out of the tub to get dried.

She poured more hot water, leaving the toys, and called Ollie and Ben. They came more slowly, Ollie more eager than Ben.

"Get your nightshirts. We'll have an early night after we're all clean," she said, and sent them off. When they returned she stripped Ollie of his clothes and popped him into the water.

"You, too, Ben. Climb in. There are toys to play with, and there's soap in the metal pot. Just make sure everything is clean. I'll come back to wash your hair, you can cover yourself with that face cloth if you like."

She left the room, and heard splashing as Ben climbed over the rim of the tub. When she knocked on the door and went back in, their faces were shiny and both were grinning.

Julia scrubbed their scalps and handed them towels. "Out you come. Put your nightshirts on, and we'll have dinner. It's just about ready."

She paused and looked them over. "I'll have to get you boys some slippers. It's nice and warm right now but come November you'll be glad to have them." As she left the room, they were both looking at their feet as if they'd never seen them before. Sometimes she felt she was dealing with wild children. Everything that she and her own kids took for granted, they found different and fascinating.

They had the roast chicken with stuffing and boiled potatoes. She added salad from the garden, lettuce from the latest planting, grated carrot, tomatoes, and lima beans. She chuckled to herself. Her salads were always filled with whatever came out of the garden at the moment, and never even remotely resembled the salads that other people ate. But no one seemed to notice at her table, they just mouthed it down with relish.

Dinner over, she organized the troops and they cleared the table, washed dishes and dried them, while Julia put the food away and cleared up.

She'd made cookies the day before. So they had tea and cookies in the parlour where she turned on the radio. The new Canadian Radio Broadcasting Commission had just started up that year and she liked to tune in on Sunday evenings. They had programmes of drama and suspense that Maggie and Jims loved to listen to.

Tonight it was *The Shadow*, and everyone was riveted with their ears to the set. The Shadow seemed to be a man who was a detective of sorts and he was able to sleuth without being seen by other people.

Ben's eyes were enormous at the end of the programme, where the Shadow had found the bad man and turned him in to the police. "Is the Shadow around here, too?" he asked worriedly. Julia laughed and ruffled his thick hair, just barely dry after the bath. "No, the Shadow is a story, he's not real at all. A made up story. But it was exciting, wasn't it?"

Julia got them tucked into bed, still talking about what they'd heard on the radio. Ollie decided he wanted to be a detective when he grew up. Julia walked back into the kitchen. It looked pretty good, considering. She put away the serving dishes, wiped down the tables and pushed the benches back in place.

Then she locked the front door and went into the bathroom to run her own bath, removing all the toys and digging out the special lavender soap she used. Such luxury. She leaned back in the hot water and breathed out a deep sigh, soaking until it started to cool. It felt so good, the room steamy and warm, the water lapping at her chest. She pinched her nose and sank. When she couldn't hold her breath any longer, she rose with a rush of water and soaped her hair. Drying off, she used the only towel left on the rack, and climbed the stairs.

She kept her lotion on the dresser in her room, a mixture of glycerin and rose water, bees wax and perfumed oil that she made. She smoothed it over her arms and legs, her face and hands and slid into her nightie. She slept deeply.

~~~**~~~

CHAPTER ELEVEN

School was to begin in a few days, and Maggie was wound like a clock. She tried on the new dress her mother had made during the summer, wore it around until Julia made her take it off before it got dirty.

Ben and Ollie were worried. They watched Maggie and Julia by turns, obviously wondering what was in store for them.

Jims was upset, the start of school meant all the children would be gone for the day and he was stuck at home with no one to play with. "Your time will come, Jims," Julia said, at least once a day. "Next year you'll be going to school, too. It's okay to be home for one more year."

Jims sulked until he forgot about it, distracted by a game of tag with Wagsy, which Ollie joined in with wild enthusiasm.

Ben stayed close to Julia in the house. "What will it be like at school?" he finally asked. She looked up from hemming a light jacket that she'd cut down from one of Stephen's. She gave him a close look, then laid the sewing in her lap. "Ben, come and sit here beside me." She scooted over on the couch.

As the boy lowered himself to the cushion, she put her arm around him and pulled him against her side. He stiffened for a minute, then slowly relaxed into her arm. She'd thought at first that this was a child who was slow to speak and maybe slow in thought.

Now she knew he was just very considered, both in words and action. It seemed a very good quality to have.

"Do you want to go to school, Ben?"

He was watching her with a serious gaze. Slowly he nodded.

Julia grinned. "Good, because I want you to go, too. You learn a lot in school. First you learn to read."

Ben interrupted. "I already know the whole alphabet, Maggie showed me." He looked proud and there was a tinge of colour high on his dusky cheeks.

Julia laughed and pulled him closer in a one-armed hug. "I know you do, and you're very smart to have learned it so quickly. But there's a lot more to reading that just knowing the alphabet. There's learning to spell, learning to write, getting an education by reading certain books that can teach you so many things."

Ben listened intently.

"As you learn more, you'll begin to see how the world works, what things have been invented and how they were invented. You can learn history, how Canada became a country, who were the people that made that happen, what it was like before we became a country. You can learn about countries that are across the sea, or around the world. There are endless things to learn. Once you can read, Ben, you can learn anything. It is all available to you in books."

She took a deep breath and looked into his dark eyes. "Then there are numbers. You'll need to know your numbers to get along in the world."

Ben nodded confidently. "I already know my numbers. I did the sales for Ma when she wasn't there, or when she was sleeping." He suddenly seemed to realize what he'd let slip, and stiffened in her arm, his gaze sliding sideways.

"What were you selling, Ben?" Julia asked.

"Jars," he said after a minute, still looking down. He hesitated. "Jars of moonshine."

"Ahhh." Julia said nothing more for a moment, feeling him relax again. So, what she'd suspected was true. His family were moonshiners, they lived in the hills the other side of Donegal, no doubt. "Well, that means you already know more than a lot of children your age about numbers. You can count money, and make change."

Just then Ollie and Jims came bounding into the house, Wagsy trailing behind. Ollie stopped. "What's wrong?" His gaze bounced from Julia to Ben and back in a worried expression. "What happened? What's wrong with Ben?"

"Nothing," said Julia. "We're just talking about classes. You boys are going to start school next week with Maggie. I'm getting a jacket ready for you." She picked up her sewing to show them the garment and then continued with her stitching. "Are you okay with that, Ollie?"

Ollie screwed up his face and burst into hysterical laughter. He spun around and Ben's grin grew. He leaped from the couch at his brother and soon the two of them were wrestling on the floor, laughing wildly with Wagsy's loud barking adding to the din.

Julia watched with exasperation. "I think I'll take that as a *yes*," she giggled.

~~*~~

The first day of school dawned clear and warm. Julia arranged to bring the children in herself and Mr. Morris would pick them up to take them home. She wanted to have a word with the teacher. She'd already told Mrs. Rasmussen that the two boys would be starting school, and given her some background on their ages and lack of schooling thus far. She wanted to make sure they settled in okay and there were no immediate problems.

Maggie's lunch bucket from last year consisted of a lard tin and lid, on which Julia had painted her name. She dug out two more tins and found a half-used bucket of paint in the basement. Ollie watched attentively as she painted his name on the lid and the side of the tin. "There," she said, holding it up by the handle. "See this, Ollie? This is your lunch pail. Can you recognize your name on it? Don't touch, let it dry."

"Where's Ben's?" he asked.

"Right here." She picked up the second pail and began to paint. Lunches were going to be more work than she'd anticipated. Before it had just been Maggie, and she would throw something together for her. She and Jims would eat leftovers at home for lunch. But now, with three lunches to produce it would mean more bread, more filling. She would have to get into some kind of baking routine. She sighed. Biscuits would work as well, and they were much faster to produce.

The school yard milled with children. The two classes in the school went from grades one to eight, so there was quite a range of ages represented. Julia saw some older boys who worked on a family farm past her place on the North Road. They were in their mid teens, but only got to school half the year due to farm work, so were still completing their grades.

Ben and Ollie slid down cautiously from the wagon, Maggie right behind them. Ben reached to tie Prince to the fence, as Julia climbed down and grabbed Jims off the seat. "Don't forget," she warned. "Your names are Benjamin and Ollie Butler. You too, Maggie." The children nodded soberly.

Some little girls screeched and ran over to grab Maggie by the hand. Julia gave her the lunch pail and watched her run after her friends. Then she herded the boys across the grass to the schoolhouse door, each of them clutching a lunch pail, pencil and notebook.

Mrs. Rasmussen was in the first room for grades one to four, printing a class greeting on the blackboard as they entered. She turned around and smiled, extending her hand to Julia. "Mrs. Butler, hello. And are these the boys you were telling me about? Hello boys, although I see Jims is here and he's too young, surely, to be starting school?"

Jims grinned, "Mum said next year. But it's a long way away," and his expression turned gloomy.

Julie pushed Ben forward. "This is Benjamin Butler, we call

him Ben. And his brother, Ollie." Mrs. Rasmussen shook hands with the boys.

"Welcome," she said. "Mrs. Butler tells me that neither of you has been to school before."

The boys looked at her, until Ben slowly nodded in answer.

"Well, that's no problem. You'll see all ages of children here. This classroom has grades one through four. Each row has one grade in it. I'm going to seat you together over here in the front row. That way I can keep an eye on you as we start. I can help you better that way, and we'll see what you know and what you might need help with."

Ollie smiled. "We both know the alphabet, the whole thing," he said proudly.

Mrs. Rasmussen looked pleased. "That's excellent. That means you already have a head start."

Julia filled out a form for each of the boys, then left them with the teacher and herded Jims outside. As the bell rang, the children lined up in front of the schoolhouse door. She spotted Maggie in the line and hustled over to give her a hug.

Jims gave her a big squeeze around the legs, burying his face in her skirt. "Don't worry, Jims," Maggie said, patting his little back. "We'll be home soon and then we can play."

~~~**~~~

CHAPTER TWELVE

Julia hurried to the general store and picked up the items on her shopping list. Yeast, sugar, tea, coffee, sewing thread and needles. She added bags of rice, flour and beans, and a few food items she could use in an emergency.

Luke Harrison was helping another customer, and when he finished, he hustled over behind the post office window to get her mail for her. There was always a newspaper, *The Vancouver Sun* this time. Stephen's brother, James Butler wrote for that paper and lived in Vancouver with his family.

She often read his column with amusement and sometimes awe, that James could write so well, live in a big city and make his living as a journalist. Sometimes there was the *Calgary Herald*, or a Toronto newspaper.

Luke got the paper in for the store's customers, and one copy for the store itself. After everyone had read it, he passed it on to her. It might be a few days old, but the news was still interesting and it kept her current with world events.

Now he came out to carry her purchases to the wagon. He chatted, catching up on her news as he deposited her parcels in the wooden box under the bench seat. Luke had been a good friend of Stephen`s, and stayed a solid support for her since his passing.

She told him about the additions to the household. Most of

the gossip of the village passed through the general store, and he'd already heard about the boys. She trusted Luke and asked him not to pass on any information. "You don't have to ask, Julia. You know I wouldn't do anything that might harm you. You can always rely on that." He smiled warmly at her.

She thanked him and headed home.

The children arrived on Mr. Morris's wagon that afternoon in high spirits. She sent them to change and then outside to do chores, they were so loud, as she got supper underway. By the time they came in again they'd calmed down, washing up with lots of pushing and noise from the boys.

She rolled her eyes and Maggie caught it. "It's noisy, isn't it?" she said. She rolled her eyes too, and Julia laughed.

"Yes, boys tend to be that way."

Just as they were sitting down to eat, Dr. Stoffard arrived. The children leaped from the kitchen table, leaving their meals hardly touched, and raced outside at the sound of his car coughing in the drive.

He came in with a large escort of children, a big box under his arm and a bag in his other hand. His eyes twinkled. "I see my timing is impeccable. I've interrupted dinner, again."

Julia laughed. "Come and join us if you haven't eaten. It's simple fare but there's plenty." She herded the children back into the house and up to the table, as he set the box on the floor inside the door.

Will placed the bag on the counter by the sink. "Just some steaks I got from a patient, too many for me to use."

Julia's eyes grew big. "Steak! I don't know when I've last had steak."

Will grinned. "Well, you do now."

Julia put the bag in the cooler and came back to rearrange the table. "Ben, get a chair for the doctor. Ollie, move everyone over to make some room. Maggie, please get an extra plate. Jims, we need another napkin."

She began to pass serving bowls to the doctor as the children settled back around the table. Potatoes, the last of the peas from her garden, leftover chicken from the night before, and cornbread. They ate amidst a lot of talk about school, where everyone sat, and the books they needed, how many pencils some of the children had. Ben was worried he might need a pen and ink after Christmas. Julia assured him that she had some and if he needed it there wouldn`t be a problem. He looked vastly relieved.

When the talk died down, Will said, "I just heard today that there was a bank robbery in Creston, is that true?" He forked a piece of chicken into his mouth. The children all paused in their eating, staring open-mouthed at the doctor.

Julia grinned. "Well, yes and no," she said. "That is, there was a bank robbery, but it was maybe seven years ago when Maggie was just a baby." The heads all swiveled as one to stare at Julia at the other end of the table.

"A bank robbery, you mean robbers in our bank, right here in the village?" Maggie squeaked, her face screwed into a question mark.

Ollie's eyes were wide with alarm.

"I'll tell you the story, but you have to eat your dinner or it will get cold." She nodded approvingly as the forks began to move again.

Will sat with his forearms braced on the table, a look of amusement on his face. She gave him a reproving look, and he laughed, lifting his fork to begin eating.

"Well, it went like this. One day around noon, two men entered the bank. They weren't from around here but later we found out that the leader was a man named Mr. Ward, John Ward."

"How?" demanded Maggie. "How did you find out?"

"Just listen, and I'll tell you. Now, they came into the bank and pulled their revolvers and waved them in the air. Then they shouted out, *Give us all the money in the vault!* Everyone in the bank hit the floor, they scrambled down on their hands and knees and then lay flat. And that's a good lesson to remember, if you're ever in the midst of a robbery, lay down on the floor."

She looked down at Jims who was tapping her arm. "Why?" he said. "Why lay down on the floor like that?"

"Well, if someone is going to shoot their gun, you don't want to be hit by the bullets, so you lie down and hope to stay out of the way. So these men demanded all the money in the vault. But Mr. Allan, the bank manager, was a veteran of the Great War, and he wasn't as alarmed as his customers were. So he dove under his desk and pulled out his own gun. And then there was a gunfight."

Ben gasped.

Julia looked at him for a second, then placed her hand on the nape of his neck. "It wasn't as bad as you might think. There were three men with six-shooters and they all emptied their guns, eighteen shots. And no one was hit."

Ben smiled weakly, and Will burst into laughter. "That was probably the best result you could have, with three men shooting wildly around the inside of a bank."

Julia nodded, grinning. "They were all probably pretty surprised. But the robbers were prepared, and they had backup guns, which they then pulled out. So Charlie Allan decided that discretion was the better part of valour, and he went into the vault and handed over the money. It was seven thousand five hundred dollars."

There was a collective gasp around the table at the size of the bank robbers' haul.

"Finish your dinner, Jims eat your turnip. So now the men ran, Mr. Ward and his accomplice. They jumped out a side window of the bank and took off. But they didn't have a very good escape plan. Because they simply ran.

"By then other people had gathered and they joined the chase. They were running and shooting at them as they went through the orchards south of town but the men didn't stop. The next day they were still searching for the robbers and they caught John Ward hiding in a ditch, hungry and cold, that's how everyone knows his name. And they recovered quite a bit of the money, over three thousand dollars. The other man was never caught, and no one knew what his name was. Mr. Ward never gave away the name of his accomplice. The mystery man. So that was the great bank heist of 1925."

Will chuckled. "That's quite a story, Julia. Who would have believed this little town had so much excitement going on?"

But the children were still caught up in the glamour and horror of the robbery. "What happened to the rest of the money?" Ollie wanted to know.

"I don't know. I doubt it's out there hiding in a ditch somewhere," Julia pointed out. "Everyone looked for the money and the second robber for quite a long time but they didn't find either. The other man probably had the rest of the money. So he escaped somewhere and kept it, it's probably all spent by now."

"That's a lot of money," said Maggie. "Think what you would do with three thousand dollars!"

Jims nodded enthusiastically.

"But Mama Julia, what did they do to Mr. Ward?" Ben wanted to know.

"Well, they took him to the jail in Nelson where the police have a detachment, and they had a trial there in the courtroom. Everyone who saw the event had to go to give evidence. You know, they told the judge what had happened. Then Mr. Ward was found guilty. I think he got eight or ten years in jail. That's a long time to spend in jail, so it certainly isn't worth robbing a bank for that."

Ben nodded. "But they didn't hang him, did they?"

Julia paused and searched his face. "No, Ben. They didn't hang him. He got some years in jail, and that tells you this was a serious crime. But they only hang someone for really serious events, where they kill someone. Isn't that right, Will?"

Will sipped his tea, studying Ben's face. "That's right. Hanging is very rare, and it always means the criminal has killed someone. It wouldn't be right to hang someone for a robbery."

Ben nodded, and snuck a quick glance at Ollie, who was keeping his head down, slowly forking his food into his mouth.

Will looked at Julia, his eyebrows raised, and she gave a faint shrug.

The doctor finished the last piece of cornbread on the plate and rose from the table. "Well, on a different topic, I have a box for you. It's come from my brother Ray in Winnipeg. I told you about his family of boys. There should be some useful clothing in here."

He set it on a bench in the kitchen and pulled a jackknife from his pocket. Cutting the string, he folded the knife again. "There you go, have a look."

The children quickly gathered round. Ben and Ollie watched wide-eyed as Julia pulled back the flaps of the box and lifted the protective sheaf of newspaper off the top. She began to unfold shirts, pants, a couple of jackets, some boots at the bottom. She laid them across the chair and straightened.

"I think they will be very useful," she said, eyeing the boys. "Too large for Jims, I'm afraid, but it looks like most of these will fit Ben and Ollie without much alteration. Nothing for you, I'm afraid, Mags. But you get enough from Betsy, anyway. Thank you so much, Will." She looked up at him with a soft smile. "This is very generous. You must give me their names and address so I can write a thank you note."

He was watching her intently. "You don't have to, I've thanked them for you, already."

Julia shook her head and went to get a piece of paper and pencil.

CHAPTER THIRTEEN

Will watched her walk away, thinking he liked every aspect of this woman. He'd heard her story, it didn't take much prodding in the village to find out about Julia.

Her husband Stephen was a carpenter and had worked in Creston and the surrounding area, mostly finishing carpentry and lathe work. He'd been held in high regard, both for the fine craft he produced and the man he was, clever and generous, a man of integrity. When he and Julia married, they'd bought the piece of land north of town and set up their household, with large gardens and a few animals to feed the soon growing family.

Then suddenly he died. Julia had been a widow since Jims was very small. She was left to fend for herself with two small children. And now she had four to feed. It was a demanding position to be in. Will hesitated to get involved, he'd just managed to extricate himself from complications of a love match before he arrived in Creston. His heart was still bruised.

~~*~~

The Creston Fall Fair was coming, and there'd obviously been a lot of talk at school about it. The children fussed round and round the event, discussing what there would be to see, who might be going.

Ollie wasn't sure what it was, and Maggie tried to explain. "It's really exciting," she said. "Everyone enters the contests. There's one for knitting and one for sewing. Sometimes there're contests for the best rabbits and the best goats. There's a contest for the strongest horses. Maybe even for ponies."

"We should put Prince in that one," Ollie interjected. "He's probably the best."

Maggie nodded soberly. "I bet he is. And then Mummy enters her preserves. She puts the garden vegetables in and her beets won last year." Her face shone with pride.

"There are things to eat, like pies and ice cream, and corn on the cob, and hotdogs. I don't think we eat those, but I'm not sure. There's horse riding and calf roping and other things, I forget."

"Wow, that's a lot," said Ben. "I wonder if we'll go to the Fair."

Jims nodded importantly. "We always go," he said. "Don't we, Maggie?"

~~*~~

Julia dropped off her contest entries on Friday, just as the Fair was being set up. Trucks with the rides had arrived in town the day before, and the midway was in the process of being erected on the far side of the fairgrounds. With Jims tagging along, she lugged her items into the big tent in the centre, where she found Betsy Whitaker surrounded by boxes and struggling, with her small daughter's help, to put a table together. Between them they managed to get all the rods inserted into the right places in the right sequence, and the table was complete, just as a crew of men came along to set up the rest of them.

Betsy wiped her forehead. "That's a relief. I can't believe they're that difficult to assemble." Her smile turned ironic as she watched the men snap several together and stack them against the wall. "Now, Julia, what have you got?"

"Not much this year." Julia lifted her baskets. "It's been pretty busy. Some preserves – strawberries, dill pickles, rhubarb chutney, plus potatoes and beets. Then I have an embroidered tablecloth, and a knitted shawl. That's enough, I guess."

She spread the items out as Betsy attached tags to everything. "I'm sorry I can't stay to help, Betsy. I have Heddie coming today instead of Monday and I need to get back."

And so on Saturday after the chores were done and breakfast out of the way, they set out for the Fair Grounds on the other side of the village, Prince pulling the cart. When they arrived, the pony was tied to the fence in a long line of horses and buggies. Ben and Ollie were visibly intimidated by the crowd, but Maggie eagerly leaped down with Jims right behind her.

"Okay, everyone," Julia called. "Let's keep together please. And remember, if we get separated in the crowd, we all meet at the entrance to the big tent. Look over there, does everyone see the big tent? Don't forget. Jims, hold my hand, please."

They dove into the crowd.

They started with the animal barns, and everything elicited comments. There was every type of chicken, banty, duck, goose, pheasant, a couple of swans, even an ostrich which Julia had never seen before except in pictures. The children watched the giant bird for a long time, trying to get their heads around the size and shape of it. Rabbits were plentiful, meat rabbits, fur rabbits.

They soon moved on to the larger animals—goats, sheep, cows, donkeys, horses, mules, oxen. In the tents there was every kind of handicraft, from carved leather to woven silk, wool to cotton, clay pottery, lathe work. The children were engrossed in the displays.

The interest quickly mounted when they came to the food. The pies and cakes, cookies and pastries elicited much discussion and finger poking, which kept her on her toes restraining the small hands.

Julia decided they must be hungry. They went back to the cart and sat up on the wagon seat to devour egg sandwiches and dill pickles, sliced carrots and cold tea from a jug.

From their higher vantage point on the wagon, the children eyed the midway, anticipation rampant on their faces. Julia felt around in her purse and found enough for tickets for at least a few rides.

She had fun. The expressions as each child was strapped into their seat, the shrieks of fear-mixed exhilaration had her in stitches. She didn't prefer most of the rides but went up with the whole gang on the Ferris Wheel, which was the most she was willing to experience. As they were getting off, amidst laugher and excited screams, Julia looked up to see the doctor at the foot of the ramp waiting for them.

The horde pounced on him, amid much discussion about which was the very best ride. Jims had been on the teacup, which whirled round and round, while moving mildly up and down. Ben, on the other hand, had gone by himself on the salt and pepper, because no one would go with him. He'd come off pale and greenish in the face, and was slowly recovering. He still maintained it had been more fun than anything.

Will took them to the food tent and bought them each a corn cob stuck on a stick. They sat on the bleachers and munched contentedly.

He glanced at Julia. "How has it been?"

She laughed. "It's been so much fun. You should have seen their faces on that whirly-gig machine. Absolute terror. Then when they got off, they all clamoured to try it again."

Will chuckled and looked at the mob of children. "What about ice cream sandwiches?"

Ben stalled, then put his corn down. "What's an ice cream sandwich?"

Will winked at Julia. "Finish your corn and we'll go see."

"They'll be sick," she protested.

"Well, you haven't had a good time at the Fair until you've gotten sick," quipped Will. Ollie laughed hysterically, and Ben

70

grinned at her. Maggie had already finished her corn and was standing impatiently for the rest to come. At the ice cream stall there was a long lineup. Two men behind the table were cutting blocks of ice cream into slices, and a third was sandwiching each slice between large square chocolate biscuits. No one complained about the wait and when everyone had received theirs, Will led them over to the tables arranged to the side of the tent. There was complete silence as the children began to eat.

Will took a large bite and spoke around it. "I don't believe I've heard such a quiet group. Now I know how to get their undivided attention."

Julia laughed. "Well, you have to admit, these are very good. I've never had this before."

He looked at her mouth, as she self-consciously wiped at a smudge of ice cream. "I think it's new this year," he said and glanced away. "Someone at the surgery talked about setting it up, so I figured it would be fun to try."

She nodded and licked at the melting cream trickling down the side of her biscuit, watching as his head swung back and his riveted gaze followed the path of her tongue. *Well,* she thought, *that's different. But really, how fascinating can I be, with four children constantly around me like a flock of chickens? Besides, he may be interested, but I'm not.*

Will suddenly leaped to his feet. "Who wants another one?"

The excited cries from the children drowned out her groan of dismay.

~~~**~~~

Part Three – The Visit

CHAPTER FOURTEEN

A letter arrived that Friday from the Butlers. Stephen's brother James was older by two years, and the pair of boys had been born and raised in Creston. Written in Sue-Ann's graceful style, the missive was full of news. Their daughter Susan was eight now, one year older than Maggie, and doing well at school. She had lots of friends and liked to have them stay over on weekends.

James was thriving in his writing career. He did two different columns for the Vancouver paper and also wrote for a smaller local weekly that had come after him for his known journalistic skills.

Sue-Ann was kept busy running the house and 'with my many committees.' The last paragraph mentioned an upcoming visit to Creston in the near future. "We can stay in the old house in town, Mum and Dad's house," wrote Sue-Ann. "That way we won't be any bother, and we'll be able to get together for a nice long visit. We hope to be there for a month or more so we don't want to put you out by staying all that time at the farm."

Julia had a burst of excitement at the idea of a visit, and an equally strong shot of concern over the house in town. She immediately wrote back to say how excited everyone was that they were going to see them soon. The house in town was rented, she added, but there was plenty of room for them to stay at the farmhouse.

She mentally made plans for sleeping arrangements. Even with Ben and Ollie here, there was still lots of space. Maggie and Jims could sleep in the spare room upstairs that she used for sewing and James and Sue-Ann would have their room. Susan could sleep in the sewing room with the children.

Sue-Ann's next letter sounded as if she were confused. "The house is rented? But we're coming for a month or more, so we'll need our own place. We can't possibly put you out for so long, and it will be inconvenient to be out of town. I'll want to visit with old friends. Mother sends her good wishes to some of her own friends who are still living there. It would just be best if we were at the house in town."

Julia felt a tightening in her chest that had nothing to do with the cold she felt coming on. How was she supposed to respond to that? Hadn't she been clear about the fact the house was not available?

She let a few days pass while she puzzled it over. Then she took up her pen with renewed determination. "I'm so sorry Sue-Ann. The house is truly rented out. I can't move the renters for a month so that you can stay there. They've been good tenants and they've been in the house for quite a while.

"But you're so welcome to stay with us. We have turned out Maggie's room, and cleaned in every corner. She and Jims will be quite comfortable in the sewing room, and we are just as excited as can be for your arrival. I know it will work out just fine. Susan can sleep in with you, or if she wants an adventure she can sleep with Maggie and Jims in the spare room."

She paused and added more ink to the nib. "And we still have Prince, he's seven years old but a great little pony. He's our transportation, so you will be able to go back and forth to town as much as you like. It will be so good to see you all."

The visit became the only topic of conversation, who would sleep where, what Susan would be like, just the fact of having another child in the house to play with. But Julia detected worry in the comments from Ben and Ollie.

One night at dinner, the topic resurfaced. When would everyone arrive? What would they think about the two boys? As she guessed, they were worried that James and Sue-Ann might somehow find out that they'd been passed off as Julia's nephews from the Butler side of the family. It was tricky, and they knew it.

Julia assured them that James and Sue-Ann were good people. They'd do the right thing. But secretly she worried as well. She would trust James with their lives. He was Stephen's older brother and made of the same stern stuff, full of fun and laughter, but absolutely reliable and loyal to his family. But Sue-Ann seemed different, petulant and demanding. Julia didn't know how she would react.

Determined to meet it head on, but only when necessary, she tried to put it out of her mind. Nor did she warn James before they arrived. After all, they had not been back to Creston often since they'd married and left town for Vancouver ten years ago. They came for Stephen's funeral. Even then, they didn't stay long.

Sue-Ann's parents left Creston for Vancouver shortly after James took his small family westward. Sue-Ann was their only child and they wanted to be near her and their granddaughter.

Then another letter arrived. In it, Sue-Ann suggested that if Julia couldn't move the tenants out for a one-month visit, perhaps they would stay longer. Would it be worthwhile if they were to come for a few months? It would just be more convenient for everyone if they were in town and not getting in the way on the farm.

Shocked and somewhat mortified by her sister-in-law's lack of sensitivity, Julia sat down to reply before her temper had a chance to cool. Her short note went straight to the point.

"The tenants are not to be moved under any circumstance. However, you and James won't be in the way on the farm, not at all. I can use your help. There's a lot of work to do, and the extra labour will be greatly appreciated."

It wasn't a very gracious letter, but her patience was at an end with this silly skirmish of suggestions. She tried to put it out of her mind.

~~*~~

That weekend Julia was working at the stove, putting her jars of canned tomatoes into the hot water bath, when a knock sounded at the door. She looked up to see her brother smiling at her from the doorway.

"Sam!" She leaped across the room and threw her arms around his neck, knocking his fedora hat askew. "I can't believe it's you! Oh, you look so much better than last time."

She stood back to gaze at him. He was still painfully thin but there was more colour in his face, more life.

She grinned in delight. "It's so good to see you. Come in and sit down, let me put the kettle on. Are you by yourself?"

She peeked past his tall body and spotted the others standing at the foot of the steps. "Annie! Mum! Sam, you brat, you could have told me they were here!"

She was down the steps in a flash, throwing her arms around the small family. Annie had the baby in her arms, and little Jasmine was holding fiercely to Grandma's hand.

"Come in, come in." Julia ushered them into the house, calling to Maggie to see who had just arrived.

Julia got them seated, and Annie settled the sleeping baby on the soft cushions of the old couch by the dining table. Maggie rushed down from upstairs, followed more slowly by Jims. Jasmine and Maggie stared at each other for a few moments but soon disappeared up the stairs, with girlish chatter coming through the heat vent from above.

Everyone at the kitchen table talked over each other. "How are you?"

"Why didn't you let me know you were coming?"

"Mum, you look well."

"Yes, the visit was sudden. We had the unexpected chance of a ride into Creston, and it's been so long since we saw you."

There was a small silence. Yes, a long time. First there had been Stephen's funeral. And the next time they saw each other, Sam had been diagnosed with Black Lung. He was laid off at the mine. Since then it had been a tough time for everyone.

Sam and Julia knew all about Black Lung. Their father had died from it when they were in their teens, just after Sam himself began work down in the mine. Their mother, Sarah, had barely had time to bury her husband let alone mourn him. She'd been too busy trying to keep her family together. As a new miner, Sam's income was not equal to what his father's had been and the mining company had been making motions to repossess the house.

Julia had gotten work in the mine office, and that had helped. Between them, they pulled together and had been able to keep their home. Now Sarah lived there with Sam, Annie and their two children. The baby was almost a year old, Sam the Third, as they jokingly called him. Jasmine was five and the apple of her father's eye.

Julia hustled around to tend to her canning, taking it out of the hot water bath and leaving it to cool on the wooden sideboard, putting another set of jars into the water. As she worked, she told her family about the additions to the household. Glancing out the window, she pointed to Ben and Ollie playing with Wagsy in the side yard. Then she lowered her voice to tell what she had pieced together of where the two boys had come from.

Everyone had an opinion. Sarah was concerned about the violence the boys had seen in their young lives, and the fact that Julia might be taking on more than she could handle, already being a single mother responsible for her own two children. Sam was more worried about the family, who they were and if they were coming after the boys.

Julia told them about the concocted story, that these boys were her nephews. She'd registered them at the school under Butler. There hadn't been a whisper of interest so far.

"After all James is almost never here," she said. "He's coming shortly for a visit, and I'll just play it by ear. But I couldn't pass them off as your sons, Sam, everyone in town knows you, and you're too close over there in Sparwood for that story to be believable."

Sam had heard rumours recently of families living in the back woods around Sparwood, running stills and selling moonshine. No one had talked of a black man, however. Ben obviously had a parent who was dark.

The talk died abruptly as the boys came in from playing, Wagsy trailing behind. Julia introduced Ben and Ollie and the boys sat quietly, watching but not participating in the conversation, even when Sam tried to draw them out.

~~~**~~~

CHAPTER FIFTEEN

With Sarah's help, Julia produced dinner, and as they seated themselves around the dining room table, heads were bowed and Sam said grace.

"Thank you, Lord, for my family, and for the chance to visit with them. Thank you for each person around the table here tonight. In Jesus' name, Amen." It was a simple prayer but Julia felt great gratitude for the comfort of her family.

Seated beside Sarah, Ollie became fascinated with the idea of a grandmother. "I have a friend who has one," he said, as Sarah cut his meat into bite-sized pieces. "But I don't."

Sarah laughed. "Well," she said, "you could have me for a Grandma, just like Jims and Maggie. Would you like that?"

Ollie nodded, satisfied for the moment. But then he questioned her. "What do grandmas do besides cut up your meat?"

That produced a lively conversation between the children. Jasmine had a lot to contribute as she lived with her grandmother, but Maggie was not to be outdone. The list they produced was long—tie your shoes, brush your hair, wash your face, cook your dinner, feed the dog, do the wash, read you stories, sing you songs. Sarah was in stitches.

Ollie was fixated by the idea of reading stories, so Sarah promised to read them one that night.

After dinner, the girls asked permission and got out the gramophone. Maggie put on her record of Snow White and the Seven Dwarfs, and the children gathered round, trying to sing along with the tunes as they looked through the large pages of the book that came with the record. They played it over and over, till Julia mentioned in an undertone to her mother that she might have to break it, even if she was the one who had bought the record in the first place.

Over tea, Julia grilled her brother. "How are you actually feeling?

Sam grimaced. "Better, I think. I'm still wheezing."

She nodded. "Yes, I can hear that. But otherwise, how has it been?"

His gaze tracked Annie as she changed the diaper on a sleepy baby. "I think it's been good. I've put on weight. Not a lot, but moving in the right direction. I've been able to cut firewood and split it, if I take it easy and rest often. Annie does a lot, too much really."

Julia took his hand. "You look better. You sound better, more optimistic. What does the doctor say?"

He shrugged. "Haven't seen him in a while. Not sure what he'd have to say."

Ben had come over to sit on the bench beside Julia. As he leaned on her arm, he looked at Sam across the table. "We have a doctor," he offered. "He'd listen to your heart, if you wanted him to."

Sam smiled. "Thank you, Ben. That's a nice idea."

Julia laughed and ruffled his woolly head. "Yes, he would. He listens to your heart, doesn't he?"

Ben nodded and blushed a dull red.

~~*~~

The Grants could only stay two days. Their ride would stop to take them home to Sparwood early the following morning.

It was a school day and Maggie thought it was grossly unfair that they had to attend class. But Julia was firm, they'd never get an education if they stayed home from school every time there was company. There'd be plenty of time to play when they got back and she promised to pick them up early. Jims, on the other hand was ecstatic. He finally had a playmate at home when the other children left.

Julia had a good day with her family. Sam did some repair work on the barn with Jims underfoot, and the women put on a baking frenzy that produced bread, cake, and crackers which could be stored away for later use. The baby was good as gold. Sam the Third was a good natured little chap who hadn't started walking yet, but could crawl at speed anywhere, then pull himself up to grab stuff down with an astonishingly long reach. Julia had a lot of fun watching him maneuver around the house getting into much more trouble than she would have imagined possible.

Julia left Jims at home with her mother and Annie, and took Sam to town in the cart when she went to pick up the children. She stopped at the Doctor's office. Sheila, the nurse was there, and she fit them in to see Will. Julia introduced her brother, and left Sam to be checked over.

When they came out, Will looked grave. "Thank you, Sam, for stopping in. I'll get back to you with that information as soon as I can." He shook Sam's hand, and smiled at Julia before heading back into the clinic.

"Well," Julia demanded, "what did he say? Are you getting better? Can you get better, or do you just have to live with it?" Her eyes were sparkling. "Honestly Sam," she hounded him as they climbed back into the cart. Julia tugged the reins and backed Prince into the road, before heading across town to the school. "You're as close mouthed as a…. Why, I don't know what!"

Sam burst out laughing. "Julia, you never change. You're so busy fixing everybody, I'm surprised you have any time for yourself. Here I am in town for two days and you drag me off to see the doctor."

He gave her an exasperated look that slowly softened. "Dr. Stoffard said that my lungs sound fair, not good. He could hear the fluid in them. I can expect to have continued improvement over the next couple of years and then I'll just have to live with it. Over time, I might recover most of my strength. He thought there might be a new treatment and he'll find out about it and write to me. He said it was good that I didn't have too many years in the mine, not like Dad. Obviously, it's an advantage that I left the mine so young. Starving to death has some merit to it after all," he added bitterly.

"Oh, Sam. I'm sorry. I always put my foot into it, don't I? You haven't starved, but you could certainly use a bit more weight. You know, you and Annie and Mum could come and live with us. It would be a bit crowded, but we've lived in worse, haven't we? It'd be a lot easier in some ways. I wouldn't have to drag Jims out every day when I go to town to get the kids. I wouldn't even have to go to town everyday to get the kids. Because there would be someone else who could do it sometimes."

She glanced at her brother. He was staring off into the distance, as if he couldn't even hear her. She bit her lip and pulled the cart over to the side of the road in front of the school. She put her hand on his thigh. "I'm glad you're getting better, Sam, even a little bit. This doctor is good and he knows the latest stuff, not like old Doc Farley. Maybe he really can help you. If there's something out there to find, he'll find it."

Sam swung his head slowly around. "I know, Julia. And thanks for the doctor visit. I haven't seen a doctor since I left the mine. I haven't been able to afford it."

Just then the school room door burst open. Ben and Ollie were first out, heading straight for the cart. Maggie was right behind them.

At the dinner table that night Sam told them about the Relief Camps that the government was setting up in western Canada for the unemployed. The men would be housed and fed and given work. They'd be paid twenty cents a day. There was to be a project near Sparwood to clear land and deliver logs to a nearby sawmill.

The men would produce firewood with the leftover wood which would also be sold.

"Maybe it's a way to help," Sam pondered doubtfully. 'I just don't know. Can you imagine, if a married man had to go to one of these camps? It doesn't solve the problem of how his family would be fed, does it? But I guess if a man's single, at least he can eat and be housed. And he won't get physically weak or mentally discouraged from not working. Maybe it's a good thing, in the short term anyway."

They were interrupted by the sound of a mad scramble in the parlour accompanied by fierce yowls from Cat. At that moment, the animal emerged from the parlour with a large mouse in her jaws. She jerked her head forward and got a better grip, parading proudly into the kitchen.

Sarah laughed, and Julia smiled weakly. "Good kitty, good kitty. Here, take it outside," and she opened the door as Maggie and Sam got behind the animal and herded her onto the verandah.

Julia closed the door firmly. "Well, that's a first. I hope it just ran in while the door was open, rather than came in through a hole somewhere. I haven't heard or seen any sign of mice in the house."

"Don't worry," said Sam. "I'll look around in the basement tomorrow morning to see if there are any signs. The boys will help me, won't you?" The boys nodded enthusiastically. Jims seemed taken by the idea, and leaned on Sam's leg as they talked.

Her heart contracted in her chest. He had barely known his father before he was taken from them. And Uncle Sam lived far enough away that they didn't see him often.

She smiled at her brother. "Good old Cat. She's a very accomplished hunter. I see her with mice all the time, out of the barn or shed, and around the hen house. I can't imagine having to feed her, because she eats so well on her own. Although," and here she looked at Ollie, "sometimes we do give her a bit of milk." He blushed, and gave her a shy smile. Ollie had a soft spot for Cat.

The evening was fun filled. Sam was feeling pretty good and he ended up wrestling with all four boys on the floor, albeit gingerly, before Annie picked up Sam the Third and left the rest of them to it. Ben seemed awkward at first, but he soon got into it and tried, with help from Jims and Ollie, to pin Sam down. Sam flipped them all, and pinned the three of them under him, holding them down till they cried uncle.

The house was full to overflowing, with pallets on the floor, little bodies bookended on the sofa in the parlour. It was a good feeling and ended all too soon.

Their ride appeared the next morning, a big old truck pulling a wagon that was headed north, back to Sparwood, at the same time that Mr. Morris, headed south, stopped at the gate to pick up the children for school.

Pandemonium ensued, with many long hugs and heartfelt goodbyes. Jasmine and Maggie both cried, and Julia couldn't seem to let go of Mum, holding on until she realized she was probably strangling her. When the noise and confusion died down, Julia and Jims were left by themselves in the otherwise empty house. She sat down in sudden exhaustion and cried her eyes out, with Jims on her knee patting her hand.

~~~**~~~

CHAPTER SIXTEEN

That afternoon, Sue-Ann's latest letter arrived at the post office. She informed them that Susan would not be coming on the visit, after all. She would stay at Granny's to make sure she didn't miss school. Perhaps she could come another time.

This caused a huge letdown among the children. Maggie was inconsolable. She'd been so excited to think there would be another little girl to play with. Having Jasmine there just whet her appetite for some female playmates in the midst of all these boys

The day of the visit arrived. In the late morning, Julia and the children were waiting at the station when the train pulled in. Amid all the smoke and noise, she spotted James alighting from a rail car. He looked almost foreign in his long tailored wool coat and fedora hat, his polished leather shoes.

But he also looked so familiar. She'd forgotten how much he was like Stephen, the same tall, lanky frame, the shock of wavy auburn hair as he took his hat off, even the tilt to his head. There was a sudden catch in her throat and tightness in her chest at the impact of the memory.

She ran forward to throw her arms around him. He grinned, and hugged her back with his long arms. "Julia, you're looking well," he grinned at her. "I hadn't forgotten what a lucky find

Stephen had in you, and such a beauty too." Julia felt herself blushing and swatted at his arm. "You're just as handsome as Stephen was, and almost as charming," she said. James laughed again and turned back to the door of the car to offer his hand to his wife. "Here's Sue-Ann."

Julia smiled up at Sue-Ann and waited for her to descend the stairs. Her outfit was astonishing, and Julia suddenly felt dowdy in her serviceable dress and coat. Sue-Ann wore a beautiful cherry-coloured wool suit, shiny brass buttons marching down the front of the jacket. Her navy overcoat was slung over her arm, and her hat was of rich crimson velvet with a wide black satin band. Her shoes were like nothing Julia had ever seen, with buckles and raised stitching that matched her hand bag.

Sue-Ann's smile seemed strained, but slowly warmed as she took in her sister-in-law, with arms out waiting to give her a hug. "Oh, Julia," she said. "It really has been too long." She returned the hug with warmth. "And where are the children?" Her eyes looked beyond to search the platform.

Julia pulled back and turned. "Here they are," she said gaily. She waved them over. "This is Maggie, look how big she is. And Jims, four years old now. Haven't they grown?" She pulled them forward. "And these are Ben and Ollie, my nephews." She took the boys' hands and led them forward for introductions. "Benjamin, Ollie, this is James Butler, and Sue-Ann, his wife. James is my husband's brother. And oh, how you look like him, James. You just gave me such a start. It's been too long, but the same hair and smile. I'm just so glad to see you both."

And that's how Julia passed off the boys, without time for anyone to make a comment or wonder why they were living with her. She hustled Sue-Ann down the platform, as James went off to get their luggage. It turned out they had two large cases and some smaller bags that wouldn't fit in the pony cart along with all the people. As it was, Ben and Ollie had volunteered to walk behind the cart. Poor Prince simply couldn't be expected to haul half the town home, as Maggie put it.

In the end, James hired Marcus with his car to bring the cases and Sue-Ann out to the house after he had finished his taxi service around town. Sue-Ann looked relieved that she wasn't going to have to ride in the cart to the farmhouse.

And so they headed home, Prince moving along at a steady pace, Julia driving. Maggie and Jims were on the seat with her, Ollie on the tailgate with the smaller bags, and James and Ben walked behind. Julia heard them talking as they went. She hoped Ben would keep his head, and not choke up on any questions James asked.

When they got home, the house was still warm and Julia stoked up the pot belly stove with more wood, and put the kettle on the gas burner. She sent the kids off to change out of their good clothes and sat James at the kitchen table while she began to lay out sandwiches for their lunch.

James looked bemused as he watched her work. "This makes me think of home with Mum and Dad before Stephen and I left," he said, glancing around at the kettle humming on the burner and the old dining table across the room with the six chairs, more battered now, tucked against it. "Mum was always working in the kitchen, making bread, making soup, making dinner. It seemed she never stopped. What are you making there?"

"Just roast beef sandwiches," Julia answered. "We had a roast Friday night and this will take care of the last of it. I'll add pickles and some coleslaw and that will do for lunch. Are you hungry? I know the kids will be in here any minute looking for something to eat."

She glanced at him as she worked. "They're like bottomless pits. If one isn't going through a growth spurt than another one is. I spend half my week planning ahead to make sure there's enough food in stock to keep them going. Oh, I'm so glad you're here, James. It's really good to see you."

Sue-Ann arrived just as Julia put lunch on the table. The children rushed outside to watch Marcus pull into the yard, with the two large cases tied on top of his Model T and Sue-Ann seated primly in the passenger seat. They wrestled the cases into the house, and Marcus helped James carry them up the stairs and into Maggie's room.

Sue-Ann felt faint and sat by the pot bellied stove to warm her while the lunch was laid out in the dining room. Under Julia's direction, Ben and Maggie quickly set place settings and pulled out chairs. The table was full. Maggie and Jims shared the piano bench at one end and that left enough chairs for everyone. The sandwiches and coleslaw salad were passed around. Julia opened a new jar of her dill pickles and saw Ollie's satisfied grin. They seemed to be his absolute favourite.

As they settled, Julia and the children held hands for grace and the guests joined them. As James ate, he commented on the furniture. He recognized the piano from his parents' home, and the large framed painting of the dogs, terriers, that had graced the entrance to his folk's place all the years he was growing up. Julia pointed out the picture of Stephen on the bureau, and even the platter that the sandwiches sat on that had been his mother's.

"We did sort of take over what was left in the house, James. But if you notice anything that you want to take home with you, then you're welcome to it. I know what it's like to see your mother's things. It is a comfort to have them around."

James smiled, but Sue-Ann frowned and shook her head. "No, really, Julia. We have everything we need. Thank you, though." Sue-Ann picked at the food on her plate, then excused herself to go to her room for a rest.

Later, Julia sat with James over a cup of tea at the cleared table and listened to the chatter as the children washed and dried the dishes from lunch. She smiled to herself. It was good to have them here. James gave her such a feeling of home and comfort, if a pang of heartache, too.

"Well, what do you think?' he said, smiling.

"You remind me so much of Stephen," she murmured. "And as time goes by, I don't think of him as often. I've been so busy, and with the boys here, I don't dwell on the loss as much. I feel guilty in a way," she admitted, tears starting in her eyes. "I mean, I don't want to think of Stephen all the time, and feel sad. But I don't want to forget him either."

"You won't forget him," James said, patting her hand. "Look at little Jims. He's already looking so much like his dad." They both watched the children for a few minutes. "And Maggie looks like you, doesn't she? With her wide eyes, and serious little chin."

Julia laughed. "How is Susan?" she asked. "We were so hoping to see her. I can tell you, Maggie was in a deep despondency when she learned she wasn't coming. She's inundated with boys right now. Is Susan well? Does she like school? Who does she look like? We haven't seen her in forever, it seems."

James sobered as he gazed at her. "Susan is well, she spends a lot of time at Granny's. She's very fond of her, and Sue-Ann is busy with other things a lot of the time." He paused awkwardly. "And she likes it there. So she spends the night a couple of times a week, and that gives Sue-Ann a break."

He took a deep breath and looked around determinedly. "On a different topic, Ben and Ollie seem like fine boys. They're a bit shy, not too talkative. How long do you think they'll stay with you? It must be a great burden to be looking after more children when you're on your own like this."

Julia looked at the boys to avoid looking at James. She'd always been greatly fond of Stephen's older brother and she didn't want to lie to him. But at the same time, she had to protect these young men if she could. "Well, I hope they stay for a while," was all she said. "My brother Sam is quite sick, he has the Black Lung. You remember him, James. He used to visit often, and he was at our wedding. Now he's too sick to work. Annie, his wife, is at her wit's end caring for him and the younger ones."

This much at least was true, and Julia found she could look at James as she explained. "Annie has two little ones, a boy and girl who are one and five and her hands are full. They were just here a couple of weeks ago, a surprise visit. And Sam is actually looking better. He doesn't have much energy, and you can still hear him wheeze, although he says he's mending."

"As for these boys, they are such a big help, and very willing to do whatever I ask. They are just the best boys."

Ben looked over at her just then and gave his shy smile as if he'd heard her words. And she beamed back at him.

"But what about you, James? How are you? It's nice that you've taken the time to come for a visit. But I wonder that you would come for so long, a month or two, Sue-Ann mentioned in her letter, and not bring Susan. What is this trip really about?"

She watched the colour come and go in his cheeks. "Don't get me wrong, I love having you here. I'd visit you in Vancouver if it was possible. But there must be something that has brought you suddenly back to the old town where you grew up. Sue-Ann doesn't look thrilled to be here," she added doubtfully.

"It was actually Sue-Ann's idea to come," James stated in a slow drawl. "And to be fair, the trip has worn her out. She'll be better tomorrow, I'm sure. It's just that things are not so great in the big town right now. I'm still working but my earnings aren't enough to keep us in the way that Sue-Ann would like to be able to live."

His mouth firmed. "She thought if we moved back to Creston, I could continue to write from here, and it would be cheaper to live in a small town. We could sell our house and move into the folk's home on Maple Street here. Maybe live a little cheaply for a while, just until the economy picks up again. It has to pick up at some point, doesn't it? Everyone keeps predicting soon, but soon doesn't seem to come." He ran an impatient hand through his hair and it sprang back in waves, just the way Stephen's used to.

Julia watched him for a moment without saying anything. Finally she asked, "You know the folk's house is rented, don't you? I told you that in my letters."

James nodded and looked away. "She thought you could get rid of the renters and we could live there for a while," he said.

Julia glanced down as heat filled her chest. "I could, of

course," she said. "And if you really have nowhere to live, I'll do that. But they're nice folks, a husband and wife and little boy just a year younger than Jims. And they don't deserve to be moved if there's another alternative."

She gave him a level look. "And I can't afford to let you have it rent-free, James. If you need a free place to live you're welcome to live with us here. I could certainly use the extra pairs of hands around the place, and to have a man here would be a God send. I mean, when it comes to the heavy work I have to get someone in each time, and it costs money. But with Sue-Ann to help with the garden and the laundry and baking and all," she paused meaningfully as she saw James grimace, but plowed on, "and you in the yard and field, it would certainly make a difference. And Maggie would kiss your boots for bringing her cousin Susan to live with us."

When James didn't reply, Julia gathered her resolve. "But the rent from the house in town pays for the taxes on both places, the house and the farm, and it gives me the bit of extra cash I need for things like shoes for the kids. It's my income just like your writing is yours. We wouldn't even be able to keep the farm without that rent."

~~~**~~~

CHAPTER SEVENTEEN

I know, Julia." James patted her arm. "And I know that Stephen and I divided things fairly when Mum and Dad died. I wanted the shares in the railway, and neither I nor Sue-Ann had any interest in keeping the house. Stephen took it and I thought he got the worst of the deal.

"I tried to tell Sue-Ann that it wasn't reasonable to expect you to get rid of your tenants, but she had it in her head that she could come back here and be the big girl in town. She'd be coming from the city, to this little place and she could live in the folk's house and still keep her head up."

James fidgeted in the chair. "The reality is she might have to have her mother move in with us, to help pay the mortgage, and perhaps even take a boarder. And then she could do some economies like grow a bit of garden and make clothes rather than buy them, things that you have always done, Julia. Perhaps you could show her how it works. Maybe she's just forgotten." For a moment, he looked very tired.

Julia stood with sudden determination. "James," she said, "why don't you go upstairs and rest? I think you and Sue-Ann must both be exhausted. I'm going to check on the children, and get them out to gather the eggs and feed the hens. We'll finish the chores, then we can all have a bit of a break, until dinner. Off you go, and I'll call you in a couple of hours."

She hustled out to the kitchen, taking care not to let him see her confusion. The rest of the afternoon passed quietly. Tired from all the excitement, the children were content to sit in the parlour and read, or in Maggie's case, write a letter to her cousin Susan about her great disappointment that she had not come with her parents to visit.

Julia stuffed the chicken and put it into the oven to slow roast. An hour later she added potatoes and parsnips in the pan around the bird. It would be a simple supper, with some cranberry sauce from the pantry, green beans from her jars and tomatoes from the coldframe. She'd made a cake and it was iced and waiting on the pantry shelf. The children had checked it several times already to make sure it was still okay.

When Sue-Ann came to the table, she'd changed into a day dress that was less flamboyant and actually suited her better. Her hair was pinned up at the sides and hung down on her shoulders and she almost looked like the young woman who'd been at Julia's wedding those years ago.

~~*~~

It settled into a good visit as the awkwardness slowly faded and the old familiarity reasserted itself. The children were back to school the next day. Mr. Morris picked them up as usual in the morning, and Prince pulled the cart to pick up all five children, Julia's three and the two Morrises, in the afternoon.

After the first day, James made it his job to go in every afternoon with Prince to the school. He'd leave the house a little early to have time to look around town and call on people he knew, often taking Jims with him, which delighted the little boy no end. He became James' shadow, closely followed by Ollie. Ben was still leery and stayed clear of James just to be on the safe side.

It gave the women time together. Sue-Ann began to relax and Julia decided it was time to test her mettle. She set her to work making bread and doing the laundry with the new-fangled washing machine. Sue-Ann worked reluctantly at first, but soon got the bit between her teeth and dug into the chores.

She went with Julia on the morning rounds, feeding Prince and Daisy Mae, even trying to milk the goat, although she gave up with a laugh halfway through and gave the pail over to Julia to finish. They both returned to the house with smiles on their faces. She managed to feed and water the chickens and fight off the old rooster to collect the eggs, although she arrived back at the house quite breathless after that episode.

After a few days, calm descended on the household, and Julia felt she had her old friends and loved ones back again. They were comfortable and affectionate with each other and the tension eased.

That night Julia sent the kids to bed early and pulled out a bottle of dark rum that she kept in the back of the closet. The adults gathered in the parlour and she turned the gas fire on to ward off the chill of the evening. She squeezed a couple of oranges and added water to the juice, pouring three drinks and carrying them in on a tray.

She laughed as she passed the glasses around. "I have to be honest with you. Stephen bought this rum. Can rum go bad?"

"Rum can never go bad," intoned James, who took a sip. "Perfect, absolutely perfect. But I must say, Julia, this is a bit shameful, that the bottle is still half full after four years. You're going to have to do a bit better than that. I prescribe a drink every Sunday evening, for medicinal purposes only, of course. And don't skip even one week or the medicine won't work."

"You might be right," she admitted. "I've been exceedingly serious these last few years." She took her apron off and laid it across the back of the sofa. "It might be time to ease up a little, relax instead of being so darned determined to get everything done that's on my list. The list is so long it doesn't leave much time for anything else."

Sue-Ann nodded. "I know what you mean, and yes, it's

probably time to ease up. I think I need to, no reason why you shouldn't too." She gave a rueful smile. 'I've been a bit of a pain lately, I'm sure James would agree anyway."

James gave her a tender smile. "No, no, my love. You're the best wife a man could hope for, and a wonderful mother to our little Susan."

Tears sprang to Sue-Ann's eyes as she looked at her husband. "Thank you," she breathed. "Thank you."

Julia rose to turn on the lamp on the mantel to dispel the gathering gloom.

Sue-Ann stared at the fixture. "I don't think you had electricity out here the last time I was in town."

Julia settled back on the cushions. "The electricity was strung along North Road from town a few years before Stephen died. He did all kinds of renovations to make it work in the house.

"They already had lights in town most places, the Village Hall and the Fire Hall for example. The hospital, too. They tried to get it all around the village, but there wasn't enough power from the power plant. The mill has power of course."

They all nodded at that. The mill had its own power supply, a generator that ran off the stream it was built on. "And the curling club. It had power as well, mostly just used in the winter time. But," said Julia, "They built a dam on the Goat River and put in power for the whole village. It was very exciting. Stephen couldn't wait."

Julia smiled whimsically. "It's nice to have electricity, but I often think I liked the soft light of the oil lamps, too. The evening would slow once I lit the lamp and we'd wind down the day. It was soothing."

James grinned. "You make it sound very romantic, Julia. But we don't buy it. It's extremely nice to have electric lights. I remember the Goat River. Stephen and I used to go down it with our friends, riding logs. Stephen was a phenomenal swimmer and I was a close second, if I do say so myself." He tensed his muscles to show his bicep. They all laughed. "Still, power in the whole village certainly makes a big difference. It might mean you'll get a new hotel."

The Creston Hotel had burned down a few years before in a spectacular fire, leaving the downtown area without accommodation for travelers. "That fire was incredible," she said. "Stephen had just come home for dinner when we heard a great boom, and couldn't figure out what it was. It was the hotel roof blowing off in the blaze. As it got dusk we could see the glow in the sky, so we put Prince back in the traces and went into town to see what was happening."

James took a sip of his rum. 'I remember the reports in the *Vancouver Sun* of the great fire. It was really something. The hotel had been there practically since the railway came through in 1898."

"It was called Seventh Siding, then, instead of Creston, remember?" Sue-Ann interjected. "That was the number of the railway siding. The seventh siding. Not very colourful," she added. "I'm glad they changed it."

"Well, old Mr. Long wouldn't have been pleased about the fire," said James. "He was one busy man, into a bit of everything in the old days. Although he was used to hard times. If I remember my local history, while he was busy building the Creston Hotel, he lost all his fixtures for it in the fire at Ainsworth, where he was storing the furniture for the new hotel. He must have been a real optimist to keep on with the construction."

"Or desperate," said Sue-Ann, and they all laughed, then fell silent. They knew about desperate, each of them in their own way. "So what do people do now," Sue-Ann said, "When they come to town and need a place to stay?"

"Well," began Julia, "if they don't have any kind-hearted relatives to bunk in with."

Sue-Ann laughed, a bit shamefaced.

"Actually, Luke's mum, Mamie Harrison has taken over the bunkhouse behind the CPR train station and turned it into a kind of boarding house. Some people just stay overnight, others stay for months. It's a bit chilly in the winter in the upstairs rooms, but

Luke has been working on it, putting insulation in the upper walls, and his mother runs it with his help."

"I just saw Luke today in town when I stopped at the store." James looked pleased. "He and Stephen were such good friends, and Luke was always a clever fellow. He'd be a good one to be in business with. He knows everyone, what they need, how they think, and he can find just about anything."

Julia felt herself grow warm. "That's true. He's been so good to me and the kids since Stephen died."

Her voice caught, but she went on, smoothing her skirt with her hand. "Well, I've wanted to broach an awkward subject with you, and I'm determined that now is the time."

~~~**~~~

CHAPTER EIGHTEEN

J ulia leaned to top up their drinks from the tray.

"Please don't, Julia." Sue-Ann pulled a face. "I apologize for how I've been. I know I've been demanding. It was unforgiveable."

But Julia held her hand up. 'Not that Sue-Ann, and you have definitely not been unforgiveable. I just had to explain what the rent means to our household and you haven't mentioned it since." She smiled at her sister-in-law, and cleared her throat. "I want to tell you something that you may have already guessed. But I need your complete confidence and your help in this. It is a very touchy matter."

Her guests looked mystified. They exchanged a glance and James said, "You have our word on it, we won't speak of this, whatever it is, to anyone." He gazed steadily at her face. "You can trust us."

"I know I can, and that's why I'm going to tell you this story. The only other person in town who knows any of this is the doctor, Dr. Stoffard." And she launched into her story of Ben and Ollie. As she talked their eyes grew wide and their faces still, until there was no sound in the room but Julia's voice. She told about the shivering little bodies, ill from malnutrition and abuse, of the old and new marks on their backs and buttocks, of their inability to even tell her what had happened.

Then she came to the crux of the matter, passing the boys off as nephews, Butler nephews.

"But I thought you said they were Sam's nephews," James protested.

"Well, I did and I didn't," said Julia. 'I said Sam has been very sick and Annie has two little ones to look after. I didn't want to lie to you, James, but I didn't know what to do. Sam lives in Sparwood, and there are people here who know him. I couldn't pass them off as Grants, or relatives of Annie. I'd be found out, and that could put us all in danger." She looked at them pleadingly, her gaze moving from one face to the other.

"I thought it was safest if I pretended they were Butlers. For all I know, your father had brothers, maybe they could be from that branch of the family. I had to invent something, they're very afraid. They have little security, I'm it. They're just starting to trust me, that I mean it when I say they're my boys now. It's been a big adjustment."

She saw the growing acceptance on their faces. "Ollie still cries in his sleep at night. Ben keeps his fear hidden, he's silent and watchful. They've only been here a few months. Not a long time to get accustomed to being loved and cared for." Her voice broke.

Sue-Ann rose and moved across the room to kneel against her legs and put her arms around her. "And you've been so alone, Julia, while I have been famously self-absorbed. I'm ashamed. Don't cry, please don't cry. You're so brave, my darling, and they're very lucky boys to have found you. James, say something. Surely there's a branch of the Butler family those boys could be from."

James stirred and rose. He settled beside Julia on the sofa, and put his arm around her shoulders. "I'm humbled," he said. "Julia, Stephen couldn't have found a better life partner and mother for his children if he'd looked all over the country. But he didn't, he stopped looking the minute he met you. I'm just sorry that you had each other for such a short time." He squeezed her against his side and put his other hand out to his wife, taking her hand in his. They sat there for moment in silence.

He gave a sigh. "Now," he said, sounding determined. "As I see it, we need to do two things. We need to invent a history for these boys so they can stay as part of the family." He paused as he considered that, then went on. "And we need to identify who their real family is so we can somehow nullify their potential threat. Don't forget your own safety, Julia."

"Well," said Julia. "I definitely need my drink now." She laughed a bit shakily.

"You know," said James, "Dad had a brother. They grew up in Buffalo, New York. Now and then there'd be a letter from him. Dad used to make cracks about how the Butler boys rode again, when he was talking about Stephen and me. He told stories of their horses and the antics they got up to. I think his brother was quite a rider. At any rate, there's no reason these boys couldn't come from that branch of the family."

Julia looked hopeful, but Sue-Ann said, "But why does one of them look so dark? And how did they get here? Don't forget they didn't arrive at the station where everyone would have seen. Everyone and everything arrives by train in this village, and the whole population turns out to see it."

They thought on that for a few minutes. "You're right about the train," said James, "but that isn't the only way they could have gotten here."

"We need more rum," said Julia.

Sue-Ann snorted, and rose to her feet. "Let me help. There's a better way to mix rum, I'll show you." She led the way to the kitchen. "When I don't have anything to mix it with, I squeeze a lemon and add strong tea, and it tastes great. A little sugar helps too. Here's some cold tea, readymade. And half a lemon left. Voila."

When they returned to the parlour, James had wound up the Victrola and was placing a record on the turntable. "This was Mum's favourite," he said, as the strains of the Viennese Waltz filled the air.

"Oh, I hardly ever play those," sighed Julia. "Isn't this delightful." They all sat and listened to the music, sipping their drinks.

"We don't have to solve it all tonight," said James softly, when the music was finished. "It's enough that we know what the situation is, and we can think on how to handle it. I had noticed about Ben, and he's very guarded. When you say he watches for both of them, I believe it. Ollie will talk and come with me out to the barn, but Ben hangs back. And his looks are different. That dark skin and kinky hair points to some Negro blood in his background."

"Yes. When I first cut his hair I couldn't believe how thick it was. It took me a while to get used to it so I could cut it properly. But it makes him a very handsome boy."

Sue-Ann nodded. "Yes, for sure he is. Ollie too, for that matter, with his freckles and the red hair. It's hard to see that they're brothers, but they certainly act like it. You can't drive a toothpick between them, they're so close."

James laughed. "That, too. Ollie has hero worship for Ben, which is nice. I remember that myself, and I miss it, miss that closeness." He cleared his throat awkwardly.

"But I don't see any reason why the two can't be Butler boys. There's a branch to the family, wherever it is, and it makes it a perfectly good story. It's happening all over the country. Children get help from whatever family can lend a hand."

Julia slept better that night than she had for months. It seemed in sharing the story, she'd shared the burden. It was not all on her shoulders now, there would be help in how to handle the situation. Her concerns about the boys were diminished.

Ben and Ollie would be okay. They just had to find the way to achieve it.

~~~**~~~

CHAPTER NINETEEN

D r Stoffard arrived just as Prince and the wagon were pulling into the yard. Julia heard the men's voices outside and went to investigate. "Mum Julia, Dr. Spofford is here," Ollie cried, running up the steps. He was always excited when the doctor arrived, it tickled him no end to answer the endless questions the doctor asked and open his mouth to be examined each time. Julia corrected him. "Stofford," she said, "it's Dr. Stofford," but Ollie didn't recognize the difference.

The doctor left his car parked in the drive, while the men put the wagon away and trotted Prince into his stall. Julia heard heavy boots on the verandah and the door opened to admit a swarm of people, with Jims and Maggie chattering the fastest, walking backward to address the doctor.

Julia set another plate at the table for dinner. She put the coffee pot on the burner to make a fresh pot. "Did you meet everyone, Will?" she asked. "This is Sue-Ann, my sister-in-law, and her husband, my brother-in-law, James. They're visiting from Vancouver."

William Stofford inclined his head to Sue-Ann. "Very pleased to meet you, ma'am, call me Will. James and I met at the school. Ben and Ollie introduced me as a matter of fact."

There was much jostling in the kitchen. The doctor examined

each of the children who lined up like birds perched on the bench, as he explored every mouth, the glands in the neck and behind the ears. He poked and prodded, asking numerous questions that Ben took extremely serious and Jims giggled while answering. In the end, all were pronounced healthy. After each little heart had been listened to with great concentration, and each pulse taken, the doctor put his black bag away and settled down to cup of coffee and a chat at the kitchen table.

Julia asked the children to change their clothing, and gave them each a handful of nuts and raisins and a glass of milk before sending them out to do their chores before dinner. It was Maggie's turn to gather the eggs and she needed an older helper, given the ferocity of the bantam rooster in the pen. Sue-Ann volunteered.

Will stayed for dinner. He'd seen Matt York in the village the day before, and they'd discussed a boy's hockey team. "I remember Matt," said James. 'He was a fireman when I was a kid. I was always impressed with that. It looked so exciting."

"'He's the fire chief, now," Julia said. "We have about twenty members on the fire brigade. All volunteer except the chief. Pretty good, isn't it, for a little village like ours? He was chief when the Creston Hotel burned. I remember him at the site, shouting orders and trying to keep it from spreading to other buildings."

"When was that?" asked Will.

"Almost four years ago," Julia said. "The heat was incredible. They were busy using buckets to water down the side of the general store, to keep it from catching fire, and the buildings weren't even that close."

"That lot is so overgrown with weeds, I thought it must be longer than that. I'll have to ask Matt about it. Now, as for hockey," and he glanced at the Ben and Ollie, "Mr. York tells me there are a number of boys about your age who could play, once the rink freezes. The rink is kept in shape for the men's team and we could use it for the younger ones."

Ben and Ollie looked doubtful. 'We don't know how to skate," Ben said. 'Don't you have to skate when you play hockey?"

Will nodded and added, "I think you'll catch on pretty fast. None of the boys skate well, and some of them are like you. They haven't had the chance to give it a try."

~~*~~

With the children tucked in bed, Julia was just re-entering the parlour with a fresh pot of tea and cups on a tray, when she heard the last of a conversation that James was directing. "So, you arrived here in July for the first time, and you didn't come by train. Why not?"

"I came by train from Winnipeg to Nelson to visit a colleague of mine," said Will. "In fact he's the one who told me that a doctor was needed in Creston. Doc Farley had retired because he was too ill to handle his patients. I'd never been to the Kootenays before, and it's so beautiful, quite different from the Manitoba landscape. I was totally unprepared." He smiled, his gaze lingering on Julia as she set the tray down.

"Then I took the steamboat down Kootenay Lake and travelled by lorry into Creston. My friend told me I could catch a ride with some of the logging rigs that run in and out from the Lake. It was a wonderful way to have a look at the area. And I got to arrive in Creston without the huge kerfuffle that seems to occur whenever anyone comes by train. It's town news within minutes." His smile became ironic.

James glanced at Julia to catch her eye, and then back to the doctor, a speculative look on his face. Julia leaped to her feet, hoping to avert disaster. "Goodness, it's warm in here. I don't think we need the fire at all tonight, do we?" She started forward to turn the gas fireplace off but Will got there first.

"Allow me," he said, and twisted the lever down. "There, that does it. Bit stiff, is it? Although better that than being too easy for the children to twist. I can adjust that for you next time I'm here."

Julia sat down in a fluster, glaring at James.

He grinned back at her. "It's perfect, Julia, you know it is."

103

"James, really. That's enough," she whispered and slanted a glance at the doctor.

Will Stoffard followed this conversation with some interest.

James turned to him. "What do you think of this idea, Will?"

"James!" Julia blurted.

William half rose from his seat. "What is it?" he said, his forehead wrinkling with concern, his gaze swinging between Julia and James. "What has you upset?"

"Let me tell you," interrupted James. "Suppose you were to let the story out that you had traveled here in the company of Ben and Ollie. That you traveled all the way with them from Winnipeg, Manitoba."

Will sat back in his chair and said nothing, a keen gaze fixed on James.

James continued, "You could say you know the Butler family from Buffalo, New York, and a friend knew you were coming to the Kootenays and asked you to bring their sons to Creston."

James stopped and Will looked back to Julia. "Is this what has you upset? You didn't want to ask me this?"

Julia spread her hands and took a deep breath. "We have this problem, but I didn't think it fair to ask. And we haven't had time to think about it. James, we don't know if this is the best solution. We're putting the Doctor in the middle of it, and it isn't his affair."

"But it is my affair," Will said slowly. "These boys are my patients and I'll do what I can for their safety. If by putting about a harmless story, I can mitigate the circumstances, then I'll do it. After all, what have you done to help? Much more than we're talking about here, surely."

His voice became steely with emphasis. He cleared his throat. "So what is it I am supposed to have done? If I can let it be known that the boys traveled with me from Winnipeg, that should allay most questions. It's only if someone were persistent that I might mention the friend who asked if I might escort them to Creston to stay with their aunt."

Everyone nodded.

Will continued. "What's been said so far about how they arrived?"

Julia shrugged. "Very little. No one has asked. I've volunteered that they're my nephews but I didn't say how exactly they're related. I've been asked how long they're staying. And I say things like, well, it's family. I know the boys don't say anything. If they had a story to tell, it would be easier."

Sue-Ann jumped in. "Surely they're feeling more secure by now. They seem to have adjusted quite well to living with you, Julia. They're certainly well behaved."

"Yes, and that has me worried too," she said. "Children who never quibble with the parent, let alone rebel are pretty repressed."

Sue-Ann's brows rose, but the doctor nodded in agreement. "Not very usual, for sure," he said.

"So that tells me they aren't that comfortable yet," said Julia. "The day one of them argues with me about the chores, that's the day I'll know they've accepted that they're safe here."

"However, the more crucial issue is the real parents," Will interjected.

Julia told what Sam had said about the hill families near Sparwood who supported themselves with distilleries and moonshine.

James nodded and went back to the doctor's comment. "That makes sense, Julia. That's exactly my thought, Will. Where are the parents, and what might they do in the future to try to find the boys."

The men exchanged a speaking glance. "Perhaps we can talk about that further at some point," James murmured.

Julia listened and knew that some things were about to be taken out of her hands. With a sigh, she couldn't help but be grateful. She'd been carrying a heavy load, and she felt her shoulders grow lighter and her heart less heavy.

~~~**~~~

CHAPTER TWENTY

After the doctor left and James and Sue-Ann went up to bed, Julia checked each of the children, adjusted a blanket, smoothed a sweaty forehead. She missed Stephen. Not just the physical presence but their emotional closeness. They'd discussed everything, bounced ideas off each other, laid out plans to deal with issues as they arose. She missed it all, and her chest was tight, her eyes burning as she washed her face in the small bathroom and brushed her teeth.

She checked the locks on the doors, locks that they'd seldom used when Stephen was alive. Climbing the stairs, she sat in front of her mirror, brushing out her hair. She massaged her head lightly with her fingertips the way Stephen used to do. It felt soothing, but just reminded her further of her loss.

And as she laid her head on the pillow, she heard the shifting of bodies and murmured comments from the next room. Then the pause and sigh, and the slow rhythmic bumping of the bedstead, and she pulled the pillow over her ears and ground her face into the sheet as she cried herself to sleep.

~~*~~

Friday was Julia's day at the soup kitchen in town. It was a weekly service run from the church, started by the Ladies Guild when times had gotten so hard. Teachers at the school reported children coming to class without breakfast and bringing no lunch, and everyone had seen the steady stream of hungry, transient people looking for work. They were mostly men on their own, but now and then whole families came through, small children without proper clothing, or shoes to walk in.

This week she brought bread. She and Sue-Ann had made a double batch the day before and she had five loaves to contribute. Sue-Ann came with her to help and Julia got the impression she'd never done something like this before. It might be an education for her sister-in-law. It only took a good look at someone who had nothing at all to make you value what little you had.

The ladies had most of the tables set up when they arrived, and Julia helped XXXhreadXXX the chairs while Sue-Ann took their bread into the kitchen. There she was directed to slice and butter, until the butter ran out. People began to appear outside the door, mostly men, wearing mismatched and worn jackets. Julia directed them into the hall to sit at the tables.

Word spread fast for these events. Any man who rode the rails into town on a Friday would be directed to the hall for a hot meal, and some families from around the area came as well.

They were soon very busy, ladling thick soup into trenchers and adding a stack of sliced bread to the meal. The men were lined up out the door, a couple of them on crutches. When they finished their meal, they were given something extra to take away with them. Today it was a few cookies and an apple.

The tables were quickly cleared and the dishes washed, then delivered back to the soup line for more meals to be served. Julia looked anxiously at the thinning line of hungry men and back into the soup pots. She sighed in relief. There would be enough. Just barely. She'd been there on occasion when they'd run out of soup and it was a dreadful feeling to try to find something else to fill the last empty bellies.

Looking out over the hall, her gaze stopped on a small family gathered at one of the tables. There was a mother and father, and three children. The oldest was no more than six and the youngest about two. The children had wild hair, full of hay and bits of twigs. Their shoes were the wrong size, either much too small or so big they were tied tightly around the ankles to keep them from falling off. The father had a desperate starved look to his face. He saw Julia staring at them and lowered his head.

"What do you think, Julia? Are we nearly finished? Maybe I should start the rest of the dishes." Sue-Ann stood beside her, drying her hands on a towel.

"Good idea, Sue-Ann. I'll be right back to help."

Julia approached the long table with cups of coffee for the parents and one for her, and sat across from the little family. She talked softly to the children for a few minutes, and when the father finished with his soup and bread she pushed a coffee cup over to him. She began to talk.

At first they just looked at her and listened, but then the mother began to softly reply. They'd been travelling for most of the summer. They'd lived on the prairies, but they lost their farm for taxes the year before. They were able to stay in their house over the winter, which had been a God send. But the drought and the grasshoppers had finished off most of the small farmers around their area.

There wasn't any work, not even just for food, and the bank insisted they vacate the farmhouse. They'd walked a long way, sometimes getting rides with people passing their way. They knew the grasshopper plague hadn't reached this far, and they managed to ride the rails into the Kootenay area. But they hadn't found any work.

People were just managing on what they had and could do for themselves, they didn't have any extra to hire them. Then they heard about the soup kitchen, and it was Friday, so it was a good day to be in Creston. Julia smiled into the woman's eyes and thought how desperate she must be feeling.

"Don't go away," she said, rising from the bench. "I have

some work to do here at the hall, and then I'm going to see someone in town. But don't leave. You can wait on the benches outside for me, would you do that? I'll be back to talk to you."

She and Sue-Ann helped with the final cleanup in the hall kitchen and began organizing the benches and tables. "Sue-Ann, come with me," Julia said. "I have to make a trip to the Co-op Store, to see Luke Harrison for a few minutes."

Sue-Ann walked along beside her toward the centre of town. "It's about that family, isn't it?" she asked.

Julia turned to look at her. "Yes, it is. How could it not be? Does that not just tear your heart out?"

Sue-Ann nodded and looked thoughtful. "But what can you do for them? You can't take in any more people, and you don't know if that man is reliable or trustworthy or…" Her words petered out at Julia's pointed look. "Well," she persisted. "You don't know anything about them."

"Yes, I do," she said fiercely. "I know that he didn't leave his family behind with nowhere to live. He took them with him. I know that the mother trusts him because she followed with her children. I know that he doesn't look as well fed as the children, so that tells me he gives them his own food to eat. I know he's embarrassed by his situation, yet is willing to talk to me and wait while I try to do something. I do know something about them."

Sue-Ann fell silent.

Luke wasn't at the store, so they walked over to the boarding house. Mamie Harrison was having a cup of tea in her parlour and greeted them with a grin. "Come in, have some tea. I just made it. How are you, Sue-Ann? I haven't seen you in so long, why it must have been…." Her smile faded as she realized when it had been. "It was a funeral. Of course. Stephen's funeral wasn't it? Well. But it is nice to see you on a cheerful occasion, now."

Julia gave her a hug. "Thank you, Mamie, we don't have time for tea. I actually came to find Luke, but I'm sure you can do as good or better."

Mamie chuckled.

"You see, there's a small family who came to our soup kitchen today. A mother, father and three children. They look about two, four and six years old, the babies. Their clothes are worn and ripped. The one child has no shoes and the others' are worn through. They lost their farm last year and can't find work, not even for food, with the drought and the grasshoppers. I wondered if maybe they could stay for a few days, perhaps a week in the boarding house.

"Do you have any rooms available? I can provide the food, if you provide the room. That would give them a break, wouldn't it? Just enough to catch their breath and gather a bit of strength. They could wash and get cleaned up. Maybe they can make a plan. Riding the rails and going from town to town doesn't work that well, when small children are involved. Could you help?"

Mamie nodded. "Sit down for a minute, Julia, and you too, Sue-Ann. Let's talk. Now, there are five of them you say? I have a room that would take them all. There are two double beds in it, and we can put a pallet on the floor. They'd have to have a delousing bath before they came into the building. Lice are hell to get rid of in a room, it is just too much work, and usually the mattress is finished. I have a tin tub out back and some delousing powder, so if they're willing to do that, they can stay here a few days. Then their clothes go straight into the washtub, kill anything that lives in them. I've done this before, as you can tell."

Mamie's smile remained cheerful. "They can stay out in the tent for the night tonight. We heat the water in the morning for the wash."

"That's what I do, too," said Julia. "Only it's a shed I use, so the travellers have a place to stay but don't come in house."

They finished their arrangements and Julia rose. "Okay, that's perfect, Mamie. You're a saint. I'll bring food every day for the five of them. They can eat it cold, it won't hurt. I have some clothes that might fit as well. Even a week is going to give them a lift, isn't it?"

"Yes, and don't prepare it, Julia. I have to make meals

everyday anyway, for all my boarders. Just bring what you have and I'll put it in with the mix to make enough for everyone. A week is good, I can manage a week."

~~~**~~~

CHAPTER TWENTY ONE

James and Sue-Ann were leaving on the train that arrived in Creston every Saturday at two-thirty in the afternoon from the east and departed, heading west at precisely three. The 'train platform' crowd swore you could set your watch by it. The cases were packed and Marcus had picked them up earlier to deliver them to the station in preparation for boarding.

Sue-Ann wore her cherry wool suit with the brass buttons down the front of the jacket and her black shoes with the intricate stitching, the matching hand bag over her arm. Her crimson velvet hat sat on the table, the wide black satin band reflecting light from the window. "Come on Julia, try it on. It'll look great. You'll be beautiful in it."

Julia laughed and carefully picked up the hat. She peered into the foggy glass above the dining room bureau and arranged it on her head. When she turned around, she was met with a chorus of 'oohhhhs and aaahhhhhs' from the children.

"Smashing," James declared, "it looks wonderful."

Sue-Ann nodded eagerly. "You have to keep it, Julia. Wear it today for the ride into town. It goes perfectly with your navy coat. Say you will. It looks absolutely right on you."

Julia felt the heat rising in her cheeks. "But this hat was made for your outfit. Oh, alright," she relented, laughing. "If you positively insist. I can't quite see it." She peered into the mirror again. "It's too gloomy in here. But I like it."

Julia wore the hat into town, driving the wagon with Prince in the traces, Sue-Ann, Maggie and Jims in the wagon, Ollie riding the tailgate and Ben and James walking behind.

Tucked in the cart was a large bundle for the family at Mamie's boarding house. It included a dress for the mother, a shirt for the father, some of Jims' clothes for the two youngest children, and vegetables from the root cellar.

Julia knew she could manage, she could do this, if she just took it one day at a time.

~~*~~

Julia arrived at the Co-op Store early. She mailed her letters, picked up a few necessities in the store and read the newspaper headline from the *Vancouver Sun* that sat on the counter. "Good Lord, Luke, what now? The drought is getting worse and now dust clouds are just travelling across the land? What will become of the great prairies? It's devastating!"

Luke finished writing up her order and put the receipt book beneath the counter. "I know, it seems to go on and on. It's hard to imagine what else could happen. It all seems to have started with Black Tuesday, and just continues to flow from there. A breakdown of the system as we know it anyway. At least the grasshoppers probably won't reach our area, everyone seems to think they won't get through the mountains. Can you imagine the devastation to the strawberry fields if a plague of locusts attacked?

Julia got the mail and found several envelopes, a letter from Sue-Ann, and a local note. She opened the note first. It was from Leah Luchinski, her tenant at the rental house. Could Julia please call around tomorrow afternoon around two if that was convenient. There was a matter they'd like to discuss with her.

She tucked the note into her purse with a sinking heart. The most likely matter her tenant might want to discuss would be ending the tenancy. There were other houses in town for rent, some of them empty. Times were tough, and they weren't getting any better.

Before Stephen died, they'd decided to keep the house. Stephen had worked off the farm to earn extra money, but now, with him gone, Julia didn't have that option. She was almost totally dependent on the rent. Sometimes she sold eggs, or goat milk, even raspberries at the side of the road or in the store. But with two extra stomachs to fill, that wasn't likely to happen now. It was the house rent that kept her in cash, such as it was.

Yes, she'd heard rumours about her tenants. Mr. Luchinski travelled, and his wife and their small boy lived there, often alone. They took the train into Nelson, or even as far as Vancouver, she'd heard. Julia hadn't seen the woman often, but the tenants had been there less than six months. And they were never late with the rent.

Her friends teased her about having the 'perfect tenants'. They didn't complain, they paid on time and didn't ask for constant repairs to the house.

People also made sly comments. What did Luchinski do for a living, that he was never in town? Yet he seemed to keep his family here without a thought for the cost. Julia ignored this. She didn't know what Mr. Luchinski did. She'd heard rum runner, mafia, salesman, all manner of things. But it was based on pure speculation, in a small town where people prided themselves on knowing everyone else's business.

Until she knew otherwise, she'd just assume he was a fine man who cared about his family, and wanted them to live in a small and safe community while he traveled with his work. Maybe he was a salesman. Who knew? It wasn't her business. Not unless it became her business. She counted herself lucky that she could still hang onto her small piece of land because of the rent from her tenants.

She sighed. Maybe not for long. She mentally searched for ways to rent the house to someone else. Who did she know who could afford to pay rent? Not many candidates came to mind.

Quickly, she scanned Sue-Ann's letter. They had arrived home safely and Susan had been very glad to see them. Susan was disappointed not to have had the chance to visit her cousins and hoped they could come out to Vancouver soon. Sue-Ann had dusted off her sewing machine to make curtains for the large bedroom at the back of their house. Her mother would move into it, making it more comfortable for everyone. It would be nicer for Susan as well, to see Granny as often as she liked without having to travel across town.

Enclosed in the letter was a note for Maggie from Susan. Julia smiled and tucked it into her purse. She was pleased to hear how things were going for them, and this letter was a real change from the ones she'd received before the visit.

It was bridge day and she and Jims arrived just after lunch time at Becky's house, tying Prince to the fencepost outside her front door. There was usually enough time to play cards for a couple of hours before the children had to be picked up at school. The bridge games got dropped in the summer for the most part. Everyone was busy and Julia didn't come to town on a regular basis during the summer months.

Doris held Prince by the halter while Julia climbed down and grabbed Jims off the seat. Becky's little girl, six months older than Jims, liked to boss him around when they played. But Jims was used to that, having Maggie for an older sister. They seldom caused any interruption in the card game.

The players congregated at the front door, where coats landed in a pile on the old chaise just inside. Shoes were scattered beneath. Becky's house was warm and toasty, and they settled about the kitchen table, with tea at the ready and the cards shuffled. Amid all the chatter, the women chose partners and spread the cards to see who would deal first to begin the game.

Julia had played bridge with her father when she was younger, but she didn't really know all the legalities. Becky, on the other hand, was a stickler for the rules. The ensuing discussions, even arguments, often made for a lively afternoon. Doris was a good player and Lizzie was new. They had highjacked her, needing a reliable fourth for their winter games, and she was coming along very well. She teased that no wonder she didn't know the rules, if the rest of them couldn't agree on what they were.

Lizzie started dealing cards, "I see your Mr. Luchinski is back in town."

"How do you know that?" queried Julia. "Don't tell me you keep watch."

"Heavens, no." Lizzie laughed and picked up her cards. "But I do live almost right across the street from your house on Maple. He makes quite a stir when he arrives, his car must be brand new, and I don't think there's another in town like it."

"Yes, I suppose he could keep a lower profile if he didn't want to be the topic of gossip," Julia admitted. "I'm afraid they're about to give me notice on the house. I don't suppose any of you knows of someone who would like to rent it?"

She looked hopefully around the table, to a chorus of 'no's'. She looked at her cards. "That's what I thought. I could drop the rent a bit, although I hate to. Or I could try to run a boarding house out of there."

"I'd think you have your hands full already, Julia. You can't do everything. Maybe someone else could run a boarding house for you."

The women sorted their hands as they tossed the idea around. Everyone knew Luke's mum ran something similar and it wasn't full. The consensus was that, with the unemployment situation, there should be any number of people available to do it, but no one came to mind.

They talked about children, asked how long Julia's nephews might stay. Julia replied they'd stay for a long time, as things were very tough back home. *That was no lie,* she thought. *Things were indeed tough back home, just not at the home her friends thought she was talking about, and not the kind of tough they might think. And those boys were certainly not going back to that home if she had anything to say about it.*

The game proceeded with so little attention, that in the last hand Julia scooped the final trick with two trump on the board, and no cards left in her hand. They laughed and suggested she be awarded a fictitious one thousand bonus points for such creative dealing of the cards.

~~~**~~~

Part Four – The Tenants

CHAPTER TWENTY TWO

The next day, she brought Prince early into town and tied him to the fence post at the sidewalk on Maple Street in front of her rented house. She eyed the brand new motor vehicle parked there. Lizzie was right, if Mr. Luchinski wanted to go incognito he could have chosen a less flashy car. She and Jims climbed down and walked up to the front door. She twisted the dial on the doorbell and heard the chimes sound inside the front hall.

How many times had she and Stephen come here for dinner with his folks? Stephen's dad had been built just like his sons, long and lean, with the wiry wavy hair, snow white by then. He had died unexpectedly, without a sign of ill health. His mother was heartbroken. She only lasted a year, succumbing to influenza the next winter.

That was when Stephen and James divided up the property. James took the cash and shares they held in the railway, and Stephen took the house. James had no interest in holding a piece of property that was worth so little in this little town, and with no market to sell it. He was happy to have Stephen take it off his hands.

Julia heard footsteps inside before the door opened. Mrs. Luchinski appeared in the opening. "Come in," she said, standing back to give them room. She was dressed in a lovely day dress that looked like silk, with velvet collar and cuffs. Her little boy hovered right behind her, also in velvet, this time knee breeches, and his mother almost stepped on him.

"Look out, Gerry," she scolded. "Mind where you put your feet. Now, come in Mrs. Butler. Let me take your coat. How is your little boy?"

Jims stomped in ahead of Julia, eyeing a possible new playmate. Mrs. Luchinski ushered them into the parlour and told the boys to go play. Jims promptly headed out to the kitchen followed by the smaller boy.

Julia settled on the sofa and accepted a cup of tea, served in a beautiful china cup and saucer with gold detail around the rim. She hadn't seen anything that lovely in a long time and said so. Mrs. Luchinski blushed prettily. "It was an anniversary present, from my husband," she said. "He knows I love fine china, and it's part of a set."

"Why don't I see you at church, Mrs. Luchinski? You should come and bring Gerry, there's a very good Sunday school, and you'd enjoy the sermons, not too long." They laughed together.

"Call me Leah," she said. "To be honest, I wasn't sure what kind of reception I would get."

"At church?" Julia was shocked. "I'd hope you'd get a very warm welcome. If people don't welcome you at church, there's something seriously wrong. And not with you, but with them. Do come. I can meet you outside and we'll go in together, if you like. Little Gerry is probably a bit lonely, not having any brothers or sisters to play with. It would be nice for him." She took a sip of tea.

Leah set her cup down. "I really asked you to come about the house," she said.

Julia nodded in resignation. "I thought as much. I suppose you're moving away."

"Oh, no." Leah shook her head. "No, but my husband wanted to talk with you. I'll get him now. He's just in his office." She stood and left the room. She returned shortly with Gerald Luchinski following.

He was a short compact man, stocky, with dark hair oiled

close to his head, and a heavy mustache. He bowed gallantly over Julia's hand. "Thank you for coming to see us. I know you're busy, but I thought it was better if you came here than if we called on you at your home."

Julia smiled. "Either would be fine. I'm glad to see you again. I know you aren't in town too often."

He frowned. "I suppose you hear rumours about that."

Julia shook her head. "I don't listen to gossip, Mr. Luchinski. It doesn't hold any interest for me. I deal with what I know."

Luchinski eyed her for a moment. "I hear things about you, Mrs. Butler. For instance, I understand that you have two nephews living with you now, as well as your own children."

Julia stiffened. "Yes, I do," she said shortly, daring him to say anything more.

He grinned. "I admire a woman who's willing to extend a helping hand to family." He made himself comfortable on the chair across from his wife, and crossed his legs. Julia noticed his shoes, beautiful rich-looking leather with tassels at the toe. His whole appearance spoke of money in restrained good taste. "Now, what I wanted to talk about is our rent." He adjusted his cuffs, the cuff links glinting in the sun coming through the lace curtains.

Julia nodded, waiting. She didn't know if it would be good news or bad, but all she could do was hear him out.

"I don't know how you feel, having us as tenants," Luchinski continued.

Julia regarded him for a moment, then smiled. "Well, I'm surprised you ask. You're good tenants from my point of view. You pay the rent on time, every month. That's very important to a landlord."

Luchinski smiled back.

"Furthermore," she continued, "you take good care of the house and grounds. I noticed the bushes are trimmed across the front garden, and the porch has been painted. I know that from the Morrises, their older son was hired to do it. Again, that's very important to a landlord. So, I have to say I'm pleased having you as tenants. Is there a problem that I'm not aware of, or something that I should be taking care of?"

Luchinski shook his head. "No. I just know that there are rumours, as there are wherever we go. When a man travels to make a living, people talk. And if I don't want to divulge my personal information, people talk more."

"Well, talk never hurt anyone. I don't listen to talk," said Julia.

"Good," he said. "Good." He smiled at his wife reassuringly and then turned his attention back to Julia. "I'd like to make a business arrangement with you. Here's what I propose. Leah likes it here, the town suits her and our little boy. She'd like to bring her mother out to live with us, so she has company when I'm away. If we're going to do that, we want to ensure that we're able to stay for a while, not just a short time. Otherwise it isn't worthwhile to have her mother move.

"I propose we sign a year's lease. We can pay it in advance, that way there are no questions. If Leah is on a trip to Vancouver at the end of the month, there is no worry because the rent is already paid. I know this doesn't leave you with any flexibility, and I'm willing to pay you for that. So the rent would be a little higher than it is now, to allow for your accommodating us."

Luchinski mentioned a sum that was more than he currently paid. Her eyebrows rose, but she said nothing. *I haven't heard the whole deal yet,* she kept telling herself. *I'll wait. There must be a catch here somewhere. I'll hear what he has to say before I make any comment.*

Luchinski waited for a response, but Julia just smiled. So he continued. "We'd sign a lease, and pay by banker's draft for the year. At the end of the year, we'd pay another year, or give you notice that we don't want to renew. If we don't renew, we owe you three months rent. That gives you some certainty to your income from the house, and time to make other arrangements if we decide not to renew. Does this interest you, Mrs. Butler?"

Julia continued to smile, while her brain buzzed in her head. She barely made sense of what he'd proposed. "Could you excuse me a moment?" she said, rising from the couch. "I just need to check on the boys."

She walked calming through the doorway to the kitchen. The boys were seated at the kitchen table, colouring in a book of pictures. They looked up when she came in. Jims beamed, and kept on colouring. He was telling Gerry about their horse, Prince, and how strong he was.

Julia smiled absent-mindedly as she glanced around. The kitchen was stocked with shiny new cookware, a lot of which looked like it had never been used. The table itself was new, and the four chairs painted a lovely shade of dark green, matching the oilcloth floor mat beneath. Even the kitchen windows had lace curtains. She took a deep breath and walked back into the parlour.

The Luchinskis were sitting together on the loveseat, his arm around her comfortingly. Julia sat down and did her best to look relaxed. "Mr. Luchinski, I need time to decide what I'm going to do. At this point, I can't think of any reason why I wouldn't want to accept your offer. But I've been wrong before, mostly because I didn't take the time to think it over. I can let you know by the end of the week. At first glance it looks like a very generous offer. I like your little family, and I'd like to see them stay here in town. I've just offered Leah to come to Church with us on Sunday. Gerry can go to Sunday school with Jims, he likes it well enough and would love a little buddy to go with."

Luchinski eyed her guardedly.

Julia eyed him right back. "Thank you for the tea, Leah. The boys have almost finished colouring, and I'm due at the school to pick up the children so I'd better be on my way. If you want to come out to my house for dinner Friday night, all of you, and bring your lease, I'd probably be ready to make a decision." She rose and headed for the door.

"Come on, Jims," she called. "We have to get going. Maggie and the boys will be waiting."

Luchinski rose and escorted her to the door. "Mrs. Butler, you're a surprising woman. Are you sure you want us out to your house for dinner? We aren't well received by some here in town, you know."

Julia waved in farewell to Leah and lifted her coat off the hook by the door. Luchinski held it for her as she put it on. "Mr. Luchinski, as I explained, gossip means little to me. I think you're good people, and I'll be pleased to welcome you into my home. If you think your wife is lonely here, what kind of life will it be for her, even if her mother comes to stay, if she can't go out and about in the town and bring your little boy with her? So we'll see you for dinner Friday night. Bring your lease, and we'll have a look at it then."

Luchinski smiled and gripped her hand. "Thank you, Mrs. Butler."

CHAPTER TWENTY THREE

Late Friday night, Julia finished tidying away. She checked on Ben and Ollie, and turned out the light in the hall as she climbed the stairs. Jims and Maggie were fine, and she left their door partway open, the way Jims liked it.

Sighing, she pulled the pins from her hair and lay them in the china dish on her dresser. Dinner had been quite an event. Jims had been ecstatic to have a buddy there to play with. Mr. Luchinski hadn't really known how to conduct himself. He was awkward but courtly and spent his time trying to assist in getting the meal on the table and clearing the plates. Leah had been more relaxed, chatting with the children and Julia and making herself at home. Will had been invited in advance and showed up with a huge basket of apples from a client.

And now, downstairs on the dining room buffet, lay a signed copy of the lease for her house in town, witnessed by the doctor, along with a banker's draft for the entire year's rent. She sat motionless on the side of the bed, her hands in her lap. Then she gave herself a hug and pulled the covers back to slide into bed. What would Stephen have thought of this? Never in her wildest dreams had she imagined having this kind of cash in her hands. Never!

She had taxes to pay next year, and other recurring costs, and she'd be sure to set money aside to look after those contingencies, plus even a cushion for unexpected expenses. But there was no guess work here, no constant concern that the renters would not pay or would move out without notice. Or try to negotiate a lower rent or, heaven forbid, just up and leave town. This was security, the like of which she'd never seen. Her excitement was such that she was sure she would never sleep this night. She rolled over to her side, breathed out, and fell into a deep slumber.

As one day followed another, Julia pondered her situation. She had the banker's draft hidden in her dresser drawer. The little bank in Creston was certainly as safe as any. She knew the manager, Charlie Allan, who had been known to defend his bank with a revolver, and she knew both tellers very well. She'd gone to school with one of them. They all knew her. Whenever she made a deposit, or withdrew money, they commented in a friendly way. They obviously didn't leave their comments there, because she heard little jibes about other bank clients. The banking business in town was everyone's business. And she didn't like that. Her business was going to stay hers if she could manage it. But how to handle that?

Finally by Thursday, she had her plan in place. That night she gathered the kids around the kitchen table. They were having a quick dinner of scrambled eggs and toast. There was applesauce for dessert, courtesy of Will's client. "I have a plan," she said.

All four faces looked quickly up at her at the end of the table. *What a difference in expressions,* she thought. *There was Ben, guarded and alert, very solemn. Ollie alert as well, but not as anxious. Maggie like a puppy, as if to say, oh good, will it be fun? And little Jims, not paying too much attention, but a gleam in his eyes. He's probably feeding Wagsy under the table.*

Julia sipped her tea. "I think we should go on a little trip." The expressions sharpened. "I think we should take the train to Calgary, it's three hours. We can go tomorrow, so no school."

The first reaction was stunned silence. Then Ollie cheered, and Maggie frowned. All her friends were at school. "Just this

125

once, Maggie. We take the train into Calgary, it leaves here at eleven in the morning so we'd get there at two o'clock. We find a place to stay, I have some business to do. Then we find a nice place for dinner and maybe go to see a moving picture."

The cheering drowned out her next words. *Funny*, she thought. *I'll bet Ben and Ollie have never seen a moving picture. I know Maggie has only been once but hardly remembers it, and Jims never has. What magic they must imagine.*

She looked at her little crowd and thought of them getting off the train in Calgary. Ben with his coat that she'd made over for him from an old one of Stephen's. Ollie with his hand-me-down from Will's sister-in-law. And their boots, all scuffed and borrowed. That's okay. They wouldn't be aware of it, and this trip should take care of some of that.

She was nearly as excited as they were. "There's a lot to think about. We have to take Prince over to Mr. Hoskiss. I talked to him today and he promised to look after him until we get back. And he'll stop in and feed the chickens too. We'll take Daisy Mae down to the Morrises. They'll milk her until we get home again. Dr. Stoffard said he would take us to the station, and pick us up again when we get back. Won't that be exciting? We get to ride in his car."

The children chattered non-stop, even Ben had many comments about the picture show, everything he had ever heard about moving pictures. There was a movie house in Nelson and some of the school children had been there to see a show.

Julia hustled them off to bed, saying they had to get up early in the morning to get everything done. She made a long list for herself and dug out two carry bags before she put the light out. It seemed her alarm rang a few minutes after her head hit the pillow.

She milked the goat, fed all the animals and gathered the eggs before she woke the children. They hustled around, getting breakfast quickly out of the way. Maggie washed the dishes while Ben rode Prince down the road, leading Daisy Mae to deliver her to the Morrises. On the way back, he dropped Prince at Jerome

Hoskiss' place and walked home across the road.

Julia supervised the arrangements, leaving Wagsy in the barn with some food in a bucket. She got everyone packed and into their travel clothes, ready and waiting for their ride. The gas was turned off, the fire dampened down, and the house locked up tight.

Will arrived early and they piled into the car. Julia had dressed them all in their best, which wasn't much for Ben, but not too bad for the rest. She was wearing Sue-Ann's beautiful red hat. They had two carry bags, Ben would carry one. Only a change of underwear, socks, and something to wear to bed for each of them, in the way of luggage. Plus a packed lunch for the trip. And deep in Julia's purse, next to the big house key, was folded the Luchinski banker's draft.

Will gave them a suggestion for a hotel in Calgary, 'not far from the train station, very reasonable in price and close to the shopping downtown.' The children responded with another cheer. Will looked at Julia with a grin. "You've definitely started something here. It sounds like you're taking a sports team with you, not a small family."

Julia snorted. "No one would call this a small family," she retorted.

Will looked quizzical. "It's not a big family, yet," he said and his eyes lingered on her face.

Julia blushed. *Drat the man, he was always making remarks that she didn't know quite how to take.* Was he making advances, or just being friendly? Well, as her motto was, so she would go. If he wasn't making advances that she could recognize, she'd ignore it. How else could a woman carry on? Otherwise she'd be distracted all the time, and she was too busy for that.

They arrived at the station in a great rush. Ben and Julia each carried bags, and held the little ones by the hand. There was much comment from the folks on the platform. Luke Harrison from the Co-op Store was there to pick up an order that had just come in on the train. "Going traveling, Mrs. Butler?" he called, a twinkle in his eye.

All heads turned. Julia smiled and waved. "Just a quick trip to the city, we have a few things to take care of." She kept walking, and boarded the first car she came to. They walked through two cars before they found an empty double seat, and settled themselves down.

There was much stowing of bags and arranging of coats amid a great deal of chatter. When the train began moving, the children crowded to the window to wave to the doctor, and watch as the village disappeared from view.

Even Julia was excited. She'd been to Calgary twice, each time with Stephen to do business. She knew which bank she was going to. She'd dug out some old papers and found the information, then sent a letter earlier in the week to remember herself to the banker and tell him she would be in town to see him on Friday.

The children oohhed and aahhed as the train began to thread its way through the mountains. The vistas were breathtaking. Julia couldn't help but grab the nearest child in a ridiculous attempt to keep them safe as the train travelled around some of the dizzying corners, the earth falling away straight below on one side and towering high above them on the other. At noon she pulled the packed lunch down from the overhead rack and handed out sandwiches. She had a jar of cold tea that she passed around.

She was content to let the children chatter, answering the occasional question. She had a lot to think about. This was a big adventure for her as well. Five of them, and her in charge, in a city that she didn't know well at all. But she was having fun, and when was the last time they'd done something like this? Something that was just fun, and impromptu, that they could afford for heaven's sake? She laughed out loud, and the children all looked up and laughed with her.

They made friends of an elderly couple sitting across the aisle from them, and got lots of advice. By the time the train pulled into the Calgary station, she had a lift to the hotel with the couple, and lots of directions of where to eat and shop.

The children loved the hotel. It was like watching ants explore their new nest. They prowled around the lobby, sitting on each chair, examining the somewhat dusty artificial plants in the windows and leafing through the brochures on the low table. Then they were shown up to their room. Ben was anxious to try out the big key in the door. They put their bags down and investigated further.

There were two double beds, a high-backed chair and a dresser with a mirror in the room, and the desk clerk promised to deliver a trundle bed that Jims would sleep on. They tested the mattresses, bouncing up and down till the springs shrieked, opened all the drawers in the dresser, then unpacked everything and put it away.

Once the trundle bed had arrived and been installed at the foot of the other beds, Julia took them all down the hall to go to the bathroom, and wash up before they headed out on the town. Everyone washed their face and hands, and went back to the room for their coats. Julia lined them up and brushed hair. She'd found that Ben's hair never went out of place, it was so thick and wiry. If she kept it short, all it really needed was washing. But he insisted on being brushed along with the rest of them.

She brushed her own hair in the mirror, and pushed pins into place, applied a bit of lipstick that was watched intently by four pairs of eyes. Goodness, she should make more of an effort. Obviously, she didn't put lipstick on often enough that even that was a novelty. She grabbed her coat and purse, and they were out the door.

CHAPTER TWENTY FOUR

The bank was the first stop. Julia got directions from the hotel desk clerk to the right address. They took the tram across town, another whole new experience that was commented on extensively. Julia began to feel like she was surrounded by a flock of magpies. They arrived at the institution and she ensconced the children in a row of chairs in the lobby while she went to speak to a bank officer, admonishing them to make her proud and behave quietly. They were like little mice when she left.

The banking itself didn't take long at all. They treated her with respect, brought a cup of tea and a biscuit while she waited, and quickly took her in to see the manager in his office at the back of the bank. He remembered Stephen, and expressed his belated condolences on his death. Then he helped her set up an account in her name, with arrangements for her to make withdrawals by mail, which they would direct to her by bank draft and she could deposit into her local branch.

Julia was thrilled. She knew it would cause comment back home, but no one would ever know what was in her Calgary account. She took cash with her for their shopping and a first draft to deposit when she got home. The manager shook her hand as she left.

But as she walked across the lobby, she spotted the children sitting on the chairs, and an elderly lady leaning over talking to them. "Can I help you, children?" Julia heard her say. Ben stood out of courtesy and looked desperately around for Julia but didn't see her. "No, thank you."

"But what are you waiting for, are you all alone?"

Ben's chest swelled importantly. "No, Ma'am. Our mother is talking to the bank manager."

The woman looked them over sadly. "You poor things, you poor, poor things," she said. "God bless you."

Julia's spirits fell and yet she couldn't help laughing to herself. They did look like poor little mites, with their scuffed shoes and mismatched clothes, and that nice woman probably thought their mother was in with the bank manager dealing with a foreclosure on their home. There were so many people who were losing their houses because of the loss of work and the inability to pay their taxes.

She was blessed, they all were. They didn't have to deal with that. They were dealing with something quite different and it meant they had more security than they'd had in a long time. The children didn't know it, but Julia did and it meant a great burden had been lifted.

But she'd get a chance to change how they were dressed, just not yet, not today. That could wait. Nothing was going to get in the way of the fun they had in store for them this weekend.

~~*~~

The restaurant they chose was perfect. There were fifteen different kinds of spaghetti and pasta to choose from. The young waiter was very good, teased the boys, and flattered Maggie till she beamed. He suggested the bigger boys could eat a full meal, and likely Maggie and Jims could share. And he knew exactly which movie they should see, *The Wizard of Oz*.

"It's new, and I've already seen it," he told them. "It's

fantastic. I'm going to see it again with my friends. The songs are great."

The kids wriggled in excitement. Julia looked around the table at the shining eyes, and found tears in her own. What a gift. If she weren't already fond of the Luchinskis, she'd absolutely love them for this gift of joy and excitement. Dessert came with the meal, and involved spumoni ice cream with little bits of fruit peel in it. Julia hoped there wouldn't be stomachaches to follow that might interfere with the movie.

The theatre was just a few blocks away. They trooped down the street and soon were settled into their seats by a young usher who looked very important in his uniform. They gazed around the theatre at the other patrons, chattering and pointing, staring at the lush red curtains across the front of the stage. But when the lights went down, a hush descended that wasn't broken until the movie was over.

Julia moved around the darkened hotel room, removing her clothing and laying it on the chair with that of the children. They were all sleeping now, quiet and still under the covers, exhausted after so much excitement in one day. She shook out her hair and pulled her nightgown over her head, creeping softly under the covers beside the slumbering Maggie. Letting out a deep breath, she stretched out the kink in her back.

What a day. She couldn't remember one like it. The thrill she'd seen on her children's faces as they watched that magical movie. They'd skipped back down the sidewalk to the hotel singing snatches of every song they could remember. Maybe she could find a record of those songs tomorrow while they shopped. That would be something. She shifted and drifted off to sleep.

~~*~~

Ben let his breath out softly and closed his eyes. He'd been holding his breath ever since he caught that glimpse of Mama Julia as she pulled her nightie on over her head. Just the silhouette, that was so beautiful. He thought she was the most beautiful woman in the whole wide world. He would never love anyone else, he vowed, the way he loved her.

~~*~~

The trip home on the train was more fun than the trip out. The children were giddy with fatigue, and at the same time looser with each other. They'd passed some kind of milestone together that had formed a tight bond between them all. They'd taken a trip, had fun, did 'business', and gone shopping. And now they were heading home.

She watched Ben admire his new boots, not just shoes, but real boots. They were too big, but he was growing so fast they'd fit by spring. He seemed to be checking his image in the shine on the leather.

Julia glanced out the window and sighed. It would be good to get home, get Daisy Mae from the Morrises. She hoped they had milked her so she wouldn't go dry on them. Jerome Hoskiss was a funny old fellow but he would most certainly have looked after Prince and the chickens. She'd just need to gather today's eggs. Will should be there at the platform to give them a ride home. Wouldn't he be surprised at all the bags and boxes they were bringing back?

Julia couldn't believe how much they had bought. But there wasn't a thing there they didn't need, and the prices were so much better than at the Co-op store in Creston. They barely carried it all to the train station. How would they get it into Will's car?

There was much shouting and laughter when they got off the train. Will picked up two of the kids and swung them around, and then had to do the same for the rest. He staggered under the weight of all the bags, and the boys laughed hysterically, explaining that *they* had carried it to the train.

So they trundled home. Julia cooked up some scrambled eggs, the quickest dinner she could think of and Will just happened to have bread and jam from the store that he could contribute. It was a merry supper and the children wandered off to bed without complaint, carrying new clothes carefully in their arms.

Will turned to Julia, and put an arm around her shoulders. "What an adventure you must have had. They can't stop talking about it. That was quite a trip to take by yourself with all of them. I would have gone along to help if you had asked."

Julia turned a questioning gaze on him. Now that was pretty clear, she'd have a hard time misinterpreting his comment. Why hadn't he mentioned it earlier? *And what would it mean if they took a trip like that, with Will along?* The townspeople would certainly have something to say about a single woman traveling with her children and an unmarried man on the train to Calgary? She could claim they just happened to be going at the same time. As if anyone would believe that!

"I never thought of it," she said innocently. "I just needed to do some business in Calgary, and it was a good opportunity to do some shopping. It would probably have been a lot easier with another adult along, though. Can I take a rain cheque?"

His eyes crinkled at the corners as he grinned and pulled her against his side, before dropping his arm. "I'll take that as a promise," he said.

Well, there you go, she thought. *He blows hot and then cold.*

~~~**~~~

CHAPTER TWENTY FIVE

Julia picked the children up from school and they had all climbed into the wagon, when she caught a glimpse of Ben's cheek. It was swollen and red under the dusky skin and he was obviously trying to keep her from noticing. His head was turned as he looked out of the bed of the wagon on the other side.

She paused, then climbed down again. "Bertie," she called to the oldest Morris boy, "come and tie Prince for me, will you? I just have to speak to Mrs. Rasmussen for a minute."

Bertie climbed laboriously down and grabbed Prince by the halter.

Mrs. Rasmussen was just clearing her desk when Julia darted back into the classroom. "Hello Mrs. Butler. I can't say I'm surprised to see you." She smiled wryly at Julia who was out of breath. "Noticed Ben's cheek, I take it."

"Yes," Julia puffed. "Do you know what happened?"

Mrs. Rasmussen nodded and sat in one of the student's seats, motioning to Julia to sit down. "I think it was the Postnikoff boy, he has a black eye right now. There were words in the schoolyard apparently, at recess between some of the older boys and Ben, and Nick Postnikoff was at the back of it. They were calling Ben names, like 'stupid,' I imagine because he hasn't been assigned to a class yet. Mostly it was Nick but the Bloodoff boys were involved as well I understand. Bertie Morris came running to tell me. Ben didn't say a word, but he kept his head down the rest of the morning."

Julia covered her mouth in horror as she continued. "I was inside during lunch, Miss Cusp was supervising, it's her week. A few of the older children in her class help supervise at lunchtime. But apparently Nick encouraged Ben to go around the side of the building, out of sight by the woodpile and a scuffle ensued. One of the bigger boys broke it up and brought them into the school. Nick's eye was swelling and Ben's cheek was red. They both have a few marks on their knuckles. Nick said Ben started it, and Ben didn't say anything. Ollie was very upset, he hadn't noticed Ben disappear until it was all over."

Julia had caught her breath. "That is really too bad. These boys have enough to deal with. And how like Ben not to say a word to defend himself." She looked searchingly at Mrs. Rasmussen. "What happens now? I doubt if this is the end of it."

Mrs. Rasmussen looked severe. "Well, they have both been given an assignment to hand in. They have to write a paragraph on why they shouldn't fight."

She leaned forward and put her hand on Julia's arm. "This is not that serious, Mrs. Butler. Pretty minor, really. I won't have it, of course, in the school. But much worse has happened and the boys usually sort it out between them. And it will help when Ben moves into the regular classroom, which will happen any day. Ollie has already moved into grade one, and he will likely be in grade two after Christmas or before Easter certainly.

"I've just been waiting for Ben to catch up with his reading, so he isn't at too much of a disadvantage, but I'll be putting him into grade two next week. He'll stay there until he's ready for something more. Before the end of the year, I'm sure." She looked with concern at Julia. "Are you okay? I don't see this as a serious encounter, Mrs. Butler. I hope you don't feel you have to make it into an issue with the boys."

Julia stood and held out her hand. "No, I see what you mean.

And you're more used to this than I am. I just didn't think bullying would start this young. I guess this is part of my education as much as Ben's. Thanks for talking to me."

Mrs. Rasmussen rose and walked her to the door. "Your children are very well behaved in the classroom, Mrs. Butler. And I include Ben and Ollie in that observation. It either is trained up in the family, or they're taking their cues from you. None of them disturbs the class. They're very respectful. I really feel this is something out of the ordinary, and won't be repeated. I have already spoken to Nick, and warned him about any repeat performance."

At the kitchen table over supper, Julia brought up the mark on Ben's face. Maggie promptly defended him. "It was Nick Postnikoff, Mummy. He took Ben behind by the woodpile and tried to make him fight. I heard all about it from Lisa." Lisa was Maggie's close friend, and a member of the Doukhobor community, as was Nick.

Ollie jumped in. "Ben didn't do anything wrong, Mama Julia. He went because Nick told him to, and then he got punched." There was the sheen of tears in his eyes.

Julia looked at Ben's mulish expression. "What happened, Ben?"

"Nothing," he said, his mouth tight.

"Well, obviously something happened. I can see the mark on your cheek."

"You already know. You talked to the teacher." He looked defiant.

"Well. But I'd rather hear what you have to say."

Ben pushed a meatball around his plate, then popped it into his mouth. He spoke around it. "Nothing much happened." He chewed for a while, but Julia just waited.

Finally he put his fork down. "Nick called me names, but I know all those names already so I just ignored him. Then at lunch he said he had something to show me and we went around the back of the school. And he tried to fight me. But when I hit him back he fell down, and the other guys just looked, so I left." Ben shrugged, and drank his milk, watching Julia from the corner of his eye.

Julia thought for a moment. "What kind of names?"

She knew she had him, Ben looked back down at his plate and scraped the gravy with his knife. "Homeless," he said.

Julia snorted and his head jerked up in surprise. "That's pretty silly, isn't it? Hardly homeless. This may not be the most high class house in Creston, but it's hardly homeless."

Ben nodded slowly, his eyes fixed on her face. "And 'stupid,'" he said.

"I see," said Julia. "Because you've just arrived at school, I suppose, and haven't been placed in a class yet. I'd be surprised if there are many children who can learn as fast as you and Ollie have."

She beamed at them both. "Why, you started without knowing more than the letters of the alphabet and now you're reading grade one and two books. How fast is that?"

Everyone smiled but Ben.

"And 'blackie'," he said.

"Oh," she said. "Really?... blackie. Because of your colouring, I suppose."

"I guess so." Ben gazed at his plate.

Ollie stared at his brother. "Blackie," he said, clearly outraged. "What does that mean? It's just Ben. That's what he's like. What's wrong with that?" He looked hurt and confused.

"Well," said Julia. "Did that hurt your feelings? I imagine it did. What a thing to say. What would people say about Nick if they were going to be nasty like that? Immigrant, I suppose, or Duhkie, for Doukhobor."

"Or chubby," said Maggie. Nick Postnikoff was built like his father, short and heavyset, even at age twelve.

"What's a Doukhabor?" asked Ollie.

"They're people from Russia who came to Canada about thirty or forty years ago," Julia said. "They were persecuted there.

Do you know what that means? They were driven out of their homes and out of their villages by a group of mean people who didn't like them because they were different. A lot of them live together here and farm communally and keep to themselves. But some of them have branched out and have farms of their own, the way the Postnikoffs have. But they certainly know what it's like to have people be mean to them. Nick should know better than to do that to Ben."

"It doesn't matter," said Ben stubbornly.

"You're right," said Julia. "It doesn't matter. But I hope you won't set out to start a fight with anyone. I wouldn't like it if you were to do that." She paused and looked at Ben as he shook his head.

"Well," she said again. "Good. But just for the record, I like your black hair and dark skin. It's part of what makes you a very handsome young man. Maybe Nick is just jealous. Think about that." And she rose to begin clearing off the kitchen table, feeling Ben's gaze follow her thoughtfully.

~~~**~~~

Part Five – Neighbours

CHAPTER TWENTY SIX

It had turned cold. Julia wore Stephen's old winter coat as she sat on the milking stool in the barn, tugging away on Daisy Mae's udder. They were lucky there was still milk. Daisy Mae was expecting another calf, she usually had twins, and as she got closer to her time, the milk would reduce. They were coming up on a month or six weeks of no milk, and it was going to be missed.

Those two boys were growing literally like weeds. She couldn't believe the size they were and how tall Ben was now. They never seemed to stop eating. Maybe she could make an arrangement with Mr. Dean. Lawrence Dean had a herd of goats and that was where Stephen got Daisy Mae originally. Perhaps she could borrow a goat for a couple of months while Daisy Mae had her calf.

She shivered as she headed across the yard with the milk bucket. Back in the house, she woke the children and hustled them down near the fire to get dressed. She could see her breath in the upstairs.

She'd have to start the pot belly stove a bit earlier in the morning and keep the wood stacked up on the porch. That could be added to the list of chores for the kids to share, although she tended to do a lot of it herself. These little guys weren't quite big enough to undertake everything that needed doing.

She stirred the porridge in the pot, and set a pitcher of warm milk on the table, strained fresh from the barn. As they appeared in the kitchen, she sat each child at the table to eat.

It was pretty quiet in the house in the morning. They were tired still and trooped silently in the direction she pointed. It was kind of cute. She often smiled at how malleable they were. She left Jims to sleep till he woke on his own accord. He was just that much smaller and younger. That's why it worked so well to have the Morrises pick the children up for the trip in to school in the morning. She could take her turn to pick them up in the afternoon, when the chores were done and Jims was at his best.

Mrs. Morris pulled up outside with the cart, whistling to get their attention. "Emma, are you doing the trip today?" Julia called, steam blowing from her mouth as she handed out coats and lunch pails to the children filing past.

"Yes, I've got a few things to do in town, so I thought I'd go in myself. Cold, isn't it?"

"Sure is, but we can't complain. It's past time. Our little creek is frozen solid."

They waved and the horse moved off down the North Road. Julia went back into the house and called softly up to the bedroom to see if Jims was awake

He appeared at the top of the stairs, hair tousselled and cheeks flushed. "Okay, Mum," he said, his little voice raspy. "I don't feel so good."

Julia walked over to the stairs as he tottered down toward her, and felt his forehead. A bit warm but not overly. "There are your slippers," she said. "Put them on to keep your feet warm and come and eat something. Then see how you feel."

She got him dressed and bundled him up to go out with her on her rounds to feed and water the chickens and collect the eggs. The water was frozen in the water dish in the hen house, she had to knock the ice out and bring out warm water to fill it. They checked Prince in the barn, fed and watered him as they did every morning. Then into the root cellar for some vegetables for a stew, and back into the house.

By this time Jims was coughing weakly. Julia was alarmed.

Ever since Stephen died, she'd been paranoid about the children catching something, anything. This must be just a cold. She hadn't heard of anyone being sick. But she couldn't be too careful.

"Let's have you rest on the big chair by the fire, while I get the stew going." She covered him with a blanket and turned the radio on low. She propped the door open on the potbelly stove and threw in more wood, turning the damper down low, then went back to her cooking.

She looked over a few minutes later to find that he had fallen asleep. Probably just over tired. He was still pretty little and couldn't keep up to the older children all the time.

She braised the meat and got the vegetables chopped and into the pot. Then she added tomatoes from her canning jars, a couple of diced onions and stirred it. There were still some herbs at the side of the house, in the cold frame. She slipped out and snipped leeks, parsley and oregano, and threw it into the pot with a couple of dried bay leaves. That would do for a start, let it simmer and test it for flavour later.

Jims was still sleeping, so she picked him up and carried him up to her bed. She dug out her jar of chest rub, equal parts camphor oil and eucalyptus and rubbed him down thoroughly, front and back and under his arms, put a wool sweater on him and tucked him in.

By lunch time he was still sleeping, his forehead burning with fever. Julia wasn't sure what to do, she didn't want to bundle him up and take him out in the cold air. She pulled the wool sweater off and bathed his face with water in the hopes of cooling him down. She was going to have to head into town soon to pick up the children, and she was getting worried.

She put on her coat and ran across the road to Jerome Hoskiss. She banged on his door. "Go away," he yelled. "I don't want any today."

"Jerome," she called. "Mr. Hoskiss, it's Julia Butler. Can you open up, please?"

There was a shuffling noise inside and the door opened.

"Sorry. Come on in," he grumbled.

Julia entered and looked around at the shambles of his home. There were dirty dishes in the dry sink, day's old food glued to the surface. The dishes were chipped and cracked, the mugs stained from coffee. It appeared the floor hadn't been swept in weeks, bits of bark, dirt and leaves tracked in and spread everywhere, the logs for the fire dumped unceremoniously in an untidy pile next to the stove. She had no idea when last the floor had been washed.

Jerome himself was wearing the same clothes she had seen him in for nearly a month straight. Every time she was in his cabin she thought it looked a little worse, but that wasn't her concern today.

"Jerome," she said. "Little Jims is sick. He started with a scratchy throat and warm forehead this morning, and now he's sleeping and doesn't want to wake. His fever is worse. I need your help." She had his attention now.

"Sure," he said. "Want me to go for the doctor? I can ride one of my horses in."

"That would be wonderful," she said. "But I have to pick up the children as well, could you take your wagon? That way you could stop to tell the doctor and then carry on to the school for the children. There are five of them," she reminded him, "the Morris children come too."

Jerome threw on his shaggy jacket. "I'll help you get the horses harnessed up," she said as she followed him out the door of the cabin.

The poor man looked more underfed than ever, stalking along on his spindly legs. She was sure he couldn't actually get the horses hooked up to the wagon on his own. But she had underestimated him. *Men are always stronger*, she thought, *they might look lean but that muscle seems to have more strength than a woman possesses.* She was breathing hard, pulling the traces on one side to hitch them to the whippletree. Hoskiss had his done already and was threading the reins back through the harness rings.

"You go back to your boy, Mrs. Butler, I'll look after this.

Don't you worry." He climbed onto the wagon, his face in a determined frown, and backed the horses into the yard to turn around.

"Thank you, Jerome." Julia waved him on, and ran back across the road.

It seemed forever before Will arrived. Jims was thrashing around, his face beet red. His little body was hot and dry, and his throat seemed so sore. She tried to get him to drink water, but he only took a tiny sip. Her hand trembled as she smoothed his sweaty forehead and prayed the doctor would come.

CHAPTER TWENTY SEVEN

Will knocked at the door, immediately opened it and strode in. "Is it Jims?" he asked when he saw Julia stop halfway down the stairs. "Where is he?" He mounted the steps two at a time, and stopped when he reached her to put his hand on her shoulder. "How are you? It'll be okay, don't worry." His fingers touched the side of her face in a gentle caress, and then he was past her up the stairs and heading down the hall, Julia following close behind.

"In here." She paused at the open door to her room and he walked in to stand beside the bed.

"Could you open the drapes more, just push them back. And I need light, a good lamp if you can." He sat on the side of the bed, and peeled back the sheet. "Hi there, Jims. How are you feeling?"

Jims opened his eyes and blinked slowly as Will placed his palm on the little boy's forehead. He tried to swallow. "Good," he said, his voice scratchy. "But my throat hurts. And my head hurts. Are you going to listen to my heart?"

"I sure am. Let's have a look, here." Will unbuttoned the damp little shirt and spread it wide. He pulled out a thermometer and put it in Jims' mouth. "There you go, just leave that there for a minute. Keep your lips closed, but don't bite it. We don't want that. If you bite it, it might break, it's made of glass. So just hold it carefully in your mouth."

He pressed the stethoscope to the small chest, and listened intently. He took the skinny wrist in his big hand, and placed his fingers on the pulse. "Now I'm going to check your eyes," he said. Jims nodded, holding the thermometer carefully with his lips. Finally Will took the thermometer out and checked it.

"Well, you're a little warm, Jims. I guess you could have told me that, right? All I had to do was ask you."

Jims shook his head.

"Open up, I need to look in your mouth. Julia, can you hold the lamp and shine it on his throat? Hmm, yes. And let's check the neck, now what do we have here?" and he began massaging Jims' throat.

"Okay, your mummy did the absolute right thing. You're to stay in bed for a bit. You've caught some bug and my job is to get you well. You're a good boy, Jims. I'm going to give you something so that throat doesn't hurt so much."

Will pulled the covers over the little body, and Jims' eyelids slowly closed. He took Julia's arm and led her out of the room, stopping on the landing. His arms came around her as she looked anxiously up into his face.

"What is it? It doesn't look like a cold to me. If it was bronchitis he'd be coughing more. Do you know what he has, Will?"

He pulled her against his chest. "I'm not sure, Julia. I doubt it's a cold. I think it's diphtheria. No, wait." He tightened his arms as she tried to pull away.

Julia began to cry, wringing her hands. "No," she cried, "no, no, no!"

Will rubbed her back. "It's okay, Julia, he is a strong little guy and he'll pull through."

"No, he won't," she sobbed. "Stephen didn't, and Jims won't either!" She gripped his shirt front with both hands. "I can't bear it! Do something, Will! Do something! Save him for me, please!" Her voice broke and she cried into her hands.

Will was silent for a minute, holding her tight. "Julia," he said, his voice low. "Listen to me. Jims is a strong boy. We've caught this in time, in fact, we've caught it so early that I can't even be sure yet that it is diphtheria. He's going to be okay. I promise you." He forced her chin up so he could look into her eyes. "I promise you."

She took a deep breath and held it.

"That's better." He stroked her back, his hands warm and firm. "Jims needs us to be strong to help him all we can."

She nodded, choking back a sob, and he pulled her tight against his chest.

"Now, listen. I won't know for sure for another day or so, it takes a little while for the symptoms to develop. But I heard there were a couple of cases in Donegal, and I wondered if it would appear down here. There's an anti-toxin, and I'll order it in now. It should be here tomorrow, and by then I'll be certain of the diagnosis. If it is diphtheria, there will likely be other cases in the area so I'll need a supply of drugs anyway. That's in plenty of time to get control of it. It's better to wait the day and be sure. Now, there are things you need to do."

He pulled her toward the stairs and led her down. *Better to keep her busy, anyway. Keep her too preoccupied to stew about Jims' condition.* In the kitchen, Will filled a basin with warm water and washed his hands.

"First we have to give him some aspirin to try to bring the fever down a little. Two spoons and a bit of jam, and we can crush the pills and feed them to him. Yes, that's right, a glass of water to back it up. Good. I'll take that up to him."

When he returned he stood in the kitchen, hands on hips. "Now, we have to disinfect the house. Start with a basin of warm water with soap and a few drops of carbolic acid. Do you have carbolic acid? Well, I'll bring some from the surgery. Just use soap on your hands for now, and we'll do the disinfecting when I return. Every good medicine cabinet needs carbolic acid. Now, wash the dishes with the water with carbolic acid in it. Then toss the water out, get a fresh basin and begin by washing off the table and chairs.

"Work in the bathroom, all the taps, the sink, maybe put the toothbrushes in boiling water with a few drops of iodine and let them sit in it for a while. Everything you can think of to keep the rest of you from getting it. I know the other children are coming home with Jerome Hoskiss, and they can help. I'm going to my office for supplies, something for his throat, and to make the phone calls. I'll be back."

Will paused, examining her pale face. "Julia, I didn't know that Stephen died of diphtheria. I'm sorry. I'm truly sorry."

She nodded.

He looked at her searchingly. "Things are different, now," he went on. "Even just in the last couple of years. We have anti-toxin now, and we know how to use it. It's pretty effective, as long as it's administered in time, and we have plenty of time right now with Jims. Even if some of the other children fall ill, we will still be okay. I'm sorry that Stephen didn't have that, that it wasn't here for him."

The tears sprang to her eyes, and she shook her head. "Thank you, Will. I'm okay now. I can do this."

He gave a short nod, and headed for the door.

~~*~~

When the children arrived home they came into the house with grave faces and hesitant steps. Will had explained to them that Jims was sick, and they had to be careful not to catch it, too.

He sent Ben back over to help Mr. Hoskiss unharness his horses, and set Ollie to scrubbing the tables down. Maggie was to wash the chairs and the handrail up the stairs. Julia was doing all the dishes, and Will was in the bathroom, disinfecting everything.

Jims began to cry weakly and Julia left her washing to flee up the stairs to his side. They took turns spooning fluids down his throat and bathing him for fever. Will had set up a small basin of soapy water on the dresser for hand washing.

He heated up the stew and fed the crew. Then he made Julia leave the sick room to eat. The children were anxious. Maggie hovered in the doorway, watching Jims as he lay on the bed, listening to his heavy breathing. "He can't breathe, Mummy, help him," she begged.

Julia came and cuddled her daughter against her side. "He is breathing, sweetheart. That's what it sounds like when you have diphtheria. But he'll get better. Will promised that he's going to get better." They both stood, watching Jims struggle for air.

Finally she sent the children early to bed. Maggie couldn't get comfortable, kept calling for her mother to check on her, maybe she was hot too, maybe she was getting sick, why was it so cold in the bed. She couldn't settle down without her brother beside her. She finally fell into a fitful slumber.

Will set himself up on the parlour sofa with a cushion for a pillow and a couple of blankets. He woke in the early morning, and rolled out to stoke the potbelly stove with more wood. Then he went upstairs to relieve Julia. With a great deal of encouragement, she was persuaded to go downstairs and lay down, just for a while, and in fact she fell asleep and slept till dawn.

CHAPTER TWENTY EIGHT

Julia woke in a panic, racing up the stairs, terrified that Jims might have gotten sicker or died in the night. But all was calm in the sickroom. Will dozed in the upholstered chair in the corner, and he woke when she bolted into the room. He held up his hand and walked across to her.

"He's fine, Julia, certainly no worse than yesterday. Come have a look, he slept most of the night."

Jims opened his eyes and squinted up at his mother. He tried to talk, but finally just shut his mouth and looked around the room with a vague gaze.

Julia wrung her hands. "I think he's worse, Will," she whispered. "He doesn't know who I am."

"He knows. He just has such a sore throat that it's hard to talk. The film developed in his mouth overnight. I'm able to do a positive diagnosis this morning, so we're well on our way to being able to treat this effectively. Just sit with him for a bit, and hold his hand. He'll be comforted by that. But make sure to wash your hands before you leave the room." He gave her a one-armed hug on his way by, washed his hands thoroughly and went down the stairs.

When Mr. Morris stopped to pick the children up, Julia called from the door that they were staying home. They had diphtheria in

150

the house and there would be no school for a while. Will left to pick up the anti-toxin as it came in on the ten-thirty train and to check on his office. By late afternoon, two neighbours had delivered food, fresh bread and a pot of soup to the house.

Julia kept Ben, Ollie and Maggie busy, there were chickens to feed, and eggs to gather. Prince needed to be fed and Daisy Mae to be milked, although Julia did that last job. She set them to shoveling out the hen house and the barn. She even had them washing the floors to keep them busy and get the house as clean as possible.

She made them take naps in the afternoon, convinced that Jims must have gotten overtired and therefore more susceptible to illness. She dressed them in wool to keep them warm enough so no one would catch a chill. When Will returned with the medicine, they crowded around Jims in the bed to watch him get his needle. He barely stirred, all they could hear was his breathing hoarse and ragged.

Julia covered her face with her hands. She couldn't bear it. Ben and Maggie crowded on either side of her and held on, hugging her wherever they could reach. She had to respond, pulling her hands from her face and wrapping her arms around them.

Wills herded the children downstairs and produced more medicine from his medical bag. "I have vaccine for everyone," he said. "There's no reason to get this disease, and the vaccine gives you a resistance to it. So I want to vaccinate you all. I know diphtheria has been in the house before, and Julia, you may have a resistance to it already, if you didn't get it when Stephen did. But I don't think we need to take that chance. So who wants to go first?"

He looked around the little group, and his gaze alighted on Ben.

"I think you could go first. You're a strong young man and the others will be able to see that the needle doesn't hurt that much. I already had mine, a few years ago. I'll show you." He rolled up his sleeve and pulled it higher to show his bicep. "See? No mark. So this isn't bad at all, it doesn't even leave a mark. You sit here, Ben."

Ben's eyes were wide, but he gritted his teeth and sat at the kitchen bench. Will arranged his needles on a clean cloth along with the small vials of vaccine.

Julia gripped Ben's hand. "Brave boy," she said, and smiled into his eyes.

Will swabbed his arm and sank the needle. Ben flinched and then gave a wobbly grin as Will pulled the needle out and pressed on the spot. "It's not too bad," he said, his voice shaking. "You're next Ollie."

One by one they were vaccinated. Maggie sobbed for a minute in Julia's arms after her shot, and Julia flinched as the needle sank into her arm. There was a collective sigh of relief when they were all done, and Julia made tea for everyone.

By the second morning there was more food on their porch, a bucket containing cheese and sausage, a cooked ham, a cake still warm in the pan. And Jims was a little better.

Julia could finally breathe again, instead of feeling stifled. There was hope, although Will had been telling her that all along. He didn't think Jims was that sick. The typical white membrane that covered the breathing passages, and caused swelling in the neck were quite mild to what he had seen in other patients. He had full confidence Jims would be fine. *But*, Julia thought, *this isn't his child*, and then felt guilty for thinking that.

The loss of Stephen had been all she could bear. She had just recovered from that staggering loss. Getting Ben and Ollie had seemed at first scary but then like a miracle, more children to love.

But when Jims got sick, all her old fears came back, compounded by her memory of the dreadful days after Stephen died. She'd gone into a tailspin of dread and anticipated loss. Now that Jims seemed to be on the mend, her heart eased, her spirits lifted and she was suddenly exhausted.

She checked the other children constantly but they had no signs of fever. They got so they felt each other on the forehead to check for heat and that was when Julia realized how paranoid she'd become.

Well, they could go back to school next week, and this too would pass. She had a chance to catch her breath and deal with all the food on her table. She put some of it in a bundle, donned her coat and walked across the road to see Jerome. She'd thank him for his help and give him some food, since he didn't cook much for himself.

She knocked on his door, then banged on the panel. Standing on the little porch she surveyed the yard. The horses were out in the field, but maybe he was in the barn with his prize cows. She walked across and pulled the barn door back on its track. Inside the air was warm and humid. The cows were moving restlessly and lowing in their stalls, but Jerome was nowhere to be seen.

Back at the cabin, she hammered on the door and pushed it open. Sticking her head in the opening she called. "Jerome, I want to thank you for helping with the children." She shouldered her way in and laid her bundle on the grubby kitchen table. The cabin was cold, the fire long dead in the stove.

She heard a hoarse cough and poked her head through the curtains in the bedroom doorway. Hoskiss lay in his bed in an old pair of gray wool underwear, the blankets dragging on the floor by his feet. He coughed weakly, his eyes half closed.

Julia approached hesitantly. "Jerome, Mr. Hoskiss," she called softly. His eyes tracked her across the floor. "You don't sound well. How are you feeling?"

He tried to answer, but the words got lost in a fit of weak coughing.

She felt his forehead. He was burning up. She picked up his arm and put her fingers against his pulse. It was XXXhread, his skin hot and dry. "I'm getting the doctor, Jerome. He won't be long. He'll know what this is and be able to help you." She got a cup from the kitchen and poured a bit of water in it. He tried to take some, but most of it dripped onto his chest.

Julia stoked the fire in his pot belly stove, got it going and set the kettle to boil. Then she walked back across the road. She left word with Ollie that Doctor Will was to come across as soon as he got there.

Then she checked on Jims, gathered up a basin of soap, iodine, carbolic acid, cleaning cloths, a jar of vegetable soup from her cooler, and one of Stephen's old shirts and headed back across the road.

~~~**~~~

CHAPTER TWENTY NINE

Mr. Morris stopped by that afternoon, said he'd heard old Hoskiss had the diphtheria as well, and that Doc had given him the shot he needed. He'd come to take care of his cattle while he was down. Emma had sent him with a soft stew and broth to entice Hoskiss to eat, if he could.

Slowly, Jims and Hoskiss began to mend. The children were back at school and Jims was still lethargic. He ate little and slept a lot.

But none of the others got sick, and for that Julia got down on her knees and thanked God. She was across the road every morning and evening to check on Jerome. Soon he was well enough to get up to add firewood to his stove and keep his cabin warm during the day. He was weak, but the fever was down.

When Heddie came on Monday, Julia brought all of Hoskiss' clothes across, and they did a lye soap wash. As they scrubbed, Julia thought of her conversation with Ben the night before. She'd been very tired, setting a quick supper on the table for Maggie and the older boys. Jims had been up for a few hours but was back in bed.

The conversation had turned to family, and Maggie asked Ollie where his other brother was. They didn't know, but Charlie had left home at least a year ago, the summer before Ben and Ollie ran away. He'd told Ben he was leaving because he needed to get away while he could. And he mentioned work at a sawmill in the valley. He knew someone, a young friend who'd been hired on there. He was going to try to get work there too. The boys had never heard from him again.

"What's your last name?" Julia asked. "What name would Charlie use? Charlie who?"

The boys looked at her dumbly.

So Julia changed the subject and talked about her own family. There had been three children. Her brother Sam was the oldest, then Julia, and there had been a younger sister. But she drowned while swimming in the Kootenay River the summer she turned eight. "That was just before my father died," Julia said.

Maggie put her hand in her mother's. She'd heard this story before and knew her mother still missed Maggie, her namesake. "So I know what it's like to lose a brother or sister."

Julia looked at Ben, he had an especially determined look about his mouth. She didn't push any further. She remembered clearly the day she'd had them both in tears because she asked so many questions they weren't able to answer.

Later that evening, she was knitting on a pair of mittens when she heard a lot of whispering in the bedroom where Ben and Ollie slept. Suddenly Ben appeared in the hall. He stood in his nightshirt, too short for him already with his knobby knees showing, silently watching her.

Then he padded forward until he was leaning against her knee. "Mama Julia," he whispered, "can I talk to you?"

"Of course, Ben. You know you can, have a seat here." She patted the sofa beside her and he sat down against her thigh.

He sighed and leaned into her side as she put her arm around him. "Ollie and I been talking, and we think we should tell you." He didn't look at her.

"Tell me what, Ben?"

"Tell you what our name is," he said. "It's Valadio." He looked up at her a moment, as if that would mean something to her. When she just waited, he continued. "Our Pa is Olin Valadio. Our Ma is Alanna. Ollie's name is Olin, like Pa, not Oliver. We lived in the hills, kind of behind Donegal. I'm not sure exactly. Ollie isn't either. But Charlie always said you could reach Donegal in a good day's walk anytime you wanted."

He paused and Julia waited. "Ma and Pa make moonshine. Mostly Ma makes it, and guys come up to buy it from them. Sometimes Pa takes it away to sell it somewhere else, we don't know where. The problem is bottles, how to get enough jars. But the customers usually bring some."

Ben was silent for a bit. Julia tightened her arm, the knitting sitting idle in her other hand. "What else, Ben?"

He shook himself. "Well, we had an older sister, Valerie, but she disappeared too, we don't know where she went. When Charlie left, he said he was going to a sawmill. I don't know what the name of it was, but it's on the river."

"Are there any other children at home?" Julia was almost afraid to ask. The answer could be so frightening.

"No, just Ollie and me."

She rocked him softly. "Would you like to find your brother Charlie? Do you think it would be safe to find him and let him know where you are?"

Ben's face shone. "Charlie would look out for us, no question. He said if we was ever to get away, we was to come to him. That's what we was doing in the summer when we wound up here, but we got chased by a dog, and we got afraid. And then we got lost like." Tears leaked out of his eyes, falling on the hands folded in his lap. "We didn't find him." His shoulders shook.

Julia wiped his eyes with her hand, and pulled him into her arms, rocking him gently. "It's okay, Ben. You both did very well. For two little guys to get as far as you did was pretty amazing. I'd say you did as well as any two boys I know."

They were silent for a while. "Does Charlie look like you, Ben? Does he have the dark skin and thick black hair, or is he more like Ollie?"

"Like Ollie, but more. You know, more lighter. His hair's kinda redder and he's got a few of them spots on his face like Ollie."

"You mean freckles?"

"Yeah, freckles. Our Pa's got red hair and lots of freckles and Ma has the dark hair like me, only more if you know what I mean. Her face is darker too, darker even than me."

They hugged and rocked in comfortable silence.

Finally Julia sighed. "You go back to bed now, Ben. We can talk more in the morning. Maybe there's some way to find Charlie. If he's using the last name Valadio, we might be able to trace him. It would be nice to know he's okay. And maybe he could visit, and you could see him. You'd like that, wouldn't you?"

Ben nodded.

~~~**~~~

Part Six – Christmas

CHAPTER THIRTY

The Christmas pageant at school had been rehearsed and everyone was to attend. Will had been invited, about forty times. He came to pick Julia up in his car which wasn't too steady in the snow. They slipped and slid, but went slow as they didn't have far to go.

The community hall was packed, chairs in rows all the way to the back wall. Great swags of evergreen boughs decorated the front wall and above the stage. Red ribbon in floppy bows hung at intervals. There were candles set in glass jars across the front of the stage as footlights. The children had been excited, and full of trepidation by turn. Julia could hardly get them into bed the last few nights, there was so much chatter about whether their costume would be finished, and would they remember their lines.

It was already hot in the room. The wood stove put out a fair amount of heat, coats came off, and the humidity rose. Even Jerome Hoskiss was there, coming because, 'well, Ben asked him to come and well, it just wasn't right not to encourage these young'uns.'

"I'm glad this isn't a dance," Will whispered in Julia's ear. "We'd melt if we had to dance in this heat." They were seated in a row with Jims on one side, Bert and Emma Morris, and Jerome on the other.

A great deal of noise, rustling and giggles came from behind the curtain. Finally one curtain was pulled aside and Miss Cusp, the teacher for the senior class, appeared on the stage. A hush fell over the audience.

"Good evening, ladies and gentlemen," she began. "We'd like to welcome you to the Creston School Christmas Pageant. Our students have worked very hard to bring this entertainment to you. We hope you enjoy it. There are two parts to the evening..."

Will leaned close. "Are you excited?"

Julia's eyes shone. "Very. You should have seen Ollie this last week. He has a speech to deliver and he's been locked in his room every night, practicing. I could hear him droning away in there, Ben was his audience, and critic, I might add. And Maggie has been like a bear. I think she's very nervous."

"I'm nervous too," Will said doubtfully. "I just want those boys to do well. It would do wonders for their confidence. I'm sure neither of them has been involved in anything like this before."

"I know they haven't," she whispered back. "I think they'll be fine. I've been praying all day."

Will grinned and took her hand. "That's my girl," he said.

Well, there he goes again, she thought, growing warm. *I wonder what brought that on!*

The pageant was a huge success. Benjamin played one of the Wisemen in the scene at Bethlehem, which was wise of the teacher. A child of few words, but great presence, Ben carried it off so well the audience applauded as he left the manger scene. Ollie aced his little speech, given as an angel speaking to the shepherds watching their sheep. Maggie played one of the sheep, and she obediently grazed the stage, and stared in wonder at the star hanging on a rope from the rafters.

For the finale, the children gathered on stage in their costumes to sing carols, with the audience singing along. After it was all over, tea and cookies were served at the back of the hall. The children were so excited they ran shrieking around the big room, creating pockets of mayhem amongst the adult groups.

Jims found Becky's daughter Nell, and they spent their time

trying to catch the older children. Julia finally corralled the red-faced and sweating group, herding them into their coats and out to the car.

It was a struggle to get everyone more or less ready for bed. The adrenaline levels were still high, as Will termed it. He managed to wrestle the older boys into their pajamas and then to the bathroom to clean their teeth while Julia got the little ones to bed.

He was waiting in the parlour with the gas fireplace burning when she came down. He poured her a small glass of wine and sat beside her on the sofa. "Well, that was fun," he remarked and took a sip.

She gazed at him quizzically. "Are you serious, or being sarcastic?"

"Serious," he said, looking offended. "I enjoyed that no end. The sheep were especially entertaining, with their surprised looks outlined with fuzzy fur stuck all around their faces."

Their laughter trailed off into chuckles. It was warm in here, and she was tired.

Will took her hand, and held it in his, palm up. "Julia, I won't see you until after Christmas. I leave tomorrow morning on the train for home." He looked thoughtful. "Not that that is home anymore. I think of this place now as my home."

"Do you? That was pretty fast."

His lips compressed and he gazed at her mouth. "I know. But there are a lot of good people here and I've felt very welcome."

"Yes, it's a good community." She shifted on the cushion and withdrew her hand. "Have a wonderful Christmas, Will. I hope you really enjoy your family back there. Will your brother Raymond be there with his wife and children?" Will had talked about Ray a bit, the next brother to him and also a physician. It was Ray's wife, Polly, who had sent the clothing for the boys.

He nodded. "All my brothers are there."

Julia raised her eyebrows. "All? How many are there?"

"There are five of us, five boys, and…" He held his hand up as she went to interrupt, "two girls. Of the five boys, four are doctors, like Dad, and Danny is a teamster. Don't know where that came from, but Dad seems just as proud of him as he is of the rest of us. And they all stayed in Winnipeg."

"Your poor mother,' Julia said, smiling cheekily.

"What," he bristled. "Nothing wrong with my Mother."

"Well, nothing that having five sons wouldn't cure," she murmured.

He took her hand back and gave a little tug. She fell against him. "You can hardly talk, you're well on your way, with three sons and a daughter."

Julia laughed. "Yes, but I did it the easy way. I only had to give birth to two of them."

They were silent for a moment. "So where are your sisters?" she asked.

"The oldest, Agnes, lives in Brandon, married to a doctor. The other one is still in Winnipeg. She's single, and at university. Studying to be a doctor."

"No!" Julia was astounded. "Really? Your father has a lot to answer for, doesn't he? A woman doctor. Well, I knew there were some, but I just never met one."

Will nodded. "Yep. It isn't just my Dad though, Mum's father was a doctor, so we got it constantly from both sides of the family. There is no more honourable profession." He said this sardonically, but Julia read the pride in his face.

Her expression softened. "You're a good doctor, Will. We're really lucky in Creston that you decided to come here to practice. What would we have done without you?"

Will flattened her hand against his chest. "That's what I needed to talk to you about. I don't want you to do without me. Julia, I care for you a great deal. And I've been slow to say anything."

He shook his head when she opened her mouth to speak. "Please, just let me say this. I've been looking for an opportunity to speak and there aren't many. This is one busy household.' His expression was wry.

She sat back and waited.

"I know that you come as a package. There's a whole family here, you and the children, all four of them. I know how important they are to you. So if I were to become part of the family, there would be six of us." His eyes were tender, as he gripped her hand. "I wanted to take my time, and not make you uncomfortable. I needed to see if the children would trust me. And I think they do."

His gaze became fierce. "I want to court you, Julia. I want to court you openly, not pretend I'm just a family friend, or someone who helps you out with the children. I mean, I want to be those things too, but I want to be more than that to you. Is that alright? Do I have your permission?" There was hesitation in his expression as he watched her.

"That's a fine thing to say, when you're leaving town in the morning," she whispered.

He shouted with laughter, and hauled her into his arms. "Julia, you're a brat. I'm serious here, with my heart in my hand, and you're teasing me."

He kissed her then, holding her flush against his body. She was suddenly reminded again what a big man he was, but so tender. He didn't frighten her, she trusted him completely. She kissed him back. Oh, how she'd missed this.

My goodness, he could kiss. She pulled away, flushed and breathless. He was breathing hard, his chest pumping.

He gazed at her face. "Do I have your permission, Julia? I want to court you and your family. I think that's how it should be done." He looked like he was planning a strategy to take the barricades, very determined, a bit desperate.

"What about Miss Cusp?" she asked.

He frowned down at her. "Who?"

"Miss Cusp, the school teacher." She felt a flush rise up her throat at the awkward question, but she needed to know.

His eyes narrowed. "What about her?"

"Well, she mentioned to me tonight that you'd asked her out to coffee, but she hadn't been able to go. Yet, she added. Hadn't been able to go yet."

He stared at her for a minute, then huffed a breath out. "She asked *me* out for coffee, and I said 'no'. She asked me twice, I said 'no' twice." He glared at her in frustration.

"You just said 'no'? That sounds a bit abrupt." Julia didn't know whether to laugh or weep.

His eyes flared. "I didn't just say 'no'! I was polite, I just didn't want…"

"I see," she said.

"You see? What do you see?" The colour was high in his cheeks, and his mouth a grim determined line.

"I see that you were asked out for coffee but said 'no'."

"That's all there is to see, Julia! That's all that happened. I know what it's like to be the new doctor in a small town, every young and not so young female who's available has her eyes on you. I've been very careful." His frustration was obviously mounting.

"Yes," she said.

"What?" He reared back. "What does that mean?"

"Yes. It means yes, you can court me."

He stared at her face for a minute then hauled her against him and kissed her again.

When he pulled back a while later, he looked into her flushed face. Her heart was racing and she tried to control her breath. He ran his broad hand down her cheek. "You're so lovely, Julia. Every time I come here, it hits me how beautiful you are. That day you came charging into my office with the curls falling down your neck, and four children in tow, you just bowled me over. And when I offended you, when you thought I was implying that you might have had something to do with the condition of Ben's back, you set me right back on my heels properly."

He laughed softly and slipped his hand to her waist. "And I've been on my heels ever since," he whispered. "I don't know if I can go away for Christmas, after all. It might be too long without seeing you."

"Well, I'll still be here when you come back, unless Jerome Hoskiss starts courting me. Then I just don't know." She simpered up at him. "I'm not sure what I'd do in that case."

"Don't tease, Julia. I can't bear it. Jerome had better keep his distance," he said half playfully. "And it isn't Jerome I'm worried about. Luke Harrison is always watching you, and he had you cornered for half an hour tonight at the pageant. Whatever he was saying, he looked pretty serious. I hate to tell you, I'm a sore loser." He buried his face in her hair, breathing deeply.

The feel of him against her was exciting. Julia inhaled the scent of him and leaned against the thick wall of his chest. Such a solid man in so many ways. If only he weren't going away in the morning. If only there weren't four little ones asleep in the house now. *If only....*

~~**~~

CHAPTER THIRTY ONE

C hristmas morning dawned cold and clear, frost laying heavily along the top rail of the fence and on the steps to the verandah. Wagsy had spent the last few days sniffing around the Christmas tree, looking for who knew what. Julia thought maybe someone had put a present under there that had food in it. There was a tin from the Morrises, it might hold cookies. There was a parcel from the Grants that had arrived in the mail that week.

What a treat it had been, putting the tree up. She took the children with her to cut one down the day before Christmas Eve. They walked across the frozen creek onto the old logging road that ran down the back of their property.

The search had been thorough, not just any tree would do. But finally they found a nice little spruce that everyone could agree on, not too big, just large enough to fill the corner in the parlour. Ben and Ollie took turns sawing away on the trunk until it finally gave up and fell over.

They dragged it back across the frozen creek through the snow and up to the house, taking turns, with Wagsy barking and leaping around them. Julia propped it up on the porch and let the snow melt off it. The next morning they got breakfast out of the way, and dragged the box of decorations up from the basement.

They stood the tree in a bucket of water with a bit of sugar in it, and tied the top to the picture rail. When it appeared to be standing pretty straight, Julia put the lights on it, little tin dishes with small coloured lights in the middle. They had to go on just right so that the lights didn't touch the needles.

Ollie couldn't picture how it would look. When they finished putting the ornaments on and plugged the lights in, he was astonished. He sat for hours staring at the tree. "Mama Julia, it's magic. I didn't know a tree could look like magic." He ate his lunch in there watching the sparkling decorations turn in the air.

Suddenly they all got very busy in their rooms, whispering and wrapping. Julia had helped each one of them with small things they could give as gifts, and they had brown paper that they had coloured to wrap each gift.

She had two chickens ready for dinner on Christmas Day. The Christmas pudding was made and waiting, the sauce cooked up the day before. There were sweet potatoes with nutmeg and butter, and stuffing for the birds. She'd made pumpkin pies. There was shortbread, gingerbread, sweet bread braids stuffed with candied fruit. She'd been baking for days.

Will had left a ton of stuff, including a box of chocolates. He dropped by the morning he was leaving, loaded with parcels.

Christmas Eve, they hung their socks on hooks over the fireplace. Julia had to turn the fire off to ensure they didn't go up in smoke. The children wrote notes to Santa, and everyone needed help. Jims was done first, asking for a marbles game like Nell had, and it went on from there. Maggie wanted a doll, one with chestnut hair just like her own.

Ollie wanted a slingshot, so he could shoot rabbits for dinner. Julia made a mental note to start catching rabbits again with her wire traps. She didn't know he liked them so much. Ben didn't want anything, but Julia told him that Santa was expecting him to ask for something. So Ben wrote that he would like a gift, he didn't mind what it was, and hoped Santa had a good Christmas, too.

Julia helped him write it and was amazed at how much he had

learned since he started school in September. He could spell a lot of the words, his printing was square and precise.

When the letters were done, she read them the Christmas story from the Bible, and tucked them into bed. Then she tucked them into bed again. Then she threatened that Santa couldn't come if anyone else got out of bed, so they had all better go to the bathroom for the last time.

Eventually Jims and Maggie were asleep, and Ben and Ollie were quiet. Julia had done most of her wrapping earlier in the week and she got the gifts out from under her bed and laid them on the blanket around the foot of the tree.

It seemed a lonely thing to do, to place the presents out by herself. *Well, I'm not going to get maudlin,* she thought. *This is Christmas, and the kids are going to have a good time. I'm not going to spoil it for myself, or them.* She blew out the pretty candles on the mantle, put Wagsy out and locked the door.

When she woke the sun was just rising to a beautiful morning. She quickly got dressed and put Stephen's old coat on, hugging it close for comfort as if to bring him near again on this special day. She started the fire in the pot belly stove, then went out to milk Daisy Mae. While she was out she fed the animals.

When she got back inside, the house was still quiet. She strained the milk and set it on the porch to cool, and put more wood in the stove as the house began to warm. Ollie staggered out in his pajamas and she gave him a big hug. "Merry Christmas, Ollie."

"Did Santa come?" he muttered.

"See for yourself, check your stocking," she said. She heard his gasp as he spotted his bulging sock hanging from the mantle.

It wasn't long before the children were up and talking amongst themselves on the floor of the parlour. Their little socks contained an orange, a piece of marzipan, chocolates, some nuts and a toy.

There was great excitement around the tree, it seemed more presents had appeared since last night. Julia got them all fed and dressed before they sat down to open them.

It was a wonderful day. They went for a walk in the frosty air, their boots crunching in the snow, then had lunch. Julia put the gramophone on, playing all kinds of music. The kids let her know what they liked, including the Wizard of Oz.

By the time Jerome came across for dinner, the parlour had been tidied up. Ollie wore his new sweater. The boys each had a pullover, and Maggie's was cardigan style. Jims' was a nice heather colour that brought out his reddish hair and freckles, and Ben's a dark charcoal gray with white snowflakes that set off his eyes wonderfully.

She'd chosen the yarn to complement each of them. Ollie's was a warm brown, with a horse on the front. He loved it, stroking it smooth across his stomach, straining his neck to catch a glimpse of himself in the bureau mirror. His face was red, probably from over-heat. The room was warm and the sweater was wool, but he wasn't taking it off. Julia encouraged him to hang it on the back of his chair during dinner, so he didn't get food stains on it, and he reluctantly agreed.

Julia wore a new cream-coloured blouse, lace cascading around the collar and down the front, with a pale pink ribbon threaded through it. It was a gift from Will, and she learned he'd bribed Ben to put it under the tree Christmas morning. She missed Will and wished he were there with them.

CHAPTER THIRTY TWO

Constable Alex Terasoff of the Royal Canadian Mounted Police stopped by on his weekly trek through town two days after Christmas. Will had filled him in on the background of the boys in the fall when they first arrived, and Terasoff had been keeping an eye out for anything that might shed light on the situation.

This time Julia had a name to give him, Valadio. He stayed for coffee and promised to see what he could find out for her.

"I'm not trying to make trouble for them," Julia explained. "I don't want to attract any attention. I just don't want to constantly worry about whether they'll come looking for the boys, and what they might do if they find them."

The constable promised to be discreet in his inquiries.

Will arrived back in town the next day. He came out to the house loaded down with parcels, and the children jumped around in excitement at the sight of him. He gave hugs to everyone, his arms lingering around Julia till her face was flushed and her breathing came faster.

"There is definitely a present here for everyone, so let's see how we can hand these out," he said. The noise rose to a new level, as he slowly sorted through parcels, pretending to search for names.

Julia shrugged and sat down at the kitchen table, deciding she'd stay out of it.

So, Will gave Julia her present first.

"But you already gave me a gift," she protested.

Will frowned. "Open the present," he commanded. "That blouse was what's called preliminary."

Julia blushed at his cheeky grin, and opened the package, ignoring the inquisitive questions from the children about what *preliminary* meant. Inside was a hip length jacket, made of soft wool. It was a warm red-brown, almost matching her hair, with fur collar and cuffs. There was a pair of long gloves with pearl buttons along the back to match.

"You'll be warm riding in my car this winter," Will said with satisfaction.

Julia rubbed the fur against her cheek and smiled in delight.

He stared at her for a minute, then abruptly turned back to the other packages.

He made such a production that Ollie was nearly hysterical by the time he finished. Ben tried to calm him down, holding his brother around the chest to pin him to one spot. Finally, Will got them all seated on the benches at the kitchen table and handed out a package each. They carefully pulled the wrapping off, amid excited chatter.

Jims had a building block set with letters painted on the sides. He squealed with glee and scrambled down to the floor to set them up. Maggie got a doll, long auburn hair curling around her shoulders, eyes that opened when she sat up and closed when she was laid down. Her outfit was a pretty button up dress in velvet with a hat to match. Maggie couldn't believe her eyes, and cradled the doll in her arms, oblivious to the others.

Ollie got a train set, complete with engine and boxcars. He was fascinated and quickly staked out a place on the floor near Jims to begin laying it out. Ben's gift was an air rifle. He gasped, looked up at Will with awe, and back at the gun in his hands.

"That's only for target practice, rabbits for dinner, and such," said Will. "I got it because I can see that you're a serious young man who can be trusted to use common sense and care with something like this." He sat down to show him how to load it.

In the midst of it, Will looked up at Julia with such an expression of intent and commitment that Julia knew he had begun his courtship, as he'd promised before he left. He'd begun with the children. He'd win them over, and in doing so, win Julia's heart. He knew her so well.

~~*~~

The RCMP Constable was back the next week, just as Julia set the bread to rise on the proover over the stove. While consuming his 'usual coffee and cake', he disclosed he had some news. He'd found a Valadio, but not in the Donegal hills. This man was working in a feed store in a small town called Ymir, south of Nelson. He'd come to the attention of the police because he'd gotten into a fight in a Salmo bar.

"Was anyone hurt?" Julia asked.

The Constable shrugged. "From what I hear he's pretty tough, I doubt if he was hurt. And the other guy was complaining because he'd lost the fight, it sounds like."

"How old a man would he be? And do you have any idea what he looks like?" Julia wondered if this was the father. She prayed it wasn't the son.

Constable Terasoff shrugged again. "About twenty, twenty-one, something like that. Pretty young, and full of piss… uh, sorry ma'am. He seems not to like to take an insult, is what I mean. And he's a redhead, so that may come into it." Terasoff rubbed his own close crop of graying black hair.

"I think he's just an average Joe, drank a bit too much, and got into a ruckus over something. But he doesn't sound like our fellow, so I'll still keep an eye out for you." He rose to leave. "If you should hear from the parents of these boys, make sure you let us know. Get a phone call over to the detachment, we'll keep an eye on them for you."

Julia saw him to the door, and turned back to the kitchen, lost in thought. This might be the right Valadio, the son, not the father. About twenty or twenty-one, but once a young man hit his teens and had been out working for a few years, it was hard to tell if he was seventeen or twenty-two. And a redhead, that was exactly what Ben had said. *Like Ollie, but more lighter. And with lots of those spots on his face.*

If this was Charlie, Julia wanted to be careful how they approached him. She didn't want to spook him, but nor did she want to invite into her home a violent young man. On the other hand, Ben and Ollie would leap at the chance to see Charlie. They idolized him, their older brother who would have done anything for them.

Her emotions swung back and forth all morning as she pondered what to do. She punched the bread down and got it into the baking tins. She'd talk to Will about it, and then smiled to herself. It seemed she had someone to talk things over with, now. It was a nice feeling and she hugged it close to her breast.

~~*~~

Will wasn't interested in talking at first, he was too busy kissing her in the parlour with the door closed. "I think I'm too old for this, I mean this courting business," he finally gasped into her hair. "I don't seem to have the self control this is going to take. I don't want to stop. I just want to take your clothes off and…"

"Shhh," she said. "The children will hear you."

"They better not," he barked. "They'd have to be standing with their little ears to that door." He glared toward the door.

"No, they could be standing on the other side of the kitchen, and they'd still hear you!"

He sighed, leaning back against the cushions of the sofa and pulling her down on top of him. "That's better," he said, running his hands up to her breasts and grasping her through the fabric of her dress.

"Will! Stop, before…" She seized his wrists but held his hands in place as he kneaded her gently. "That feels so good," she murmured, leaning into his palms. He groaned and reached to kiss her, just as a knock sounded at the door.

"Mum," Maggie called. "I'm ready for bed now. Are you coming to tuck me in?"

Will hung his head, as Julia slowly extricated herself from his grasp. "I'm coming, Maggie." She grinned down at Will. "Did you think this would be easy?" she teased in a whisper and pressed a kiss to his mouth.

He grinned back. "Easy as pie," he said, and heaved himself up. "I'll check on the boys."

Later as they settled back on the sofa, Julia described what Constable Terasoff had told her.

Will was sure the best thing they could do would be to go and find this man, Valadio. If he was, in fact, Brother Charlie, it would be a wonderful gift for all of them. "If he's fighting in bars," he continued, "it's probably because he's a young man who's a little lost. He needs a bit of help, and what better help could anyone offer than to reunite him with his younger brothers.

"Think of it Julia. He'd probably be thrilled, and so would Ben and Ollie. The boys would never forgive us if they found out we knew where Charlie was and didn't do anything to find him, or if we didn't let them know. I think it's very exciting."

They talked long into the night. Julia finally fell asleep in his arms, her head resting against his collar bone. He lowered his face into her hair and breathed her in. He could feel her breasts pressed against the wall of his chest, and her hip leaning against him. He knew what her shape was, and that shape drew him like a lodestone. And he came willingly, eagerly, into her magnetic field. He sighed.

This couldn't go on for too much longer. He was no young boy and he wasn't ready to wait! Yet he knew he'd take whatever time she needed. He wouldn't risk losing her because he was impatient. But he wouldn't wait forever either!

Will grinned ruefully to himself, knowing his emotions were dragging him back and forth in a kind of tug of war. And it probably wasn't just emotions anyway, it was his physical urge as much as any emotional one that was driving him. It had just been at Christmas that he'd declared his intentions, and it had only been weeks since then, not months. He sighed again.

~~~**~~~

CHAPTER THIRTY THREE

A small family walked by the gate the next day when Julia and Jims were in the yard bringing in the eggs. They stopped and stared at the house. They all looked the same, thin, brown, and dowdy. Their clothes were old and worn thin, patched in places. But not dirty, and their eyes were alive. The father had a couple of bundles on his back.

Julia walked over to greet them and they stared at her a minute, before the man swung one of the bundles down and set it on the ground. "We have some baskets for sale, Ma'am. Don't know if you can use one. They're made of reed." And he began to unpack the sack. The baskets were surprisingly lovely in their workmanship. They were large and sturdy, with solid thick rims, and a bit of design in the weaving.

"Who makes these?" she asked as she examined them.

"We do," he responded proudly. "My wife and son and I. We pull the reeds and dry them over the summer and then do our weaving in the fall and winter. They sell pretty well, and it's a way to pay for a bit of food."

Julia looked back at the baskets, they would be useful for the eggs. When he told her the price, she nodded and said, "I'll be right back."

She bought three, two for herself and one for Annie. Annie

had chickens and could use a good basket, she was sure. The little family was beaming when they left. Before they moved on, Julia gave them some cheese sandwiches and a warm jacket for the mother, now that she had a new one of her own.

~~*~~

"Well, Ray, good to see you. How are Polly and the boys?" Will extended his hand and seized his brother in a strong grip. The tall heavily-built man grabbed him back in a bear hug and they laughed together, standing on the platform of the train station.

Will was oblivious to the watching crowd that milled around them, but Raymond noticed and pulled back. "Everyone is fine, just fine. Uh, looks like we're getting some scrutiny, here," he commented.

Will didn't even glance around. "Don't worry about it. That's how it is in small towns. There isn't a thing that goes on, or a person that arrives, that everyone doesn't know about. It's both a curse and a blessing. Where's your bag?"

He hustled his brother over to his car and fired it up with the crank. A cloud of smoke billowed out the tailpipe and blew back into the cab of the vehicle.

Ray coughed. "Might be time for a new car," he remarked as Will climbed in and banged the door shut.

He shot Ray a glance. "What's wrong with this one? It came with the medical practice." He shot his brother a wry grin. "The practice is in the same shape as the car." He put the clutch down and slid the gearshift forward. The car jerked into motion and putted down the street, stopping finally at the Doctor's sign on the edge of town.

Sheila had coffee perking in the kitchen when they arrived, and there was only one patient waiting, a man who'd cut his hand with his axe while splitting wood. It was bleeding profusely. Ray washed the wound while Will set out the tools to stitch him up. They discussed the best way to ensure the tendons were not severed, and to reattach the muscle, until the man looked like he might faint.

Will chuckled and apologized to his patient, explaining that he didn't often have the chance to compare notes with his brother on medical issues. They stitched him up, wrapped the wound and sent him on his way before closing up shop. Ray tossed his bag into the spare room as Will set out mugs for the coffee. There was a pound cake that Julia had given him resting on the table.

Ray heaved a sigh and looked around. "This is pretty good, Will. I'm impressed."

Will guffawed. "Don't give me that. I know what this looks like and I know what your surgery looks like." He laughed again and shook his head.

"No, no, I'm serious." Ray looked around again. "I can see what attracted you to this town and the practice. And now that I've had the chance to look it over I can see that you've got everything you need here for a good practice. The living quarters are fine. Lots of room, they're certainly big enough. They might do with a coat of paint but basically sound. And the surgery looks old in the entry, but you've got good basics in your examining rooms. They're pretty spacious too. I actually have some stuff that I could ship out, might be of use." The two of them launched into medical talk for the rest of the afternoon.

Will finally stretched. "We might think about dinner. There's a little restaurant in town that's open until eight o'clock. We can eat there." The men wrapped the rest of the cake and set the mugs in the sink.

Over dinner Will caught up on family stuff, their father's practice, each brother's medical work, how their mother was doing, even Danny's teamster business. "It's a company now, believe it or not." Ray said. "He has five men working for him and he hauls from all the surrounding area into town to the train platform. Freight of all kinds. He's got fifteen or twenty teams of horses, and leases others from local farmers in different districts depending on where he's hauling."

Ray took another bite of his dinner. "He's talking about changing entirely to trucks, thinks that would be a whole new thing, with different equipment and drivers, mechanics. He has two trucks now, used ones that are a bit unreliable. His wife, Kimmy, was telling me she never sees him, he's so busy. And you should hear the old man go on about him. It's Danny this and Danny that." They both grinned and dug into their meatloaf.

Finally Ray laid his cutlery down and sat back. "So, Will. When do I get to meet Julia?"

Will glanced up but kept on eating. Finally he stopped for a sip of coffee and nailed his brother with a look. "I know why you're here. Don't think you fooled me."

Ray laughed. "Come on, Will. Everyone in the family is curious. No-one can remember you being quite so smitten before. You talked about her so much over Christmas, and then you left Winnipeg earlier than planned to rush back to your practice. You didn't have me fooled, either."

"So you came out to look her over for the family?"

"Well, would you rather have Dad arrive on your doorstep? Who would you rather come to visit?"

Will's grin was rueful. "Not Dad, never Dad." He shuddered and they both laughed.

"And I didn't just come to see Julia," he added. "You know that. We're all aware of why you left Winnipeg. It would have been so natural for us to set up shop together. But after everything that happened, we all understood that you weren't going to be settling down any time soon, at least not there."

Will pondered his plate. He remembered what had happened very clearly, and he saw it far differently now than when it first occurred. At first he so was mad and full of hurt pride, he couldn't see straight.

His fiancée of a year had abruptly broken their engagement and then gotten married within a couple of months to another medical student, someone he knew from his own class. Soon it became obvious that she was pregnant, but apparently not with his child.

He'd been devastated and had gone into a tailspin that almost meant losing the final classes of his degree. His brothers rallied round, and drilled him on his studies to get him through.

Now when he thought of it, he realized he'd been more angry than hurt. And he wondered what Angela had seen in him. Maybe she saw him more clearly than he did, and realized he wasn't as committed to the engagement or at least not as interested. Now, he was glad it had worked out that way, ironic as that seemed.

He shrugged. "It's not such a big deal anymore, Ray. I've left that behind. And I'm pretty committed to the west. I like the landscape, the look of the country, and I like the people. They're hardy and rugged, they don't expect a handout but are quick to offer one. It just agrees with me." He grinned.

"I'm glad," Ray offered. "I wanted to have the chance to visit you here, look the place over to see where you've settled and see your surgery. It looks promising, and it'll keep you busy, being one of the only doctors in town. But I'd like to meet her, this Julia." He gave his brother a quizzical look.

Will relented. "I want you to meet her, too. You'll be impressed. She's invited us out for dinner tomorrow night. I'm out there most nights anyway." Will felt the colour rise in his face at the thought of being with Julia.

He went on, "I told you about the children. Her two are really cute kids, Maggie is seven, and Jims almost five. Maggie looks just like her mother, and maybe Jims like his father, I'm not sure. But his hair is red and wiry, and he's built lean like the picture of his father in their house. Stephen died of diphtheria."

Ray grimaced. "That's too bad. How long ago?"

"About three years. It's possible that Doc Farley didn't keep up with the times or know about the vaccine. Maybe he wasn't here when he got sick. I haven't really gotten into it. Not sure it's my business, you know?"

Ray nodded. "How are the kids with having you around, instead of their father?"

"Well, that's just it. They don't seem to mind at all. They're very sweet, and genuine in the way they express themselves. Maggie misses her Dad. She told me that. Jims probably doesn't remember him. Julia misses him still, too, I think." Will looked down, struggling with that thought. "She's had a hard time, a lot of work to keep the family going. Then these two little guys showed up. That's when I met her."

Will told the story of the abused boys in her root cellar. By this time they were finished with dinner and working on dessert and coffee. Will paid the bill and they moved to the door of the restaurant to grab their coats from the wall hooks. He called his thanks to the proprietor and headed out with Ray to stroll back to the surgery.

By the time they crawled into bed that night, they'd finished the better part of a half bottle of brandy and neither was feeling much pain, but Will had a full heart. His brother was here and he was grateful.

~~~**~~~

CHAPTER THIRTY FOUR

The next evening, Ray, Will and Jerome Hoskiss settled around Julia's dining room table. Jerome had decided rather unexpectedly that it was Saturday, so he should come for dinner. Julia detected a gleam in his eye that indicated there might be more to his sudden interest. Perhaps it had to do with his need to get a look at Will's brother. Jerome, along with everyone else in the community, was aware that Ray had arrived from Winnipeg and was staying at the surgery.

The children were subdued, seeing a strange man the same size as Will coming up their steps and into the kitchen. But Will had brought his black bag and set about listening to all the hearts, taking all the pulses, discussing his findings gravely with Ray, and the children were soon watching intently and participating as enthusiastically as ever.

The two men looked so much alike, it was hard not to notice. The children were soon talking to Ray as if they'd known him for a long time. He responded the same way Will did, with concentrated interest in what they had to say and a gleam of fun in his eye.

During dinner, Ray told stories of his four boys and soon everyone was laughing and hanging on his every word. When the meal was over and the table cleared, he suggested a game of cards and everyone joined in, even Jerome. Amid much amusement,

Ollie won hands down and Jerome was second.

Julia looked at the two brothers accusingly but they gazed innocently back. Will winked and nodded his head toward Jerome, who had a tiny half-smile on his face as he regarded Ollie's flushed and excited face.

~~*~~

Putting Ray back on the train a few days later was harder than Will thought it would be. He missed the camaraderie of his large family, especially his brothers. Ray was the closest to him, they'd been friends from the time he was big enough to trail along behind. "Don't wait so long next time," he said gruffly.

Ray stood back and took a look at him. "I've missed you too."

Will's eyes were wet. He stared off into the distance for a moment. "I'll make the effort and get back more to see you all. I will, Ray. And you come here too. That's what life's about, eh?" They nodded and shook hands.

That night as he was washing up for bed, he remembered Ray's words of the night before. "I like her, Will. I really like her. She's a quality woman. And beautiful as well. On the other hand…." Ray had plowed ahead as only a bullheaded brother could on all the things that boded ill for them, the instant family of four children, and the constant stream of homeless that she fed at her gate, problems pending with the Valadio family, her sickly brother and children. None of this was new to Will and he let his brother talk himself out.

Will nodded to himself now as he hooked his thumbs under his suspenders and pulled them down his arms. He knew all of that, everything that Ray had said had gone through his mind more than once. And he was in no doubt of Julia's quality. It was a depth of love and mercy, of mirth and happiness, of joy and giving. And he wanted all that for himself.

On the other hand, the town had a small posse set up just for the purpose of looking after Julia Butler. Everyone made sure he knew it too. He shook with silent laughter as he unbuttoned his shirt. He couldn't count how many times he'd been warned, to be careful of the Widow Butler, poor Mrs. Butler, treat her with respect. Julia may not be aware of it, but she had a whole slew of supporters in town and the surrounding area, watching, protecting, looking out for her and her little brood. And the New Doc had better toe the line.

~~*~~

The letter from Dr. Guy Whitmore arrived the next day, Sheila brought it in along with the other mail. She'd proved very helpful as he eased into his practice. She was knowledgeable, Doc Farley had obviously trained her as a medical helper as well as a receptionist and accounts keeper. She was practical and down to earth, even tempered and very discreet.

And she'd been able to wrangle payment out of people whom Will was convinced didn`t have two pennies to rub together. "Leave it to me," she told him early on. "I know who has cash and who doesn`t, and I won`t let them cheat you. On the other hand, I hope you`ll have patience with those who can`t pay right away."

Will opened the letter first. Ahh, he had something new to tell Julia. Guy had offered to go down from Nelson and see what he could find out about the young man in Ymir who'd gotten into the bar fight. He'd visited the feed store to get a look at young Valadio. His report lit an excitement in Will, and he knew Julia would feel the same.

He tucked the letter into his pocket for later and headed back into the surgery. He had appointments late into the day, with house calls after dinner. And now he had a good reason to call at Julia`s on his way home. He smiled with satisfaction.

~~~**~~~

Part Seven – Our Brother

CHAPTER THIRTY FIVE

J ulia was just tidying the kitchen when Will arrived.

"Are the kids in bed already?" he asked in surprise.

She nodded, a slight smile curving her mouth. "Yes, it's after nine."

He chuckled. "It's been a busy day. I lost track of time." He advanced slowly into the room, shedding his jacket on a bench as he went. He moved forward until he was flush against her, his arms sliding around her waist and pulling her in. "Almost bedtime," he murmured.

Her smile grew. "Naughty boy."

He whispered a laugh into her hair and lowered his mouth to kiss her. Immediately he felt a fire in his chest, clawing at his innards. She was like lightning, shafting through his system.

"I have news," he said, drawing her down on the sofa in the parlour after quietly closing the door. "My buddy, Guy, in Nelson sent me a note. He went to see Valadio."

He arranged her against him, and lowered his voice. "I don't want the boys to hear, but he's convinced this is our Charlie. He's young, maybe seventeen or eighteen. He's got fiery red hair and freckles. He's close to six feet in height, skinny as a rail but strong. His clothes were pretty ratty, no money obviously, but he's been working at the feed store for quite a while now and the owner was complimentary, thought he was a good worker.

"When he spoke to him, Charlie was evasive about where he was from, but when Guy mentioned knowing some younger boys with the same last name, he was powerfully curious, wanted to know how he knew them, were they okay."

He squeezed her arm. "Don't worry. Guy was very cautious, didn't tell him anything about where the boys are. I was adamant about that when I talked to him. Charlie wanted to know whether the boys were with their parents. He mentioned the parents a couple of times, but in a very careful way, and he didn't admit he might be related to them. Guy thinks he's afraid. Doesn't want them to know where he is."

She shivered in his arms. "I'm not surprised if he's afraid of the parents. They sound like a horror. But to find Brother Charlie! This is so exciting! I'm not sure what we should do now."

"I think we should go and meet him, and take the boys."

"I'm not sure. I guess the parents won't know if we meet up with Charlie." She looked doubtfully up at him.

He dropped a kiss on her mouth. "We could go this weekend, take the train to Nelson. Guy offered to drive us to Ymir. It's not far, and his car is better than mine. Maybe we can leave Maggie and Jims with someone here in the village, because it's a long way and it would be pretty crowded. Plus Ben and Ollie will need our full attention, they deserve nothing less."

"Not this weekend," she said. "But soon. Maybe next weekend."

"Whenever you say." He rested his cheek on the top of her head as her perfume filled his senses. He didn't want to go home to his lonely bed, his empty house. He wanted to be here, with her. "Julia, will you marry me?" Will held her away to peer into her face, then slid off the sofa onto one knee on the carpet. "Will you marry me? You and all your children? I've asked before, but you didn't give me an answer. I can't wait much longer."

In the dim light, her face was pale and her hands clasped

tightly together. Will took them into his, gently pried them apart and gripped them in his fingers. "I love you so much. And I'll be good to you, Julia. I promise. I'll look after all of you, all of them. I'll respect you. Trust me. We'll never be rich, especially in these times. People can't pay a doctor the way they could a few years ago. But we'll be alright, we'll eat well and be secure."

His gaze searched her face. "Please, Julia. Put me out of my misery."

She smiled a slow smile that lit her face and got his heart acting funny in his chest. "Yes, Will," she breathed. "I'll marry you, we'll all marry you."

He looked into her face, reading the joy there. He lifted her hands and pressed a kiss into each palm, then pressed her down on the sofa with his body. His kiss was possessive, shifting her into the pillows. His hands found her breasts, kneading the firm flesh. His mouth slid to her throat and lower as he gasped for breath. "Let it be soon, Julia, let it be soon. I simply can't wait much longer to have you."

He laid his hand to her hip and slid his palm slowly across, pushing his long fingers between her legs. Her eyes closed, her face pressed into the damp skin at his throat. She gave a small gasp and levered herself upward against the pressure. He kissed her again, deep probing kisses as he reached to pull up the hem of her dress.

As he moved his fingers against her, around the leg of her under garment and into her wet flesh, she strained against him. She struggled then lay still as he massaged the tender area, kissing her throat and murmuring love words. When she finally convulsed against him, he muffled her cries with his mouth, and soothed her with his hands as she slowly came back to herself, collapsing under his weight.

"Oh, Will, oh, we shouldn't... I didn't mean to...." She stopped on a sob and raised her hand to cover her flushed face.

"No, it's okay baby, it's okay sweetheart. It's all right." He pulled her hand away and covered her wet cheek with butterfly kisses, pressing his lips to her face and throat. "It's okay, baby."

He rocked her back and forth in his arms. His hands shook. And so did his heart.

~~~**~~~

CHAPTER THIRTY SIX

They made the trip to Nelson two weeks later. Jims and Maggie would stay with the Morrises at their farm for the weekend.

The rest of them embarked on the journey to find Charlie. Ben and Ollie handled the train ride like old hands, commenting often on how it had been 'last time we rode the train'. But the closer they got to Nelson the quieter they became.

Julia told them what they knew about this young man named Valadio. She reassured them that if it wasn't their brother, he may be a relative. He might know how to find their Charlie. The boys listened solemnly but didn't say a word.

Guy was waiting for them at the station, bundled up against the cold, his breath a cloud in the air. He hustled them directly into his car for the short trip to his house. His wife had prepared lunch, and they were introduced then sat down to eat. After a very short stay, they were on the road to Ymir. It was snowing lightly and slow going, but the snowflakes didn't look like they were sticking to the ground.

Guy talked shop with Will in the front seat. Julia sat in the back with one boy pressing in on each side. She put her arms around them and simply held them.

"This is very exciting," she said as they entered the parking area in front of the feed store on the north side of Ymir.

Ben looked at her doubtfully. His colour was high, but his

mouth was a tense line. Ollie shivered. Julia pulled his coat closer and fastened the top button, tugging his scarf up around his throat. She adjusted her hat and they all climbed out.

"Wait here," said Will as they stepped inside the building. "We'll go and check things out. Won't be a minute."

Julia stood with the boys in the entrance to the feed store and looked around. It was a fair sized building, sacks of feed piled ceiling-high around the perimeter and bins for grain built in a line down the middle. There was a small office off to the side, Will and Guy had headed in that direction.

The boys scuffed their boots in the chaff on the floor, Ollie holding the parcel that contained the scarf and mittens that Julia had knitted as a gift from them to Charlie. A young man approached from the gloom of the huge shed.

"Can I help you, ma'am?" he inquired.

Ben looked up and caught his breath. "Charlie," he whispered. Then louder, "Charlie!"

The young man looked down, his red hair catching the light. "Ben?" He stalled. Then his gaze swung to Ollie and back. "Ben and Olin? Is it you?" The boys crowded around him, hanging onto his legs, and he was suddenly crying. He gripped his brothers round their necks in a bear hug, then lifted one hand to swipe at his nose.

"What the heck you doin' here? What you thinking? God, you're both so big now. I can't hardly believe it." But he hugged them harder.

Julia walked to the far wall of the shed and slowly back. By the time she returned, Charlie was standing straight with his arms gripped around his brothers. He looked directly at her as Will and Guy came out of the office, the manager right behind them.

Charlie squared around to speak to his boss. "I'm still workin', sir. I just got taken by surprise, like. Them's my brothers. But I won't be slacking off no more, sir. I'll get to stackin' them sacks."

The manager put up his hand to halt the flow of words. "It's okay, Charlie. I just got told about it. I wondered if you want to take the rest of the day off. That way you can visit with the boys and get a chance to catch up. I'll see you tomorrow morning, those sacks can wait until then."

Charlie paused, his mouth half open. "But, sir. I ain't finished getting that big order ready, there's still about twenty-five bags to add to it."

"That's okay, son. It can wait. They don't arrive until about ten most mornings by the time they get over here to do a pick up, so we'll have time to finish it tomorrow. Go on with you, now."

Charlie stared after his manager, then, seeming to make up his mind, grabbed a shabby coat from the top of a stack of hay bales, and turned to Ollie. "Come on, little brother." He gripped Ollie by the hand, laid his other hand on Ben's nape and headed out of the shed.

Will stepped up beside him and put his hand on Charlie's shoulder to slow him down. "Charlie, I'm Will. I'm a doctor and a friend of the boys. This is Julia, the boys have been staying with her. And this is Guy, a friend of mine. We thought we could go to the hotel in town and have supper with you. That way we'd have some time to get acquainted and learn a bit about each other."

Charlie stopped. "Glad to meet ya, ma'am," he said to Julia, then eyed Will mistrustfully. 'Yessir, good to meet you." He paused in thought, then looked down. "Supper sounds fine, what do you think, boys?" His brothers nodded against his side.

The dining room of the Ymir Hotel was definitely warmer than outside, but no less awkward. The boys didn't seem to know what to say to their brother, and Charlie was embarrassed in front of these other adults that were strangers to him.

Julia told him about finding the boys, omitting the terrible injuries she'd seen, just complimenting them on having looked after themselves and travelled so far on their own. She told Charlie about the boys going to school, and how they were both learning to read, how clever they were at arithmetic.

Charlie listened but had no comment. Ben and Ollie stared at the tabletop.

"Will," she said, "wouldn't it be wonderful if Charlie and the boys sat together at that table over there by the window? They could catch up with each other, and we could talk about your practice with Guy and the changes you want to make."

Will raised his brows, and nodded.

"That's what we'll do," she continued. "Come on boys. Ben, Ollie, come and sit over here with Charlie. You tell your brother everything you've been doing. And you, Charlie, the boys have been wanting to see you for so long. They were looking for you when they left home. They had headed out to find you. We'll join you with our dessert. And Ollie, give Charlie his gift. I'm sure he'll like it."

Guy grinned when she returned to sit down with the men. "I see how Will needs you to keep him organized. He didn't even know he was making changes to his practice until you told him just now."

Julia laughed. "Will should pay attention. His practice needs a lot of changes, have you seen it?"

The Valadio boys started out pretty quiet but the gift seemed to thaw the air, Charlie was quite taken with the mittens and wrapped the scarf around Ollie and Ben to weak laughter from the boys. They were talking non-stop by the end of dinner.

When dessert arrived, Will asked for it to be served along with a couple of pots of tea at the table with the boys. They all settled into new chairs in the window together. They asked about Ymir and Charlie's work at the feed store. He lived onsite, in an upstairs loft above the office. It was nice and warm up there. The owner lived in a house in the back and his wife fed him his meals. He joined them for supper each evening. Charlie was pleased with the arrangement. "I've even put on some weight since I came here," he said.

"Can I see your place?" asked Ben.

Charlie looked down at him. "Sure, I'll take you up there."

Julia dug in her purse and pulled out a piece of paper and a stub of pencil. "Now, Charlie," she began and Will grinned but she ignored him. "What do you know about birthdays? Do you know when Ollie was born, what month?"

Charlie frowned. "Sure. He was born in October, 'cause the old man kept saying he was getting a Hallowe'en baby, but he come early. Nine days early."

"That makes it October twenty-second, right?"

Charlie nodded, smiling shyly at her.

"So, how old is he? Eight, nine?"

Charlie frowned again and counted on his fingers under the table. "He's nine, Ma'am, on his last birthday. 'Cause I'm sixteen now, and I was seven when he was born."

"You're sixteen," she pondered, making notes on her envelope. "When is your birthday, then?" After some discussion, it was decided that Ben was almost eleven, his birthday being in February, on a leap year. Julia wasn't sure how they agreed on that, but now she had some dates to work with. She had been about to simply assign birthdays to them. The look on their faces when Maggie had her birthday in the fall, full of longing and a kind of helpless envy had broken her heart. Jims' birthday was coming up in March, and it would be even harder if they didn't have their own birthday celebrations to look forward to.

But there were other things she needed to know. "Where are you parents, Charlie?"

The talk around the table stuttered to a halt and Charlie looked like a deer in the headlights. He shook his head uncertainly and glanced at his brothers, who were studying their hands in their laps.

"Don't know," he finally muttered.

She nodded. There would be no help from that quarter. The parents were feared by all, it seemed. "The boys have been pretty excited at the chance to see you."

Charlie blushed as Ben and Ollie leaned into his side.

"Could you come and visit us one day?" she persisted. "We'd love it if you could come. I know you don't get much time off work, but even an overnight would be wonderful. They miss you."

Charlie's head bobbed up and down. "I miss them, too," he

mumbled. "I'd like that. I haven't seen them for so long."

"If you could get yourself to Nelson," Will said, "I can get a train ticket to you."

"And send us a note to tell us when you're coming, Charlie." At his doubtful look, Julia added, "Get your boss's wife to write a little note for you, I'm sure she wouldn't mind. Let me give you this." She tore her envelope in half. "I'll write my name and address on it so you'll know where to send it. Then we'll know when you're coming. We can meet you at the train station because we live a little way out of town."

When they dropped Charlie back at the feed store, there was nothing for it but the boys had to go up and see his loft. So they trooped up the back stairs to a dark door and Charlie ushered them in. He found the string for the electric light and gave it a tug.

It was actually a pretty nice space, fairly roomy. His bed was a mattress on the floor, but he had a table and a couple of chairs by one low window, and an old dresser against the crooked wall. Someone had pounded a couple of big nails into the wall by the door to hang his coat. It was a bit chilly, but Julia noted there were lots of blankets on the bed.

Ben and Oliver admired the fact that he had electric lights and his own accommodations. They told him about Prince, and Daisy Mae the goat, even about the feisty old rooster that they had to fend off every time they went to get the eggs out of the henhouse. Charlie listened to it all, a bemused expression on his face.

The boys were quiet on the drive back to Nelson. They seemed to be exhausted. They were bundled into a small bed on the floor at Guy's house and quickly fell asleep. Julia thanked Guy and his wife for their hospitality, and then headed for bed. She'd been given the guest room, and was suddenly very grateful for the privacy. She was so tired she could barely manage, just pulled her clothes off and fell under the covers.

~~~**~~~

194

CHAPTER THIRTY SEVEN

I t's Charlie this, and Charlie that," she remarked to Will. "I hope he doesn't have too much influence over them, I wouldn't want them to think it would be better to go live with their brother. That wouldn't be good."

But that didn't seem to be what was on Ben's mind later in the week. When she picked the kids up from school, he asked if he could learn to drive Prince. She gladly moved over on the seat and handed him the reins. "This way, I'll be more useful to you," he said with a determined look on his face. "Soon I'll be able to drive places for you. Then you won't have to do so much work."

As they passed their house and started up the hill to the Morris farm, he said, "I could even let you get off at home with Jims and Maggie soon, and take the Morrises home by myself and you wouldn't have to ride all that extra way."

They dropped the Morris boys off, and Julia backed the wagon around in their drive to go home. "You know, Ben, I don't mind doing this work. I used to do it even before you came to live with us."

"That's right," he said. "But I been thinkin' that now you won't have to do all of it yourself. That would be a 'vantage of having us live with you. Less work. Why, Ollie and I talked and he can do the chickens all the time, feed and water and muck out the

195

hen house, then you won't have to be worrying about that either. That would be another 'vantage of having us living with you."

Julia smiled to herself. 'Advantage' was one of Will's favourite words and Ben had just started using it recently.

Tucking the children into bed, one by one, that evening, Julia stooped to smooth Ben's forehead. "Ben, you're a good boy. I appreciate all the things you do around here to help out. But you don't have to work your way into a place here in my house."

Ben frowned up at her. "But you can use the help. And then you won't want us to go live with Charlie. We like Charlie, and all, but we want to live here with you, if that's okay."

Julia hugged him tight, then leaned over to give Ollie a hug. "You both live here, this is your home. Don't ever doubt it. Why, I was afraid that you'd rather live with Charlie, and I didn't want you to leave."

Ben huffed a sigh of relief. "Nah," he said. "Ollie and me, we like it here, we want to live with you. And Maggie. And Jims. We like it here. Don't we Ollie?" And so it was settled and both hearts were relieved.

~~*~~

The next week Julia organized a birthday for Ben. She offered him to have a friend from school over, but he said, no, just the family thanks. But he was excited, peeking at the cake with his name in icing, looking out the window for Dr. Stoffard to arrive.

The other children had been busy making birthday cards, and they were waiting in the parlour, along with the good tea service set out on the tea trolley. They sang 'Happy Birthday,' they had cake and tea with the children kneeling around the low table in the middle of the room.

Then Ben opened presents. They hadn't had much time to prepare so the gifts were impromptu. Ben was touched by Jims' gift, one of his favourite toy trucks. "Don't worry, Jims, I'll look after it, and you can even borrow it sometimes." Maggie gave him a pin with a Canadian flag on it, and he promptly pinned it to his shirt. There was a pen from Ollie, that Julia had helped find, and a set of cuff links from Will.

"Now all you need is a proper shirt, Ben, to wear them with. They are the first set of cufflinks I ever had as a young man, and I want you to have them."

Ben stared down at the dull gold of the pattern and nodded his head. "Thank you, sir. I won't lose them, nosirree."

Julia gave him a book, *Tom Sawyer* by Mark Twain. "I think you'll really like it. It's about a boy who's around your age and he has some wonderful adventures. You might not be able to read it all yet, but it won't be long before you can." She opened the cover to point to the inscription, and read it to him – *To Benjamin, with all my love, Mama Julia.* They played a game of charades, with Will and Julia as the head of each team, and their team members rolling on the floor laughing at themselves and each other.

By the time Julia tucked everyone in that night, the children were all flushed and sighing. Ollie whispered to her, "Wasn't it fun, Mama Julia? I can't wait till my birthday."

Ben watched her with his dark eyes as she adjusted his pillow. "What have you got under there? It's a big lump." She fished around under the heavy blankets to find a book. "What in the world?" She hauled it out.

Ben grabbed *Tom Sawyer* back, and shoved it under again. "It's just for tonight," he said. "I just want to think of it there, just for tonight."

"I see," she said. "Then later, when you're ready, you can keep it on the dresser over there, with your cuff links and other presents. Did you have a good time, Ben?"

"Yes, Mama Julia, it was the best day of my life."

~~*~~

Ben got his second black eye the first week in March. Julia wormed the story out of the children, but Ben denied that Nick

197

Postnikoff had given it to him. Some of the boys had tripped him and he hit the fence with his head, and his eye got hurt.

Will examined the shiner with care but said not to worry. Julia was upset by how offhand he was about the injury to Ben's face. But by the end of the week, Will had organized the boy's hockey team. Matt York from the fire department and some other men who played in the men's league were eager to get on board.

The plan was to meet after school on the ice rink the men used for their own hockey games. The field had been cleared and flooded, with boards installed at each end to contain the puck.

Other men who had volunteered included Mr. Morris and Mr. Postnikoff. Before anyone knew it, the boys were struggling to learn to skate. Will held practices and coached everyone who came. He found a source of used hockey equipment, including hockey sticks, and the interest exploded. Julia tried to tell them that the ice would be gone by the end of the month, but Will ignored that.

"Maybe it will," he said, "Maybe not. It could be a late spring. Besides, then there'll be baseball."

Julia's mouth opened in an 'O' of surprise and he used that excuse to kiss her silent.

Soon there were eleven or twelve boys showing up for the games. Julia was kept busy making banners for them to wear, so they could tell one team from the other. At the school, Mrs. Rasmussen exclaimed one afternoon, "I've never seen so much excitement. The boys are buzzing with hockey. And," she added in a quiet aside, "Ben and Nick are talking to each other. It is as if the fights never happened. Ben has been accepted, I think."

Ben had been put into the grade three class and was doing fine in arithmetic and struggling to keep up in reading. Mrs. Rasmussen wasn't concerned. "He's come so far this year, it doesn't matter if he doesn't understand everything we cover in reading. It'll gel for him over the summer, especially if he reads at home while school's out, and he'll be more than ready for grade four in the fall."

Later that week, it was very loud around the dinner table. Ollie as trying to eat with a splint on his finger, which he'd sprained playing hockey. He kept banging it on his plate, which prompted a fit of giggling. Julia finally cut up his food and gave him a spoon.

Will dragged her into the parlour while the children cleared the table and the older ones settled down to homework. "Julia," he said, "We need to make a decision. It's time to set a date for the wedding. I spend all my time here, then I have to go drive home in the dark."

She made a moue with her mouth. "Are you afraid of the dark, Will?" she teased.

He tugged a curl beside her ear. "No, minx, I'm not afraid of the dark. I'm tired of the dark, when I'm alone that is."

She glanced at him sideways. "I told you we can't marry right away. The kids…."

"It's not the kids, and you know it. The kids are fine with me here. It's you. You're dragging your feet. We don't have to do a big wedding. We can do something small. I know you'll want your family here and your friends so we'll get married in Creston, but my family has to come from Winnipeg and they need a bit of notice to arrange the trip. I've already spread the word so they can…." He ground to a halt as she looked up at him in horror.

"What, you didn't want me to tell anyone?"

"No, it's not that, it just means I have to…." She trailed off, her mouth closing tightly.

"Get moving, you mean. Julia, have you changed your mind? Don't change your mind, sweetheart. Getting married is the right thing to do. You know it is. You don't know how much I love you. And you love me, you told me so." He kissed her softly on the mouth.

"Honestly, you're driving me crazy. I don't see that we should wait. We need to get organized. And that doesn't mean you have to do everything yourself. It just means set the date. I'll handle everything else."

He gave her a stern look. "We can get the restaurant in town to do food so you don't have to do all the cooking to feed the relatives who are coming. We can have the reception in the community hall. People who are coming from out of town can stay at my place. My folks can bring clothes for the kids to wear to the ceremony, we just have to send a list of sizes, or measurements."

He put his hand up to stop her as her mouth opened. "Just listen. Your brother-in-law, James and Sue-Ann will want to come. And your folks from Sparwood. And our kids need to know what we plan so they understand that they can depend on me."

Her mouth was set in a stubborn pout.

"Just think about it," he pleaded. "If we fix a date, then the uncertainty will be over. We can tell everyone and they can quit trying to guess what we're planning."

She didn't say no, so he decided that could mean 'yes'. "April is a good month for a wedding."

He paused at the look of panic on her face. "Okay, April is a bit soon, but May is good, it'll work for me." She just shook her head and went back to the kitchen to begin the dishes.

Before he left, he took her back into the parlour.

"I can't make a decision right now," she said, the colour high in her cheeks.

"I understand," he said. "I just need a kiss." As he lowered his mouth over hers, he had a tight feeling in his chest. *Would she change her mind?* Not if he could help it. The thought gave him heart palpitations. He put all his powers of persuasion into that kiss. Her hands clung to the front of his shirt, and he pressed his knee between her thighs, rubbing the tender spot.

If she wanted him as much as he wanted her, they'd set a date soon. He didn't stop for a long time.

CHAPTER THIRTY EIGHT

Julia sent a letter to Charlie with notes from the boys and drawings from each of the children. She invited him to come for a few days over Easter weekend. She planned egg dying, hot cross buns, a ham if Mr. Morris had any.

Then she got a letter from Sam and Annie saying they were coming to visit over the holiday. That raised the level of excitement in the house over the next few days, and as hockey stopped because of a lack of ice, the focus was replaced by the new holiday event.

Julia worried where everyone would sleep, with such a houseful. But Ben and Ollie said Charlie would like to sleep in their room. Ollie volunteered to sleep on the floor so Charlie could have his bed. They dragged the old ticking mattress out of the shed where the two boys had slept when they first arrived and aired it out. Then the two of them stuffed it with fresh straw for Ollie on the hard floor.

Sam and Annie arrived first, bringing Mom and the two children. Maggie dragged Jasmine off straight away to her bedroom for the afternoon. Sam brought large cheese-cloth wrapped rounds into the house that he thumped onto the table.

Julia stared, then leaned over to sniff.

"Goat cheese," he said. "I've taken to raising goats. An old fellow in the hills behind us died and his herd was wandering wild. I went up there to see, and found they were in good shape, he looked after them much better than he looked after himself."

"He brought them all home," Annie added. "And they don't take much care. They eat anything, as you know from having Daisy Mae. Sam's taken them down the side of the road for the early grass this spring, because we don't have a pasture. We've had five kids already, two sets of twins and a single kid, and four more of the nannies are pregnant."

"Not pregnant, Annie. In foal," her husband said.

Julia laughed. "So, you're a goatherd."

Annie said, "They're a cross of cashmere goat, we're told. Their hair is fabulous, long and soft. So we sheared them last week and I found someone who can spin. It's beautiful and very strong and warm. I've been trying to decide how to use it. I don't know if it would be better to knit with it or do weaving. But I'm taking lessons from the lady who spins and Sam is making me a spinning wheel in his spare time."

Julia laughed delightedly. "Spare time? I wouldn't imagine either of you has any of that. This is fantastic, you've got two or three different businesses going at once. I didn't even know you could shear goats."

Annie shook her head, smiling. "Neither did I, but you can."

Julia grabbed a paring knife from the counter, carved off a piece of cheese and popped it between her lips. Her eyes widened in appreciation at the flavor that filled her mouth. "This is delicious, Sam. It's absolutely wonderful."

Sam looked proud. "Yup. We've got sixteen goats. I've been selling the cheese in Sparwood."

Julia poked the bundles with her finger. "I've made it myself, but was never very good at it. It was hit and miss, sometimes it turned out, sometimes not. But this is wonderful, it's almost creamy but still firm."

Annie beamed. "Well, Sam has it figured, it works out every time. Of course, Mum helped, she's made it lots before."

Julia looked over at her mother, seated on the sofa teaching the boys how to finger knit. Sarah glanced up and smiled at her and Julia ran over to give her a hug. "I miss you, Mum," she said. "I'm so glad you're here."

Over tea at the kitchen table, Annie prodded her husband. "Sam, did you tell her about what's been happening in the hills behind Sparwood? Lots going on, Julia. You should hear." She nodded her head in emphasis. "Lots. It's become almost unsafe to live there."

Julia whirled around to confront her brother. "What? What's going on, Sam? Are you talking about the Relief Camps?"

Sam sat and braced his elbows on the table. "Well, partly that. The Relief Camp was set up in the bush and that's good. There must be more than a hundred men, all working pretty hard from what I hear. And the few stores that are left in town like it, because the men have a little bit of money and need somewhere to spend it. But the men soon found the moonshiners in the hills and started spending their money up there. And right away there were problems with fights and drunkenness in the camp."

"Even in town," Annie interjected. "There were drunken men staggering around in town, and one woman was accosted. Not hurt," she added hastily.

"So, the police were called in," Sam continued. "They interviewed people, and the next thing we know there are raids into the hills. They were trying to clean out the moonshiner camps. For days, there were posses going back and forth. We would hear shots sometimes."

"But that could have been hunters," Annie said.

Julia glanced over to see Ollie and Ben sitting still on the sofa, no longer knitting with their fingers, but their gaze riveted on Sam. She looked back at Sam and made a shushing motion with her hand.

Sam nodded, looking ruefully at his wife. "That could have been hunters, it probably was. I thought you asked me to tell this story, Annie? So, Julia, the long and the short of it is, things have been busy out our way. By the way, Jasmine loves looking after the goats, and they mind her well." As the conversation passed on to other things, the boys relaxed.

~~*~~

Will came to dinner that evening, and announced to the family that he and Julia were getting married. Julia flushed to the roots of her hair, and Will hugged her tight in front of everyone. "Someone has to tell them," he whispered.

She nodded against his chest.

There were knowing looks exchanged among the adults, but everyone lent their congratulations as if they had never suspected anything of the sort. The children were especially astonished. Ben wanted to know what that meant.

"'It means, I'll be your father," said Will. "I know you all have other fathers. Ben and Ollie already have a father but he's just not here. And Maggie and Jims have a father who died. So I won't be that father, but I'll be the father that's here now. I can look after you, and help you when you need it. That's what fathers do. Right, Sam?"

Sam smiled encouragement. "That's right. And it's not an easy job, either," he added. "Sometimes the job goes on long into the night, but that's what you do." He patted the Sam the Third's diapered bottom and rose to put him to bed in the old crib upstairs. "Congratulations, you two. I'm sincerely happy for both of you."

Julia shot him a trembling smile.

Sarah leaned forward. "So, when is the big event?"

Will grinned and pointed to Julia. "We're still deciding, but as soon as possible."

Julia flushed again and shot him a look.

"Is she dragging her feet?" Sarah smiled at her daughter. "I'm not surprised. This a big step to take for someone who has children. You always worry about what is best, how will it work.

And you're already working as hard as you can, right, Julia? So the idea of actually getting married seems exhausting to think about, let alone start planning. That's where we come in. We can help, can't we Annie?"

In the middle of the roving conversation, the table was cleared and the children tucked into bed. The party moved into the parlour.

Julia's headache, which had started early in the evening got progressively worse. All she wanted to do was go to bed, but she couldn't just walk out and leave her guests, especially with Will there. Finally, she couldn't wait another minute. "I'm sorry. I just have to lie down. I'm so tired I can't think straight and I've got a headache now."

Will was on his feet at once. "I'm sorry, sweetheart. I've overstayed my welcome. I should have seen how tired you are. We can talk about all of this later. Let me help."

He hauled his black bag from the floor by the door and pulled out a couple of headache pills for her, then helped her to the stairs, giving her a gentle hug farewell. Sarah took her arm to help her up as Will watched her disappear around the landing. He stood pensively for a moment longer, his face turned toward the second floor. When he looked around, he found Sam watching him.

"She's a wonderful woman, isn't she?"

Will nodded. "Yes, she is. And I know I'm pressuring her to set a date, but it's hard to see her doing everything by herself. I could do so much more for her if we were together. Four children, that's a lot. You've seen how much food she has to prepare, for a meal." He sighed.

"And it's hard to go home at night, right?" Sam's clear gaze seemed to look directly into him.

Will looked right back. "I won't deny that. She's beautiful, I want to be her husband in every way, not just to give her children a father. I love her deeply." He knew his cheeks were ruddy with colour as he held Sam's gaze with his own.

Her brother nodded. "That's good. Every marriage needs

passion. It can get you through some very tough times, if you love each other that way. You don't have to tell me." The men shared a look of understanding.

"If we can just set a date, I can put everything into motion." Will gestured in frustration. "My family's in Manitoba, they need time to arrange their travel. They can't all stay with me, there isn't room."

Sam raised his eyebrows. "Hmm. Sounds like a job for Luke Harrison."

"Luke Harrison?" Will lowered his voice with effort. "I don't want him anywhere near this wedding. He's around Julia all the time. I feel like I have to keep an eye on him, just to keep her safe."

Sam laughed. "Have you told Julia that? I think she'd be surprised. Luke was Stephen's best friend, the best man at their wedding. The two grew up together. When Stephen was dying, Luke made him a promise he'd help Julia and the children all he could. He keeps an eye on the rental house in town for her, he watches for any deals at the store, whatever he can do. That wood stacked behind the house was from him, he got it delivered then came out and split it."

Will watched him intently. "Hmm. Well, I'm not sure that the promise is all there is to Luke's interest in Julia. How did Julia and Stephen meet, if he grew up here and she grew up in Sparwood?"

"Haven't you asked her that?"

"There's been so much going on, it hasn't come up, but I've wondered."

"Stephen came to Sparwood with his team to play in a baseball tournament. Julia was my main cheerleader. We won, by the way. The only year we beat the Creston team. But Stephen laid eyes on her, and never looked away. You can see why. They were married the next year."

Will nodded, staring wordlessly at the dark window. Sam hitched his chair around to face him. "Will, we had this conversation before you arrived, but I want to make sure you're aware. The police have been very active in the Sparwood area.

There's been trouble between the Relief Camp and the hill people, the moonshiners."

Sam rose and walked over to close the parlour door before continuing. "There's been lots of drunkenness and disruption and the moonshiners have been more or less the root of the problem. When the police were called in, they began to clear out the hills."

Will spoke. "So Ben's folks may have been dislodged."

Sam nodded. "I thought I better make sure you knew. I guess the shacks were pretty basic, part log, part corrugated tin, some with grass thatch roofs. The children had few clothes, they said some were naked. No clothes at all. They were making rotgut in washtubs and the like, although there was a bit of sophisticated equipment. But the moonshiners are gone, at least the ones the police found.

"Who knows? There are mine shafts and gullies all through those hills that no police posse could find unless they fell into them. But we don't know what might have happened to the Valadios."

Will sighed and stood to go, grabbing his coat from a hook by the door. "I'm worried about that headache. It sounds like she's overtired. Maybe she could sleep late tomorrow morning, or have a rest while the kids are at school." He left with a feeling of frustration dogging his steps.

CHAPTER THIRTY NINE

Charlie arrived next. Will picked the children up from school, crammed them into the car and went to the train station to fetch him. He was one of the first people off, his expression anxious as he looked around the platform, his new scarf tied securely around his neck.

But Ollie broke free and ran to tackle him, Ben right behind. There was a bit of good-natured pushing and shoving. Will introduced Maggie, who put out her hand. Charlie didn't seem to know what to do with it at first, but finally grabbed it and gave it a short shake.

Will had to suppress a grin, Maggie had looked just like Julia at that moment.

They tumbled back into the car, where the Morris children were waiting. After swift introductions, they headed out the North Road, driving past home to deliver the Morrises. Ben and Ollie made sure to point out their house as the car went by.

By the time they arrived home, it was nearly dinner time. Julia came out on the verandah and waved. She gave Charlie a big hug, and he blushed to the roots of his hair.

"He gets even redder than Ollie," Maggie said, and everyone burst into laughter.

The men did the chores, looking after Prince and Daisy Mae.

Ben and Ollie took Charlie around the yard, showing him the barn, the hen house, the big garden which was bare now under small patches of lingering snow.

They showed him the root cellar where they'd hidden when they arrived at Julia's house, and the shed where they'd slept for the first nights. Charlie helped them bring in wood to fill the wood boxes, and more for the stack on the side porch.

Meanwhile the kitchen and dining room tables were arranged end to end to seat everyone. The kitchen benches came into use as well as the piano bench. It was quite a crowd. Sarah had done the cooking.

Will was relieved to see Julia's colour was much better and Sam reported that she'd slept for two hours that afternoon. He supervised the washing up, then declared it an early night and directed Julia to bed. He left with the promise of coming over at lunch the following day.

When he arrived he had his black bag in hand, as usual. He went through his ritual with the children, taking every pulse, listening to every heart, checking all the ears and throats. Then he took over the parlour and asked Sam and then Sarah to come in to see him. He even checked out the baby, and finally Charlie. He told the young man that he looked good and healthy but needed to eat more.

"I don't know," he said. "I don't want to wear out my welcome. Food costs a lot and I don't take more than my share."

Will clapped him on the shoulder. "Your boss is pleased with you, he told us that you're a good worker. I can see it's true just by watching you around here. Any worker, especially a good one, is worth the food to keep him going."

Charlie's gaze darted around the room. "I guess so," he mumbled.

"It's true," said Will. "A young man your age is still growing, Charlie. And you need to ensure that you get enough nutrition to keep yourself in good health while you grow. When you work hard, that burns up a lot of food, so eat for that too. Don't eat like a pig, but eat until you're full. Then you can gain a bit of weight and that'll be good for your health."

Ben heard the last part of this conversation and his eyes grew big. "Is Charlie still growing? Wow, he's going to be even bigger. He might get as big as you, Will. That would be something."

Will grinned. "That would be something, alright. Maybe you will too. Think of that."

Ben grinned back.

When Charlie left he was wearing a new coat, one of Stephen's that Julia had adjusted by moving the buttons to make it fit better on his lean frame. They could always be moved out again if he gained the weight Will wanted him to.

~~*~~

During the Grants' visit, Julia seemed to settle with the idea of the wedding, and Will seized the opportunity to push for a decision. After much discussion and bantering, the date was set for the middle of May.

That gave them six weeks to plan the event. Julia mentioned that the bridge group would help, and Sarah went into town to have a visit with Betsy and arrange what she could. They offered to take care of the food for the reception. And they'd make the wedding cake.

Although Will was confident most of his family could stay with him, Julia had seen the condition of his house and knew that, although it was roomy, it still looked like a house that an old man had lived in.

Will had never taken the time to fix it up and there simply weren't enough rooms to house all those in the Stoffard family. Sam talked to Luke and together they visited the boarding house behind the Co-op Store. Luke's mother, Mamie, had closed off the upper floor during the winter months. Luke agreed to open the rest of it up and get it cleaned and set up in plenty of time for the wedding.

By the time the Grants left for home, the process had begun. Sarah measured the children for size and gave the information to Will, over Julia's protests. "Let him, Julia. If he wants his family to help like that, then let him. Think how much time and energy you'd spend coming up with clothes for all the kids. We just have to worry about your gown, and we'll sort that out too before long."

Julia was sorry to see her family go, and at the same time relieved. She was tired and was looking forward to a couple of days rest. Heddie came Monday as usual, and helped with the loads of laundry that had stacked up with all the visitors. She made a batch of bread for the week, and washed the floors before she left.

By mid-week, Julia was beginning to feel better. She and Jims had a nap every afternoon, and she was starting to get some energy back again.

Maggie was chomping at the bit to stay overnight with her best friend, Lisa, from school, having just gotten her feet wet with the short visit from Jasmine. When Julia mentioned it at bridge, Betsy suggested that Jims come at the same time to stay at her house, and play with Nell. It would give Julia a bit of a break, and time alone with the older boys.

Jims couldn't believe he was to have his own adventure. He was pretty sure he'd never stayed overnight away from home before, not without his mum.

Will tried to suppress his own excitement but couldn't stop his comments. "Don't worry," he whispered, "you won't be lonely, I guarantee it. Once the boys are off to school I'll be here. Nothing is going to keep me away."

~~~**~~~

Part Eight - Pa

CHAPTER FORTY

B en, quick! Around the corner!" Ollie grabbed his brother's sleeve as he whipped past, heading for the side of the school building. Ben looked startled but Ollie kept going, his head down and legs pumping. Alarmed by the panic in his brother's voice, Ben abandoned his game of ball and ran after him, past the duty teacher and into the shadows of the woodpile at the back of the school.

"Ollie, hold it! Where are you going? What is it?"

His brother had stopped, holding his side, his eyes wide and unfocussed. "Ben, he's here, we have to hide!"

"What are you talking about?" Ben shook his shoulder and peered into his face. "Who's here? Ollie, stop it!"

Ollie shook, holding his arms against his thin chest. "He's here, Pa's here. I just saw him." He pointed a wavering finger in the general direction of the front yard.

Ben's jaw dropped. He lowered his voice. "Are you sure? Was it really him?"

Ollie nodded, staring into his eyes, panic written on his face.

Ben's head swiveled around and he looked back the way they'd come, then he moved to the corner of the building and peered cautiously around.

"Ben, don't do it. Come back, he'll see you!"

He waved Ollie back and stuck his head further out.

"I don't see anyone," he whispered. He slowly eased around the corner.

"Ben, he'll notice you more than me. Don't go out there!"

They stood still, breathing shallowly as Ben scanned the schoolyard, then he snuck back toward his brother. "What should we do?"

Ollie shook his head, "I don't know." His legs suddenly wobbled under him and he sat heavily on a stack of firewood.

Ben crouched beside him. "Do you want to see him, Ollie?"

He shrugged, uncertainty shining in his eyes. "I'm afraid he'll take us back there. Back home."

"That's not home, not anymore," Ben said fiercely. "We've got us a new home, a real nice one, with a Mum and everything."

Ollie whimpered. "We had a Mum before, didn't we?"

Ben shook his head, "Not really." They fell silent.

When the bell rang by the schoolhouse door, both boys jumped, then rose and cautiously joined the throng of children lining up at the entrance. Their heads turned this way and that, but they couldn't find their father.

"Are you sure, Ollie? I can't see him."

Ollie hung his head. "I don't know. I'm pretty sure, but I don't know."

Ben's arm snaked around his shoulders for a quick hug, then dropped to his side.

~~*~~

Ollie was quieter than usual that afternoon. He spoke in monosyllables and couldn't meet Julia's gaze when she talked to him. She gave him a dose of cod liver oil, and sent him to lie down before dinner, but he didn't feel any better when she woke him for the meal.

Both boys were jittery the next morning, and they went off to school with Mr. Morris, worried about what might happen. At lunch in the playground, Ollie stood near the schoolhouse door in the shade, hoping he wasn't noticeable. He kept watch and felt safer if he was near enough to dart through the door if danger approached.

Then he saw him. Pa stood beside the trunk of the large fir tree down at the end of the schoolyard, just outside the fence. He was so still, he was almost unnoticeable, but Ollie knew the tilt of his head, the way he leaned on one leg and cocked the other knee. He knew the exact shade of gray of his old faded leather coat and the length of its sleeves on his father's long arms.

Ollie froze, but his heart thundered. "Ben," he whispered. He looked around madly but his brother was nowhere to be seen. He shrank back into the shade of the entrance, yet he could feel his father's gaze on him, the burning intensity of it. He was pulled yet terrified by Pa's presence.

Maggie walked past with her girlfriend. They held hands and talked together in low voices.

"Maggie," he hissed.

She turned, looking around to see who was calling.

"Maggie! Over here."

Maggie broke into a smile and waved. "Ollie, what are you doing? Are you playing hide and seek?" Her voice lowered as she glanced around. "I won't tell."

He beckoned frantically. "Come here!"

Maggie twisted to look around the yard, then turned back and trotted over. "What are you playing?" she whispered.

"Listen, find Ben and make him come behind the school. Tell him I'll meet him there. Tell him it's the same as yesterday."

Maggie looked puzzled. "What does that mean, the same as yesterday?"

"Never mind. He'll know." He left her, darting around the other side of the school and over the fence, fighting his way through the brambles to get to the back of the woodpile.

There were a few boys there, throwing marbles against the wall. He ignored them and stood nervously on one leg, waiting for Ben. The bell was just ringing as Ben came around the corner.

"There you are. What do you mean, the same as yesterday? Maggie told me, but I still don't see him." He stood aside to let the other boys pass as they headed in to school. "Ollie, I think you're just spooked."

Ollie shook his head. "He's here, alright. He was standing under the fir tree at the end of the yard. He had on his old gray leather jacket, the same one!'"

Ben nodded, sudden fear in his eyes. "Yeah, the gray jacket. I remember." They looked together down the playground, wondering what to do.

Behind them there was a rustle in the brush. "Well, boys."

And they knew. They didn't even have to turn around and look. They knew it was Pa.

~~~**~~~

CHAPTER FORTY ONE

Julia waited in the wagon, holding Prince with the bit tight in his mouth. Maggie sat on the bench on one side, Jims ensconced on the other. The two Morris boys lounged on the low seats along the wagon bed.

"Where are they?" she asked. "Were they kept after school for something?" The children shook their heads.

Bert Morris piped up. "Ollie left the classroom in the afternoon to go to the bathroom and he never came back."

"Well, that doesn't make sense," Julia muttered. She sighed and got down from the wagon, tying the reins to the fence. "Stay here, nobody move. I'll be right back."

Mrs. Rasmussen wasn't in her room, and Miss Cusp didn't have any information. She hadn't been as friendly to Julia since it became common knowledge in the village that the doctor was courting out on the North Road at the Butler residence.

But she was genuinely concerned when she heard Ben and Ollie weren't waiting to be picked up as usual. "Maybe they've gone into town, to the store perhaps. Sometimes some of the children go there for candy after school."

"They don't have any money," Julia said, feeling flustered "and they've never done anything like this before."

Miss Cusp pursed her lips. "Well, Mrs. Rasmussen has already left. Her husband is sick and she needed to get home. You could stop by and ask her if she knows anything. Do you know where she lives?"

Julia nodded and thanked her. Mrs. Rasmussen's house was on the south edge of town, and Julia left Prince tied to the post in front. She rang the doorbell. The teacher came to the door looking anxious. Her face brightened when she saw Julia. "Mrs. Butler! How are you? What can I do for you? Oh, it must be the boys... Come in, do."

Julia stepped into the front hall. "I won't keep you, Mrs. Rasmussen, I heard your husband is unwell, and I don't wish to disturb him. But Ben and Ollie weren't at school this afternoon, and Miss Cusp mentioned you might have some information as to where they might be."

Mrs. Rasmussen frowned. "I don't know what actually happened. With about an hour to go in the day, Ben asked permission to take a note over to Miss Cusp. Something about the boys baseball team. After he left, Ollie asked if he could go to the bathroom. Of course, I said yes. They're both such good boys. But neither of them came back.

Her look was sympathetic. "I didn't notice right away, but when I did there was only ten minutes or so left of the school day and I just assumed they were busy on their errands, so I left it. And I needed to get home. I'm so sorry. Where do they go when they leave school like this?'

"That's the thing," said Julia. "It hasn't happened before. Thank you anyway. I'll look around the village and keep my eye out. They can always walk home, I guess. It isn't that far."

They weren't at the fire hall, which was a favourite hangout for small boys. They weren't at the restaurant or any of the stores. Luke at the Co-op promised to keep an eye out for them and bring them home if they showed up.

Back in the wagon, Julia pointed Prince up the North Road toward home. "Did you see them in class, Maggie?"

"Yes," Maggie nodded.

"Well, where did they go when class was out?"

"Nowhere." She looked confused. "They weren't there after class. It was in class."

"What did you see?"

"Well, Ben put up his hand and asked if he could take a note to Miss Cusp. Mrs. Rasmussen said he could."

"Okay, then what?"

"Ollie asked to go to the outhouse. Usually Mrs. Rasmussen won't let more than one person leave the room at a time, but Ben wasn't going to the bathroom, he was going to see Miss Cusp, so I guess that made it alright. They just didn't come back, and when the bell rang, they were still gone."

"They wasn't out in the schoolyard either," piped up Bert Morris. "I was looking for Ollie 'cause I had his marble and we was going to play, but he weren't there. Neither one of them."

It was just starting to rain as Julia dropped the Morrises off at their house, then headed home. She cooked supper, and was serving up plates from the stove for Maggie and Jims, when the door opened. Ben and Ollie sidled in and stood dripping water on the doormat.

Julia dropped Jims dinner before him on the kitchen table with a loud bang that made everyone jump. "Where have you been?"

The boys cringed in unison at her sharp tone. She softened her voice. "Where have you been? I was worried. I couldn't find you, I didn't know if you had run away, or…"

She looked them over swiftly. "Are you hurt?" Her voice was thick with tears. She reached over and pulled the wet jackets off them and hung them to drip on the back of the door.

Neither of them said a thing, their expressions hangdog.

"You're soaking wet, and your feet are soaked. Take those boots off and we'll put them on the proover. They might be dry by morning. Go and put dry pants on and then come to the table. Your dinner is ready." She turned back to the stove to hide her consternation, and the boys trooped silently down the hall.

"Eat your dinner, Jims, before it gets cold."

Julia served up two more plates and set them on the table for the boys, then served her own. The stew was surprisingly good, but she'd lost her appetite. Tears stung the backs of her eyes and she wiped them with her apron.

There was silence in the back bedroom. She couldn't even hear them moving around. Had she been too harsh? After all, they'd been good as gold up till now. They'd never stepped out of line, and at nine and eleven years old, they were certainly old enough to walk home together the mile and a half from the village if they wanted to.

She'd just been so shaken by not finding them there. They were so solid and obedient. And in the back of her mind, there was always that faint idea of the threat to their safety represented by their parents.

But the parents hadn't shown, and they were safe here. So, then… *Well, take it with a grain of salt, Julia.*

After all, who had said the boys weren't being regular kids until they challenged her? Here it was, a challenge, and a minor one at that. The boys came out to their supper and Julia shoved a plate of potatoes and stew under each nose.

CHAPTER FORTY TWO

L ying in bed that night, Ben stared at the faint square of light that was their window. "Ollie, are you awake?" he whispered.

"Yeah."

Julia had just put out the last light in the kitchen and gone up to bed. It was quiet in the house.

"What do you think we should do?"

"I dunno." Ollie's voice sounded weak, as if he were crying.

Ben thought back to the encounter with Pa. He hadn't been threatening, not at first. He'd grabbed them both by an arm to stop them from running off. "I want to talk to you boys, but I guess school is called, with that bell."

They nodded, watching him fearfully.

"Then here's what we'll do," said their father. "You go to your class. But do what you have to, the both of you, and get back out here to talk to me. I'm going to wait right here, and you better be here before school gets out. This is going to be a private talk. You got it?"

Ben nodded again, eyeing Ollie beside him.

"If you're not here, there'll be hell to pay, and I mean it. Someone is going to get hurt."

Ben nodded more emphatically and turned to race into the

schoolhouse, Ollie right behind him. They slid into their seats at the last possible minute.

Mrs. Rasmussen seemed harried and hadn't noticed. Getting out of class wasn't too difficult, and they eased open the front door to meet their father by the woodpile at the back of the building, where no windows looked over the space.

He was sitting waiting for them, gazing into the bush. His head turned slowly and he scrutinized them up and down. "You've grown," he said. "You must have fallen into a nice spot that you've grown that much in the three months that you've been gone."

Ben bristled. "It hasn't been three months, Pa. it's only been eight months, coming up on a year."

"Is that so?" Pat looked him in the eye. "You've been gone long enough to learn how to correct your Pa when he's talking to you, I see." His eyes narrowed, and Ben hung his head.

"Sorry, Pa."

"What about you, Olin? You know how to correct your Pa, too?"

Ollie shook his head dumbly.

"Didn't think so." There was a pause.

"Well." Their father straightened, and adjusted the collar on his gray leather coat. It hung looser on him than Ben remembered. Pa seemed older. His skin was deep brown, with a gray tinge, lean and lined. His hands shook as he tugged at his cuffs. "What I've come to tell you is, your Ma and me, we's leaving this country. It's got too hot up in them hills, so it's become time to move on. We're leaving."

The boys stared at him silently. Finally Ollie muttered, "How did you find us?"

Pa threw his head back and laughed out loud. "It was easy, son. Your brother Charlie told us. Well, not in so many words. But we found Charlie because of that fight down in Ymir. We got a friend close to the cops, so we knew where to find him. And when we needed to, we did."

Their father looked away again. "He didn't want to come with us, though. Too high and mighty now, I guess. Too high and mighty." He fell silent, a long pause that left Ben feeling uneasy. He remembered those long silences after his father made a statement. He always felt he was being tested, did he have the right answer to what was said, was he falling short of expectations? They gave him the pins and needles, no less now than before.

Finally Pa turned back. "So, are you going to disappoint us, too? Are you so big for your britches that you don't want to come with your Pa to a new place, a good place where we can make a right good living and no one will bother us? Is that how it's going to be?"

He glared into their eyes with a blood-shot gaze. "Because I wouldn't want anything to happen to that nice lady who took you in, and those two brats of hers. We wouldn't want that, would we?"

The boys shook their heads dumbly. No, they wouldn't want anything to happen to Mama Julia.

Maybe it wasn't meant for people like them anyway, children like them. Maybe that kind of life, where the meals came regular, and the clothes kept you warm, where there was a fire in the stove, and a hug as you went by, maybe that was only for those who were born into it, after all. Ben and Ollie looked at each other.

"We borned you," Pa declared. "We raised you, we gave you the food out of our mouths and the clothes off our backs, and is this the way you repay us? By running away when we need your help? Your Ma is right pissed. We need runners, we need scouts and watchers. We've got the gear in a wagon, but it's damn heavy to pull and I ain't as young as I used to be. I need help pullin' it."

Ben nodded, and Ollie's mouth opened in horror. His big brother laid a restraining hand on his shoulder. "Pa, we need to get our things from the house. We got stuff that's worth money, so we shouldn't just leave it. Otherwise we'd come right now, but it don't make sense. Better to get back there and pack up what we can, 'cause it's worth something, right?"

Now Ollie rolled on his side and looked at his older brother in the bed opposite. "I was sure scared when you started agreeing with Pa, telling him we'd go with him."

Ben shifted restlessly on the sheet. "Yeah, I just wanted to put him off, give us time to get home and come up with a plan. We need a plan."

"I know. I'm scared, Ben. I can't think of a plan, and I don't want to run away again. That was our plan last time, but I don't want to do it anymore. I like it here." Ollie began to cry.

"It worked, Ollie. We ran away and it worked. Hush, or Mama Julia will hear you and come see what the matter is. We came up with a good plan last time, and it worked. I know we can come up with a good one this time, too. You'll see."

Ben was silent for quite a while.

"Ollie, you awake?"

"Yeah."

"What if we run away just long enough for Pa and Ma to leave town? If no one can find us, they'll most likely just give up and go on without us to wherever they're headed. I mean, they can't stay here. The cops are probably looking for them already. If it got too hot in the hills, that means the cops are trying to shut all the businesses down. So, they must be looking for the stills, don't you think?"

Ollie was silent.

"And Pa doesn't work like other men. He wouldn't just get some kind of job, I don't think. He never has. His job is stills, that's what he knows. You can't get a job making moonshine in the village, can you?"

Ollie giggled , and soon they were breathless with laugher, trying desperately to keep the noise down. One stopped chuckling, the other would suddenly break out in more giggles and they'd both set off again in hysterics.

Finally they ran out of steam and Ben said, "Well, we don't have to have a plan tonight. He did say he'd give us a couple of days to get our stuff out of the house and hidden, so we don't get caught taking it."

"What stuff, Ben? What stuff do we have that's worth

something?"

"Why, nothing," said Ben. "What we got here that's worth something isn't anything we can take with us. But Pa don't know that."

They both finally drifted off to sleep.

~~~**~~~

CHAPTER FORTY THREE

Julia dropped Jims off at Betsy's in the afternoon, saw him safely inside with his little cloth bag in hand, holding pajamas and clean underwear. Then she picked Ben and Ollie up from school and waved goodbye to Maggie as she headed off down the street with her friend. Ben and Ollie were quiet as they travelled up the North Road with the Morris children.

When they got home, Julia said, "Well, this is a treat. Just the three of us. Let's see what we can do." She had biscuits and sliced meat with carrot sticks waiting for dinner. Then she popped some corn and broke out a deck of cards.

It was a good evening. The boys loved to play cribbage, and had gotten pretty good at it. Ben kept careful score with the pegs on the old wooden cribbage board. Later she read them the first chapters of Tom Sawyer, knowing Ben had already struggled through them with mixed success. Then she got them early to bed, hoping they had recovered from the episode of leaving school without permission. They'd been so subdued since then, she gave them reassuring hugs as she tucked them in.

Next morning, Mr. Morris picked the boys up in his wagon and Julia was alone in the house.

She could count on one hand the number of times she'd been alone since Maggie was born. She put away breakfast, washed her hands and face and tidied her hair. The next thing she heard was

Will's car in the yard. She followed the noise down the side of the house. Opening the door, she walked out on the verandah. He had driven around the back of the barn, hiding his car from sight of the road.

Will walked up the steps with a bag in his hand. "Hello, sweetheart."

"Will," she said softly.

He wrapped his arms around her and pulled her against him. The comfort was immediate. "Come inside, Julia," he said. "We're finally alone. Can it be true? I hardly think it's possible." He pulled her through the door, and closed it. "Can we lock it? Yes, that's right."

He hung his jacket on a hook and turned around to pick up his bag and take her hand. "Come upstairs, Julia."

She followed him willingly as he tugged on her hand. He rounded the landing and entered the dimness of her room. The curtains were filmy and let in filtered light. She'd made up the bed, covering it with her corded throw in deep green. Small embroidered pillows lay across the head of the bed and were tucked onto the upholstered chair in the corner. The wool rug beside the bed mimicked the greens of the throw.

Will shed his sweater and shoes, then slowly undid the buttons on her shirtwaist, rubbing the tips of her breasts with the backs of his fingers as he worked. A shiver of anticipation traced its way down her spine.

"Julia," he said, "look at me."

She raised her face and he placed his mouth over hers, his lips hot, his tongue seeking. A warm glow began in her mid-section as his hands roamed her back. The kiss grew until they were both breathing heavily. He threw back the covers and pulled her down on the bed. "Oh, baby," he said. "Oh, my darling. I've waited so long, it seems forever. I love you so. Let me love you now."

She kissed him back, the heat rising. It had been such a long time. She pulled his suspenders down and began on the buttons of his shirt. Her clothes came away piece by piece under his nimble fingers and were tossed to the floor. He wrestled with the tiny pearl buttons on her camisole, easing it off her shoulders and his breath caught in his throat. "You're so lovely, like a China doll. Look at these shoulders, so straight and strong, but fragile too."

Julia ran her fingers over his heavy shoulders and down his chest, tangling in the curly mat of black hair. "Make love to me, Will. I miss this so much."

He eased back and opened his trousers, pulling his underwear down at the same time. His erection was already standing at attention. She reached for him, laying a gentle palm against his manhood.

He grabbed her wrist. "Not yet, Julia. Just a minute, I'm so ready…"

She laid back and he ravished her with his mouth, slowly moving his tongue down her body, performing torturous patterns on her tender flesh. She panted, her fingers tangled in the sheet. "Make love to me, Will."

He grunted and crawled back up, pressing a knee between her legs. "Are you ready? Because I can't wait any longer." He entered her then, pushing his way slowly forward.

She tensed and gasped a breath. It had been so long. She used her hands on his chest to hold him back. He slowed, pressing a kiss to her mouth, then surging inward until he was lodged in her. Their gaze met in a dawning recognition, his face dark with blood.

Then he began to move again, and she felt everything inside loosen and warm until her body hummed in pleasure and anticipation. She didn't see his face any more but felt the heat of his presence and focus as her eyes slowly closed. She moved with him, hanging onto his shoulders, her fingers slipping on his slick skin.

The tension grew and swelled and she pushed her head back against the pillows as the feelings flowed in a slow progression from mesmerism to climax. She dug her fingers into his biceps as he increased the pace, pounding into her, forcing his way until she stiffened and shuddered in his arms.

He grunted, groaned and seemed to lose his hold on control, following her over the edge.

~~*~~

They lay amid the tumbled bedding, the filtered light falling across her hair. Her arms were alabaster in the dimness, her breasts wonderful mounds of flesh peaked in rose. Will placed his hand over the nipple and felt it abrade his palm, then lowered his mouth to suckle her gently. She stirred in his arms, pushing her fingers through his hair and holding his head in place as she sighed.

She raised her hips against him and he felt himself begin to stiffen again in response. He met her gaze with a fierce look that caused a blush to spread up her throat. He placed his lips there, over her collarbone, planting kisses. She sighed and gripped his shoulders.

Then he slid his hand between her legs and began a gentle massage as she pressed upward, more insistent, more consuming. When he eased into her again, she was slick with moisture. The second time was slower and at the same time more intense. She cried out at the finish, and he held her as she shook and shuddered, sobbing in his arms. He wiped the tears from her cheeks, then took his own release with a deep groan, his face buried in her softly curling hair. They collapsed together and slept.

When Julia stirred some time later, Will sat up and reached for the bag he'd brought with him. He opened it and she looked inside. Nestled on the bottom were meat pasties and little cakes from the bakery in town.

Will settled her back against the pillows, and went downstairs, returning with a pot of tea and two cups. He fed her morsels, one for her, one for him between sips of tea, until they were both spotted with crumbs.

"I have to keep your strength up," he said with a meaningful look.

She giggled.

He kissed her. By the time he put the tea things on the floor she was ready for him again.

~~*~~

"Have you ever been married, Will?" she asked, as she lay languidly in the curve of his arm.

"No, never." There was a pause, he turned his head toward her. "I was engaged once."

"Oh." She waited, but he didn't say more.

"What happened? Did she die?"

Will snorted a laugh. "No, she didn't die. Sorry for laughing. She broke the engagement and married a fellow from my class at university."

"Oh, my goodness." Her eyes mirrored her concern for him. "I'm so sorry." She placed her hand protectively on his arm.

"Don't be," he said. "She did the right thing. Although at the time I was angry and hurt. I didn't love her enough, you see. I was possessive of her and I thought it was time for me to marry, but I didn't love her. And she must have known that there was something missing in the relationship. That there was more to being in love than just being attached. She was right to break it off. My pride was injured more than anything else, but it took me a while to realize that."

Julia studied his face for a minute. "That's sad," she finally said.

Will took her face in his hands. "I used to think it was sad, Julia. But since I met you, I thank God every day that I didn't marry her." His kiss was the sweetest she had ever tasted.

He left in time to pick up the children in his car, and grab a takeout meal from the Chinese restaurant. When they all returned, Julia was bathed and dressed and looked tired but luminous, greeting the children as they came in, then giving Will a kiss that curled his toes. His eyes were fierce on her face. "It's a good thing we've set the date," he growled.

She laughed softly and turned away to put the food on the

table. His gaze lingered on her waist and the swell of her hips. He wondered if there would be consequences to their love making. He didn't think so, given the dates she'd given him for her last period, but there could be. As a doctor, the one thing he knew for sure was there was no certainty in predicting whether a woman would get pregnant.

Well, if there were consequences, he could handle it. The wedding date was set, just over four weeks away, and by the time they were married she wouldn't be showing, would barely be started.

He pulled out his chair with a sense of profound satisfaction, as much to do with finally claiming his woman as the wonderful loving they'd had.

~~~**~~~

CHAPTER FORTY FOUR

Will lay in bed with his hands clasped behind his head. His eyes were focused on the dim ceiling above him in the early dawn light, but his thoughts were inward.

One of the first things he'd done when he arrived here was to go back to Nelson to an auction to furnish some of the rooms in the house to his liking. He'd come across a wonderful handmade bed frame which he'd purchased along with some other pieces.

The bed was large, built to accommodate someone of his size, and he'd ordered a mattress from Winnipeg specially made to fit it. His brother Ray had had a mattress made and he used to rave about finally being able to stretch out in bed. Will had been pleased with his purchase, and once he wrestled it into the bedroom and onto the big frame, he couldn't believe how much better he slept. There was finally room to lay straight without having some part of him hanging off.

Now he lay in it alone, thinking that it wasn't quite as perfect as he'd thought. It needed something else, someone else. It needed Julia in it to make it perfect.

He cast his mind around the house. It was a nice place, all things considered. Old Doc Farley had raised his family here, and he'd only moved out after his wife died and he'd given up the medical practice. When Will first saw the place, he thought it was a waste, much too big for him. He even thought of renting it out and living somewhere smaller.

But his perspective on life had definitely changed since then. Now he was thinking in terms of adding on to make room for a growing family, an already good-sized family that would undoubtedly get even bigger.

He understood that Ben and Ollie were a permanent part of the family. He wouldn't have admired Julia as much as he already did if things were any different. He was mightily attached to those two young men, so there was no question that they belonged. There were also Maggie and Jims, and they'd no doubt have a few of their own, if his brothers were any indication.

Although he didn't want to burden Julia with too many pregnancies. He resolved to be careful, but knew Julia would welcome however many they were gifted with.

He turned his mind to the problem of the house itself. It was bigger than Julia's so it made sense for them to live here after the wedding. It was right next to his surgery, so that worked. It was one thing to drive to work in the morning. It was something else entirely to have someone knocking at your door in the middle of the night with an emergency, and you weren't anywhere near your office. They needed to live here.

There was a bit of land around the house, not as much as at Julia's place, but they didn't need a farm. There'd be room for a barn at the back of the property and the two sheds that ran down the side of the yard would certainly come in handy. There was also a garden out there. It hadn't been worked in a while, but he could see the vestiges of what it had been. The lettuce and chard continued to seed itself. There was a flower garden in the front that was going to wrack and ruin, because he hadn't paid any attention to it.

They'd certainly need the vegetable garden. They might need a second goat, or a milk cow. Those boys were growing like weeds, and Julia was hard pressed to keep enough on hand to meet their needs along with all the cooking and baking she did. Of course, Prince would have to come. Even if they didn't need him for transportation, he was as much a pet as a work horse and Will understood that.

He rolled to his side. There was no reason why that woman, Heddie, who came once a week to help Julia, couldn't come more often if she was willing. Julia looked tired lately and he worried about her.

Maybe she needed complete rest. After the wedding, he'd find a way for that to happen. He'd find a man to come a few days a week, do the things he didn't have time for, like dig over the garden, scythe the hay in the field below, repair the buildings. There were numerous tasks that needed to be done, that he might never get to.

And then there was the house. Why couldn't they add another wing on the south side to balance the one to the north that housed the surgery? They might not need it right away, the house was certainly big enough to handle the four children. But when more began to arrive….

There was a heavy pounding and shouting at the surgery door, just as his alarm sounded. He thumped the alarm clock, shutting off the ringer, and leaped from the bed. Pulling on a pair of trousers, he grabbed a shirt on his way through to the hall.

Some days started earlier than others.

~~*~~

The next day when Julia stopped to pick up the children, Ben and Ollie weren't at the school. Again.

She was first perplexed, then furious. By the time she reached home, she'd calmed down, but was determined to handle the situation differently this time. She wanted answers and when they showed up at home, by heaven, she would get some.

They could just explain what they were up to, and why it was alright to worry her with their behavior. She'd make sure they knew how she felt.

She thought of what Maggie and the Morris boys had said. Yes, Ben and Ollie had been in school that morning. They'd eaten their lunch in the classroom with the rest of the kids, and went outside to play. But they hadn't come back to class when the afternoon bell rang. They weren't in the playground, no one saw them leave. And they didn't show up later in the day.

Nor did they show up at home that evening. Julia finally gave up, left the front door unlocked and settled down on the sofa with a blanket wrapped around her, hoping to hear them if they came in during the night. When she woke to the dawning light, she checked their room but the boys were still missing.

The moment after Mr. Morris stopped for Maggie the next morning, Julia got Jims into his coat and out to their cart. She had Prince harnessed in a jiffy and on the North Road heading into town. Julia stopped at the doctor's house and barely took the time to tie Prince up before she dragged Jims off the cart and raced him up the path. Will opened the door before she could knock.

"Well, you're a sight for sore eyes," he said, his eyes crinkled at the corners with his slow smile. "No one's here yet, so we can go back and have a cup of coffee." He stopped as he took in her expression, then reached to take her arm and tug her into the house. "Come inside, sit right here. Jims, you too. Now, tell me, what's wrong."

"The boys," she whispered. "Ben and Ollie, they didn't come home last night."

"What do you mean, last night? Where were they?" Will looked astonished.

"They weren't at school when I went to pick everyone up. But this time they didn't come home at all. I think they've run away. I'm so worried, I don't know if they went because they didn't feel welcome or because someone came to get them. I just..." She collapsed in his arms.

"Julia! Hold on a minute." He held her away from him for a second to look into her face. "Here, sit down here. Jims, you can play with this construction set, right here at the table. Now tell me again, Julia, from the beginning." He sat beside her and chafed her hands as she talked.

Will took a deep breath as she wound down. "That gives us a lot to think about. Did they say why they were late the first time?"

Julia looked stricken. Her eyes glazed over with tears. "I was so shocked, I didn't get an answer from them. I just sat them down to the table and gave them dinner. They whipped out and did all the chores and took themselves off to bed, without talking about it. Maggie told me that Ollie stopped her in the playground and asked her to find Ben, and have him meet behind the school. He said, tell him it's the same as yesterday. I don't know what that means."

"Why didn't you tell me? I could have talked to them."

"Well, because the next time I saw you was when you came... you know, to spend the day with me."

Will's gaze heated, as she looked down at her lap.

"Yes, and it feels like a year ago already. Julia, this is eating me up, this waiting." There was a heavy pause, then he sighed and rubbed his jaw.

"Let me think. These aren't the kind of boys to play dirty tricks. I haven't seen any sign of that, they always do their level best. They want to be with you, and they do everything they can to make sure that you want them there, too. This isn't just boys being boys. Were they belligerent when they came in, were they cocky?"

"No. I think they were humiliated. They hung their heads and didn't say a word."

"Yeah, that's what I think. They aren't doing this to cause trouble. Maybe they aren't doing this, maybe they don't have a choice. Maybe their folks have come for them after all this time. Let me call Guy." He walked across to the desk.

Julia watched him for a moment. "What will Guy know?"

"Well, probably nothing, but maybe he can find something out for us. Let's see." After a few minutes on the phone with the doctor in Nelson, Will came back across the room. "He's going to see if he can get down to the feed store in Ymir today and talk to Charlie. Maybe he knows something. We can only hope. Meanwhile, I have appointments all afternoon and some house calls later today, so let's do what we can this morning. I have to stop in at the hospital and then I'm free."

Together they combed the town, searching and asking questions. No one had seen anything, but after a call to the Nelson police detachment, Constable Terasoff said he'd be happy to help. He was planning to be in town later that day anyway.

By the time he arrived, Will had headed back to the surgery. But Terasoff offered to search south if Julia wanted to head back up the North Road and talk to her neighbours.

She stopped at the school to make sure the boys hadn't suddenly turned up there, then drove toward home. What was she searching for now? Was it two small boys, or a family with a black mother, a redheaded father and their sons? She stopped at every house along the road for close to eight miles before she had to turn around to do the pickup at the school.

They all went home, Jims exhausted from the constant travelling. Maggie was disconsolate. She kept asking why Ben and Ollie would leave, where would they go. Perhaps they hadn't even had anything to eat today, because where would they get food?

Julia sliced bread and added cheese and pickles for dinner as her heart ached. They munched quietly at the table. She fed them tea and cookies. Not her finest hour for nutrition, but she was too tired to do more.

~~~**~~~

CHAPTER FORTY FIVE

J ulia was tucking the children into bed when Will arrived. The children rushed back down the stairs to see if he had any news, but there was nothing to report. Julia shepherded them back into bed.

When she came down, Will had put the kettle on and was eating a slice of bread and cheese. "I missed dinner," he said, grinning. He walked over and gave her a hug.

"That's what we ate, too," she said, resting her forehead against his chest. "So, what do we do now?"

Will lifted his head, listening to the sound outside, then went to the door to usher in Constable Terasoff. They sat down and Will made tea.

Terasoff leaned forward at the table and placed his thick hands around his cup. "I think I have something, but I'm not sure what it means. Someone on the South Road saw a family walk past his place this afternoon. There was a mother and father and two boys about seven and nine. He noticed because they were pulling a small cart piled high, with a cover tied over it. He thought it was sad that they had everything they owned in the cart. And then he saw that the mother was black. He said he'd never seen a Negro before. The father was fair, maybe gray-haired, he couldn't tell. I've seen the older boy and I imagine one of his parents is Negro, don't you?"

Julia nodded. "Yes, that has to be them." She caught back a

sob. "Ben said his father was fair like Charlie, red blond with freckles. I can't believe they'd just leave like that. Can you, Will? It doesn't seem possible.".

Will shook his head. "I don't think for a minute that they just left like that. After the mess I saw on their little bodies, I don't think so, not unless they were blackmailed or threatened. We have to find them and ask. We can't keep them if they don't want to stay with us but we need to have them tell us that, don't we?"

Terasoff shrugged. "If the parents want them, not much we can do. I went down the South Road all the way to Wynndel and I didn't see anyone on the road. They can't have walked far. They left here this afternoon, the boys didn't disappear until after lunch. Makes me think they took off into the bush."

He paused and gave Will a level look. "You might have heard about the police action up near Sparwood and the Relief Camp. They've been cleaning out the hills, shutting down the moonshiners."

Will nodded and Julia looked stunned. "Sam told me that when he was here, that a lot of people had been arrested and stills broken up. That's probably what they're carrying on the cart. They're taking it somewhere else to set up shop."

Julia covered her mouth with her hand. "Ben told me he did sales for his mother when she was away or too drunk to look after it."

Terasoff raised his bushy gray brows. "I don't know if we'll find them. If they've gone into the bush, we don't know in what direction, or where they're headed."

Julia lowered her head to hide her tears.

Will ran his hand over her hair and addressed the Constable. "We don't have to give up yet, I'm thinking. We can still do a search, and maybe the police could question people in a wider circle, see if there are any more sightings. They're pretty hard to miss, anyone who gets a look at them will remember, just like that man on the South Road today."

Constable Terasoff stood to go. "I'll keep you posted, and you let me know if you turn up anything that might help. Just call the Nelson detachment and leave a message."

"Thank you for your help, Constable. You can see how upset Mrs. Butler is to lose those boys. We don't think they left voluntarily. We appreciate any help you can give us." Will closed the door and came back to the table.

"Sweetheart, come over to the sofa. We'll turn on the fire in the parlour for a bit, and I'll get the brandy." He lifted her from the bench and carried her into the other room. When he finally got her arranged on his lap, a glass of brandy in her hand, he pulled her close and whispered in her ear. "It's okay, Julia. They aren't our boys and if they want to leave they can. But if they didn't want to go, we'll do everything we can to find them and give them the right to make that decision."

He pressed a kiss to her temple. "Hold your head up and listen now. I have some more news. I didn't tell Terasoff because I didn't want to bring Charlie into it. He already had his bar fight and got the attention of the police, he doesn't need any more. But Guy got down to Ymir and had a talk with him. Charlie's Pa paid him a visit a couple of weeks ago. He said they'd been kicked out of the hills, and were lucky to escape with their still. They threw it into a cart and pulled it out the back roads and down into the valley near Donegal. Then they went to earth until the raids were over.

"Then they started asking around for Charlie. Remember, Ben thought Charlie was working in that sawmill in Donegal? Well, that's what the parents thought too, but he was long gone by then. But apparently, Olin Valadio has a friend in the police. That's why they knew enough to get their still on a cart and hightail it out of there before the raids began."

Julia choked on the brandy. "Oh, no. That's awful. That means we can't trust Constable Terasoff with any information."

"Not necessarily, but we have to be careful. I'm quite sure Terasoff is on the up and up, and it could be that Valadio's friend will only help if Valadio can give him moonshine. Now that he doesn't have any, he might find it harder to get favours. At any rate, because of his friend, he learned where Charlie was, just like we did. So he went to see him, and leaned on him. He told Charlie they needed his help. The father said, and I quote from Guy, 'they gave him the food out of their mouths, and the clothes off their backs, and all they got for it was an ungrateful son who ran off and didn't give them any of his money or extend a hand to help when times were tough."

"Charlie told him to leave, and never contact him again. The father said he'd tell his employer that Charlie was a thief and a liar and he'd better watch his back. Charlie said it took him all night to get him to leave. He didn't see his mother, although the father said she was nearby.

"When Guy called in, Charlie got worried when he heard the boys had gone missing. He's sure they didn't go because they wanted to. He figured the father did the same thing to the boys as they did to Charlie."

He held her close and pressed his cheek to her head. "We just have to find them. Charlie didn't know where they were headed, but they used to live near Kingsgate when he was younger. He thought they'd know the woods."

Julia gulped. "Kingsgate? That's on the American border. If they cross over the border our police can't follow. We have to go there ourselves, and set up a watch on the road to see if they pass. What if they leave Canada before we get there?"

She was losing control, she could feel it. "Will, it's only been one day! How can we can possibly find them?" She burst into tears, sobbing on his shoulder while he held her. When she stopped, he tightened his arms.

"Sweetheart, I'm going to put you to bed, and I'll sleep here tonight, on the sofa. I'll call Nelson in the morning to let Terasoff know that they may have headed for Kingsgate. We don't have to tell him it was Charlie who told us. With the police looking in that area, that's a start. We'll think of more to do tomorrow. Come on now, let's go."

CHAPTER FORTY SIX

Ben lay on the ground under a blanket, Ollie plastered to his side. He shivered, still damp from crossing the stream. He'd stumbled halfway across. The cart was heavy and Pa had been helping, but he'd let go just as they started through the water. Ben tugged on the rope around his wrist, it was too tight and burned his skin. It hurt his shoulder lying like this with his hands bound. Ollie had fallen into a dead sleep, twitching now and then in his unconscious state.

Pa tricked them. He'd appeared at the school during lunch time, waiting by the same tree, then signaled to meet him around the back. When the other boys left, he'd called them from the bush. "Come here, boys. I want to show you something."

They had peered nervously into the shrubbery and he grabbed them, yanking them through the trees. Ma stood on the other side, hands on hips, smiling slyly. "Well, well.," she said. "My two boys, back again. Don't you look good. Come and I'll show you something."

With their father holding each of them by the wrist, they followed Ma along the trail. By the time they got to the cart, Ben's wrist was red and raw, but that didn't stop Ma from tying their hands to the cart, one on each side. From a distance, anyone would think they were walking beside her, one hand on the handle to help pull the weight.

They travelled like that for most of the afternoon, down the

241

South Road. Then they headed straight into the bush. Pa knew his way around pretty well everywhere, and he'd found a faint track that led them east through the woods toward the low hills. By the time they got to the stream, it was pitch black and Ma wanted to camp for the night.

There was nothing to eat but stale bread, nothing to drink but water from the stream, and moonshine. Ma went on and on about how lucky the boys were to go with them. They were going to make money, good money. And it was a family business, so the boys would be part of that, learn the trade. She needed lookouts, she needed runners, she needed salesmen. She'd train them on the still, and she had plans. Ma finally wound down, having emptied a jar of moonshine, and went to sleep. Then Pa brought them a blanket and settled down himself.

Now everyone slept but Ben. He saw no way out, he and Ollie were trapped. He didn't even know where they were any longer, somewhere in the bush, east of the South Road out of Creston.

~~*~~

Julia moved slowly through the days. Maggie was cranky, argued with her mother and cried easily. Why would Ben and Ollie leave without saying goodbye? She remembered how sick they were when they arrived. She didn't understand, and she stewed unhappily.

Jims was subdued, Julia would hear him playing quietly under the table, using different voices imitating Ollie and Ben in his games.

There was no news. Constable Terasoff reported once to say there'd been no more sightings, but they were keeping an eye on the Kingsgate area, and would inform them if they heard anything. He warned Will—the parents had the right to take their children with them, and it was possible they'd never know where they went.

This was the worst news Julia could have received. She was in an emotional spin, and the fact that her wedding to Will was coming up in a matter of weeks nearly sent her over the edge. She wrote her mother that she wanted to postpone the wedding, but didn't know how to tell Will.

Will knew life had turned precarious. He fought to keep things on an even keel with her. He tried to persuade her to take Heddie on for an extra day each week, he'd pay for it.

"I can pay for my own help, thank you," she said. Her tone was sharp. "And I don't need Heddie for an extra day."

Will backed out of that discussion as gracefully as he could.

But he didn't give up. He dropped by to say he'd bring meatloaf from the family restaurant in the village, and yet when he arrived Julia had already cooked dinner. She was despondent and cranky. Will bided his time.

To his vast relief, Sarah arrived at the end of the week, having gotten a ride with a lumber lorry that was going through. She brought greetings from Sam and his family and another round of cheese. She hugged her daughter, did a little baking, a lot of reading to Maggie and Jims, and calmed the household.

Will wanted to kiss her. She kept a cheerful countenance, and it gave him someone to talk to where he didn't start an argument with every topic he came up with.

He spent his spare time at home, telephoning everyone he could think of, asking the police detachments to keep an eye out. He talked to Guy Whitmore in Nelson to see what he could unearth, to the supervisors at the Relief Camp near Sparwood regarding any new stills, or sightings of small families in the hills. He even found a way to phone Ymir, and have Charlie talk to him from the phone in the general store. But Charlie had no more news.

Still they waited, worried and watched.

~~~**~~~

CHAPTER FORTY SEVEN

Ben pushed Ollie to wake him, and slowly crawled from under the blanket. He had a cough deep in his chest, and it caught him at odd moments, bringing him to his knees with the force of it. Ever since he fell in that creek, he didn't feel well. His eyes were swollen, and he seemed weak.

Ollie rose and rubbed his eyes. They wandered off into the brush to pee. They were both grimy, but there was no soap. Just a dip in the creek now and then, but Ben was always too cold now to want to get wet in water that was coming straight off the snowcapped mountains around them.

Pa was cooking this morning, for once. He had a fire going and had mixed flour and water to make pancakes. He had the big cast iron fry pan heating over the coals, propped on a couple of rocks. He promised them lard to spread on the pancakes, and a bit of jam. They'd been in this clearing for a few days, waiting. Ben didn't know for what.

At first they'd continued on through the bush, pulling the two-wheeled cart as best they could. Sometimes all of them worked on it, two pulling and two pushing. Ma would yell for them to try harder, and they'd put their shoulders into it and lean their weight. Pa found old logging roads with no traffic on them, grass and small trees growing out of the centre, and they followed those for a while. But the moonshine ran out, and Ben wasn't keeping up no matter how loud Ma shrieked. She finally said they should stop for a bit, get some meat, maybe make some moonshine.

Yesterday, Pa caught a pair of rabbits with his wire traps and made a stew, adding wild onion. Ma tried to start the still, but she soon discovered Pa had used most of the cornmeal for food. She was furious, but there was still a bit left and she made do with that. But when she went for the sugar, it was gone. She wouldn't leave it alone and flailed out at Pa for ruining her plans. Pa had used the last of it with the wild berries Ollie picked.

Ma was just waking up now as Pa flipped the first flapjacks out, so she ate them as he added more batter to the pan. Then Ollie and Ben sat down to eat. They each had their fill, licking their plates for the last taste.

Pa ate a couple when they were done and cooked up the rest of the batter to keep for the next meal. Then they went down to the creek to wash the dishes, a bit of sand scrubbed around in the bottom to scour out any grease, then a swish in the water to finish.

Ben lay on the blanket, panting from the exertion. His head was dizzy and he wished Mama Julia was there to give him some of her medicine. She always knew exactly what was needed, producing it from her medicine cabinet in the kitchen. Or maybe Doctor Stoffard could listen to his heart and take his pulse. He could look in his eyes, and get him to stick out his tongue to tell what was wrong. He finally rolled to his side and dozed.

He woke to the sound of shrieking above his head. Ma batted Pa away and grabbed Ben by the leg. "Get up you lazy shit!"

Ben lifted his head and looked at her in a kind of daze. Her face was distorted, almost like he was still in a dream and couldn't see her properly. "What, Ma?"

"Don't 'what, Ma' me," she shrieked. "You bin lazy all your life, and I'm not going to put up with it one more day!"

"He's sick, Ma," Ollie whispered. "He's got a bad chest and Pa thought…"

Ben looked at Ollie in confusion. *Pa thought what?* But Ma didn't let it go.

"Pa thought nothin'! Get your sorry behind off that blanket, and start packing up this stuff. We don't got no sugar, I can't do nothin' with that still without supplies. And we're going to get us some. We're out of money and we're out of cornmeal! Now git!"

Ben got to his knees, his head swaying.

"I don't think we can go just now, I don't think he'll walk." Pa spoke in a moderate tone from somewhere behind him. "I, for one, don't want to carry him. I think it's best we sit and rest for a bit. We can catch a few more rabbits…"

Ma reached over and hit Pa square in the face, banging him back a few steps. "We go when I say we go!" She was breathing heavily and foam glinted in the corners of her mouth. "Don't you tell me when he can walk. I say he walks, he walks!"

Ma stamped back toward the fire. "Ollie, git over here and take care of this." She pointed to the coffee pot, tipped over on its side. "Pick it up and get more water from the creek."

Ollie sidled past her and reached for the handle, just as Ma hit him across the back of the head. He pitched forward straight into the fire pit. He shrieked as Pa leaped and Ben staggered to his feet to wobble toward him. Pa grabbed Ollie by the collar and yanked him up, dragging him out of the coals. His shirt was burned to the elbow, the scorched cloth welded to his flesh.

Ma reached out and grabbed the edge of the sleeve, peeling it slowly off the burned area as Ollie cried out in pain. The large oval wound was singed around the edges and raw in the middle, bleeding where the cloth had ripped the skin off. "You stupid git," she snarled. "Can't you even do a simple thing like fetch some water? What good are you?"

Pa held Ollie upright as he huddled over his arm, sobbing. "Go sit on your blanket," he said quietly. "You and Ben, sit on the blanket."

Ma turned on him, her hands like claws. "Don't you protect those little shits. They aren't worth the food we give them, they're no use at all. Same as their Pa." She grabbed the coffee pot from the edge of the fire and stormed off to the creek.

Pa looked thoughtful, and leaned down to get the cast iron fry pan. He was polishing it on his shirttail when she returned and set the coffee pot amongst the coals. He lifted the pan, drew it back and took one full swing forward. It connected neatly with her skull in a dull *thunk*.

Ma pitched forward onto the dirt. Pa turned and tucked the pan into the back of the wagon, and walked over to the blanket.

"Okay, boys. Up you get. We'll walk in this direction while Ma takes time to have her coffee."

The boys rose unsteadily to their feet, Pa grasping a wrist on each side of him. He walked them back out to the old logging road. He went slowly, supporting Ben with his arm. "This way, boys," he said.

They walked in silence for more than an hour, not fast, just steadily. When Ben bent over to cough, they stopped and waited for him. Ollie's tears fell silently down his face and he shivered convulsively.

"No crying," said Pa. "I ain't got nothin' for that burn, we ate the last of the lard."

On they walked. They eventually reached a trail that crossed the old road at an angle. Pa stopped and pointed. "Down there about a mile, there's a farm. Look. I can see the smoke from the chimley."

They looked dully down the ridge where a spiral of smoke was visible in the distance above the canopy of trees.

Pa nodded. "Down you go. They'll give you some help. They can find your other family. This isn't going to work out for us, so you need to go. Bye, boys."

And he turned and walked back the way they had come.

~~~**~~~

CHAPTER FORTY EIGHT

No," said Julia. "I don't need to wait. I already know. We have to call the wedding off. I can't do this right now. It's too much. Will understands, don't you, Will? And you have to, too, Mum. I've just got too much to handle right now. Surely you don't expect me to do everything?"

Her voice rose steadily through her tirade and ended in a thin shriek. "Everyone thinks I should do everything! Why? No one else has to. Just me, and I won't do it, I can't!"

Will took in her flushed face, her hands fisted at her sides, and glanced fleetingly at Sarah. "Julia, no one expects you to do everything. All we have to do is appear at the church and say our vows. It would be nice if our families came, but they don't have to be there. We can go by ourselves."

"'No, no, no! It's too much and I can't do it. You understand, Will." She turned her back and gripped the edge of the sink with white fingers.

Sarah raised her eyebrows at him. Will laid his hand on Julia's rigid back. "I don't understand. Why can't we just go and get married? No fuss. That's fine with me." He ran his hand around her nape and she pulled away from his touch.

"I can see you don't understand. It's a good thing we aren't married already, it might have been the biggest mistake of our lives right now," she sobbed.

Will felt alarm zing through his gut as he tried to pull her into his arms, but she fought him off.

"Don't! Just don't! I can't, don't you see?" Her voice shook.

He stepped forward and crowded her against the sink with his body. "Julia, listen to me. Listen!" She went quiet, and he pulled her into his arms.

"We can do whatever you want. It doesn't matter." He pressed her head to his shoulder and surrounded her with his body. "Anything at all," he murmured. "It's okay. It's absolutely okay. I'm not in any hurry, and we can take as long as you need. We don't even have to decide right now. It's all right." He continued to murmur into her hair until she sagged against him.

He carried her over to the upholstered chair that Sarah had vacated on her way out of the room, and sat her on his lap. They breathed in and out together, while Will rubbed his hands softly over her back and along her arms, till finally she fell asleep against his shoulder. He sat with her softly limp in his arms, staring at the cold potbelly stove.

What to do now? Not much, he guessed. *Just breathe.*

~~*~~

When Will arrived the next evening, the smell of baking bread filled the kitchen. He took a deep breath as he stepped inside. "Smells good in here."

Jims looked up from the picture he was colouring at the table and grinned. "I know. Mummy says I can have a bun as soon as they cool a little bit."

Will raised his brows. "Hmmm, do you think she'll let me have one, too?"

"I bet she will," he whispered.

Julia smiled at him from over by the stove, then stooped to pull the baking sheet out of the oven. "Okay, you two. No whispering. I know what you're up to. And you'll just have to wait five minutes for them to cool a bit."

"See?" said Jims. "You have to wait five minutes."

Will skirted the kitchen table, and came up behind her. "Can I have a hug while I'm waiting?"

She turned into him and wrapped her arms around his waist, laying her cheek against his chest. "Oh, Will." She hugged him hard. "I'm sorry about yesterday. I just got so…."

"Shhh, it's okay. Don't apologize. Please don't. It's been really hard, I know." He kissed her temple and watched Jims watching them. "Is it okay if I give your Mum a kiss, Jims? Sometimes Mum's need kisses."

Jims shrugged. "Yup. I guess that's okay." He chose the red crayon and went back to his picture.

Will angled his head to look her in the eyes. "Is the wedding still off?"

She chuckled and tilted her head for a kiss. "Well, Mum thinks we can pull it off, just not so organized."

Will nodded. "I agree. Not so organized. I don't think we should do anything but have the ceremony in the church, and serve a lunch. And the food's already arranged. That should be more than enough. Sarah left this morning, right? But she'll be back in a week."

She nodded against his chest, as Maggie galloped into the room.

"Will!" she cried. "I didn't know you were here. Oh, the buns are ready!"

Jims leaped up and the two of them stood with their noses an inch from the pan where it cooled on the sideboard. Julia pulled a knife out of the drawer and got the butter dish from the cupboard.

"'Here we go," she said. They settled around the kitchen table, two on each bench. There was silence save for the sound of contented munching.

~~*~~

Will had just gotten home, pulling the door closed behind him as the surgery phone began to ring. He got across the hall in three strides, snatching the receiver from the wall. "Hello," he barked into the speaker.

A scratchy voice said, "This is Constable Terasoff."

"Yes, Constable. Thanks for calling and keeping us updated. Is there any news?"

Terasoff cleared his throat. "Yes, I think there is. The boys have shown up at a farmhouse south of Wynndel, and the farmer and his wife are looking after them. They arrived yesterday around dusk. The fellow had heard we were looking for these boys so he took the time to get into Wynndel this morning to make a call to us here. I'm convinced these are the boys, one very dark, the other lighter with some freckles."

Will couldn't speak, the relief was almost overwhelming. He'd thought they'd never find them, or see them again. He coughed a few times, then choked out, "Thank God, thank God. Give me a minute here." He wiped his eyes, and coughed again.

"That's better. Okay. Well, that's good news, believe me. How are they?"

"They aren't in great shape, the farmer says. One has some kind of chest illness, and the other has a severe burn, but they're resting and they haven't said much at all, except they're asking for you all. They wanted to know if the farmer knew Mrs. Julia Butler, or Dr. Will and would they be able to go see you soon."

Will took a deep breath and let it out slowly. "Can we go and get them? Tomorrow morning hopefully."

"Well, not just yet. I'm going out there first thing, and I want to talk to them before they're moved, but I can give you directions about how to get there, and if all goes well, they'll be free to leave after I finish my interviews."

Will took down the directions for the farmhouse and thanked the Constable again before he hung up. He stood there for a few minutes, his head hanging. Relief. Thankfulness. Exhaustion. He was overwhelmed.

He staggered to the old waiting room couch and sat down. He'd go and tell Julia, just as soon as he gathered himself. They'd make plans about getting the boys back. He ran over a list in his mind of medical supplies to take with him.

~~~**~~~

CHAPTER FORTY NINE

When Will and Julia arrived at the old farmhouse south of Wynndel close to two o'clock the next afternoon, a police car was still parked in the driveway. Jims had been dropped off at Betsy's house, with arrangements to spend the night. Maggie was to go over there after school. Will didn't know when they'd get home tonight and what condition Benjamin and Ollie would be in when they found them.

Two sheep dogs circled the car, barking loudly, until the heavily bearded farmer bellowed at them from the doorway to calm down.

Will helped Julia from the car and held her arm as they walked to the front steps. He felt the tremble in her muscles as they climbed the stairs.

"Come in. I'm Robert Malekoff, this here's my wife Rose. The boys are sleeping right now. They're just in the bedroom there." Malekoff gestured down the hall.

They shook hands and greeted Constable Terasoff seated by the stove. Tea was offered and they sat at the table as it brewed.

Terasoff shifted his chair legs on the bare wood kitchen floor. "I've been here a while and I guess I've gotten all I'm going to get in the way of information out of them. They don't say a lot." He shook his head. "The younger one looks to the older to talk, and the older one isn't a talker. I couldn't get much, perhaps you will

253

have better luck."

"What did they tell you, Constable?" Julia's voice was unsteady.

"Very little. They were travelling with their Ma and Pa. That's what they told me. They went down the road a ways, then into the bush. They said their Pa knows all the old roads. There wasn't much to eat, and their Pa tried to cook but there wasn't much to put in the pot. He caught a few rabbits and made stew. Then Pa said they weren't going to be much good because they were both sick, so he brought them down the trail and pointed out the farm, told them to go there."

Julia looked confused. "He said they weren't going to be much good? What in heavens name could he mean?"

"Maybe he meant they weren't going to be able to help their parents in the condition they were in," Will suggested.

Terasoff nodded. "That's the way I took it."

"So where have the parents gone?" Will was concerned about the continued security of the boys.

"They didn't seem to know where they were headed." Terasoff finished his tea and set the mug on the table. "But their Pa said that he wouldn't be back for them. He said, he might send them a note one day to say where he was, and they could write back if they wanted. But he wouldn't be back." He kept his gaze on Will. "So, that's that."

He rose and gestured toward the bedroom with his beefy hand. "Doc, you should have a look at those youngsters. They don't seem in great shape to me, and could use a little attention, I'm thinking."

"Of course." Will rose and grabbed his medical bag.

Rose Malekoff led them through the doorway and down a short hall. The boys lay in bed side-by-side, eyes closed, still as death. The window cast a dim light in the room, and Ollie's pale face shone like a beacon among the bedclothes. All they could see of Ben was the back of his fuzzy head, the hair longer than when they'd last seen him. His breathing was hampered by a wheeze deep in his chest. Will crossed quickly and looked at the faces of the sleeping children, placing a hand on each forehead.

"Julia," Will said, turning to her. "I want you to go back to the kitchen with Mrs. Malekoff and see if there's anything they can tell you about finding the boys. I want to be alone with them."

Julia began to shake. "They aren't dead, Will. They can't be dead. Constable Terasoff just talked to them. I can hear Ben breathing."

"No, they're not dead, but I'm serious. I need to be alone to examine them." He set his medical bag on the foot of the bed and took her by the shoulders, turning her toward the door.

"Please. You have to trust me. Mrs. Malekoff, can you help her to the kitchen? Thank you so much." He pressed a kiss to Julia's forehead, gave her a small shove toward the hall, and closed the door firmly behind them.

He peeled back the covers on Ben's side of the bed. The boy was pale and clammy but fiery hot, his breathing labored. Will listened to his chest and back, took his pulse and covered him back up. He'd deal with that later, and it would likely be a long process.

Then he rounded the bed to Ollie. When he pulled the covers back, the boy moaned. His arm was held protectively against his chest and the blanket dragged across the injury. Will picked his arm up and turned it to the light so he could see the burn. Ollie turned with the arm, trying to pull it back against his rib cage.

"It's alright, Ollie. It's Doctor Will here. I've got you and we're going to do what we can to make this better."

The boy relaxed and squinted his eyes open in the feeble light. Will smiled at him and put his hand on his chest to reassure him as he examined the wound. At least second degree burns, as he'd feared. Third degree in the center where the flesh was swollen and red. All around the burn site were bits of wood and debris glued to the flesh, the main area covered with a white mucous-like coating. The skin was missing entirely. A real mess.

The injury must have occurred at least one full day ago, as the boys had been at the farm almost that long, and likely a day and a half. So better not to wait until they got them home before he treated it. He'd have to do it now for best results of healing and protection against infection. He opened his bag and pulled out the laudanum, measuring a careful dose for a little body this size.

"Open up, Ollie. This is medicine for you. It's going to make the arm feel a lot better. Drink it all."

Ollie opened his mouth willingly, then grimaced as the liquid hit his taste buds.

"It's okay, Ollie. It tastes bad, but it works well. Swallow it, that's a boy. Here's a bit of water to wash it down." Will slid his arm under the boy's shoulders to help him drink, then lowered him gently to the mattress.

"That's good. I'll be right back." Will poked his head into the kitchen, where everyone was still sitting around the table talking in low voices. Their conversation stalled when they saw him.

"Constable, can I have your help please, just for a few minutes. And Mr. Malekoff, do you think you can have your wife show Julia around the garden for a half hour or so, maybe out there?" He pointed to the other side of the yard.

Malekoff looked at him intently, then nodded. "Sure, sure. Rose, why don't you and Mrs. Butler take a stroll down to the brook? It's nice and shady down that way and the new calves are in the pen."

Malekoff hustled the women to the door and Terasoff edged his big body around the table toward Will, with Malekoff trailing behind him.

Will led the men into the bedroom. "What we have here is a septic wound, a burn of second and third degree. You've both seen it, I imagine. It doesn't look good."

The men nodded.

"Well, the treatment is a liberal wash of iodine across the whole area, taking away all debris and covering the wound completely."

The men blanched. "Iodine," breathed Terasoff, his face pale.

Will nodded. "It's the recommended treatment and the most

successful, but the pain is intense for the first couple of minutes. I've given the boy laudanum, which will have worked by now, but I need help holding the patient down and the arm immobile while I work."

Terasoff hesitated, then moved to the side of the bed and pulled the bedclothes away to reveal the thin little body. "I can hold the boy, perhaps it would be better if I have him in my arms, maybe in that chair."

Will nodded, and picked Ollie up, depositing him in Terasoff's lap. "That's good. The light's better here as well. Now, Mr. Malekoff, if you could hold his arm, by the wrist and the elbow, firmly. He'll struggle and will be hurt more if your hands slip. I have my solution set out right here on the night table."

Malekoff gripped the arm as directed and held it carefully to the light.

Will examined it closely, picked up his swab in the forceps and began. Ollie gasped and groaned, he gave a high scream of pain that seemed to go on and on. Malekoff's knuckles turned white.

Will continued to work, closing his ears to the noise and concentrating on the wound. The debris around the edges came away with the skin in strings. The mucous was a bit harder to remove. He swabbed with quick sure strokes and was finished in minutes.

They all paused for breath. By this time Ollie appeared unconscious. Will peered into his face, and touched his chest. "Poor little tyke," he said. "He's been through enough without having this to deal with as well."

The men were all breathing heavily.

"You'll be glad to know, that's the end of the treatment," Will said.

Malekoff grinned weakly and wiped the sweat from his forehead.

Will wrapped gauze loosely around the arm, securing it above the elbow and around the hand. They lay Ollie back on the bed. Will bathed his forehead with cool water and covered him loosely with the sheet. "Okay, everything else can wait until we get them home. Thank you, gentlemen. I couldn't have done it without you."

~~~**~~~

CHAPTER FIFTY

The journey home was more difficult than Julia could have imagined. Will drove, and Ben sat in the front seat. Although he seemed semi-conscious, Will wanted him upright, his body moving with the motion of the car. They tied his upper torso with a belt under his arms to hold him in place. Julia travelled in the back seat, supporting Ollie.

They stopped the car every couple of hours to ensure the condition of the boys. It was well past dark when they reached the Butler house. Will carried the boys into their room, as Julia turned on lamps and set the kettle to boil for a steam treatment for Ben.

The night was long. They took turns sitting Ben up, massaging his chest, pounding his back to move the congestion. Will sent her to bed at two and instructed her not to come back down until at least seven.

Julia was so glad she'd sent her children off to stay at Betsy's. She wouldn't have to get them till school was out in the afternoon when the Morrises would need a ride home as well.

Will slept the morning away, then took a trip in to his surgery to see to needs there. His nurse, Sheila, had kept everything under control, judging from the calm in the waiting room and the small number of patients. He returned in the early evening with the children, having dropped off the Morris boys and picked up some supper at the Chinese restaurant.

It was a subdued evening. Having Ben and Ollie back was a turning point for Maggie and Jims. They'd mourned their going and rejoiced in their return, but the relief was heavily tinged by fear. The children tiptoed in to see the boys, Ben opened his eyes and croaked a greeting, then closed them again. Ollie lay still and pale.

Yet, Ollie was on the mend first. The burn was soon heavily covered with a brown crust that protected the wound. His fever disappeared the next day. Each day he was better, until he was sitting at the dinner table, his burn covered by loose gauze and his eyes bright.

The outer layer of the burn fell off the wound in pieces and beautiful pink skin began to show through, with very little pain. There was one small area in the centre which still required an antiseptic dressing. Julia covered it with honey every day.

It was healing well. Will was pleased with the results. He'd heard of the iodine treatment from a young doctor in Winnipeg who'd trained in Vancouver. "It's not accepted by everyone," he'd said. "It's a bit new, but the evidence is overwhelming. There's no kidney or liver damage, as long as you use the right iodine solution, not with methylated spirits, but pure alcohol. It sounds brutal, but the pain is short-lived, only as long as the application in duration."

He'd directed Will to the medical journals describing where the procedure had been developed in Notre Dame Hospital in Montreal, and as Will sat in his surgery the night he heard the boys were found, he thought back to that impromptu lesson and prepared himself to give a treatment that he, himself, had never used before.

Ben took longer to recover, his chest remained tight and burning, his breathing shallow. He was warm to the touch and listless. Julia gave him a steam inhalation twice a day, and between her and Will, they continued to manipulate his chest and back every two hours, loosening the congestion and keeping him breathing freely.

But he, too, finally began to respond to their care. Soon, he was sitting up in the upholstered chair in the dining room, with a rug over his knees and the others playing nearby. The healing of the whole family began.

~~~**~~~

CHAPTER FIFTY ONE

Julia was in the yard when Will dropped by. She and Maggie were raking the garden and planting the spring crop. Even Jims helped, holding the string for Maggie while she drew a straight trench in the ground. Ollie had the basket of seeds, waiting to see what was needed.

Will waved to them as he walked down the yard. "It's looking very good. What are these? Ah, carrots. Those will be tasty this summer, won't they?" He gave Julia a hug and whispered against her hair. "I'm just going to go in to see Ben. Give me some time, will you? Maybe an hour if you can."

She straightened from digging and gave him a questioning look. "Yes, of course. Well, we have lots to do out here."

Will nodded and headed for the verandah steps. He took them two at a time, walking into the kitchen to find Ben seated in the upholstered chair in the dining area, Cat on his lap. "Oh, good boy," he said. "Cat's a good companion, isn't she?"

Ben nodded. Will opened the boy's shirt and pulled his stethoscope out of his bag. He listened to various spots on the chest and back, while Ben huffed and blew on command. Finally, he folded his scope away and stashed it in his bag. He looked in Ben's eyes, in his throat, felt behind his ears and around his neck, then took his pulse.

"You're amazing, young man. You look better every day. A quick healer, that's what you are. I've been wondering…" Will pulled a dining room chair close and sat down beside him, reaching to give Cat a scratch behind the ears. "I've been wondering how it was that you two left town with your folks. Can you tell me about it?"

Ben looked up at him with wide startled eyes, then down at Cat as he smoothed her coat. "Pa got us at the school and this time he took us."

"What do you mean, this time?"

"Yeah, we saw him before." Ben glanced up. "He come to the school the week before. Ollie saw him first, and I didn't believe him. But Ollie was right. Pa found us behind the schoolhouse and told us to come back to see him. Anyway this time…"

"Just a minute, Ben. Perhaps you can tell me about the first time, then about the next time."

Ben nodded and told him what had happened, how they had put Pa off by promising to bring some items worth selling, thinking it would give them time to form a plan.

Will pondered the story. "Does this have anything to do with when you were late getting home from school? You know, the day Julia went to pick you up and you weren't there?"

Ben nodded. "We were trying to avoid Pa. Ollie said he'd seen him and I didn't, and we didn't know if he was waiting for us or what, so we went in a different direction. Like a decoy. We didn't want him to follow us home, see. He's not a nice man and he might do somethin' bad to Mama Julia or Maggie, or Jims." Ben looked at him earnestly, trying to make him understand their dilemma.

"But the next day, he found us anyhow. He caught us where we were hiding behind the schoolhouse, and told us to meet him back there by three o'clock, 'cause he wouldn't wait any longer." Ben told about their delaying tactics, but they hadn't come up with any plan before their father was back.

"So he just grabbed us. He said he had something to show us, and when we got into the bush he took us to Ma."

"Was she glad to see you, Ben?"

263

The little boy looked blank. "Well, she wanted us there, that's for sure. She needed our help. They had to move 'cause all the stills up in the hills was pulled down or burned. And they saw it coming, 'cause they had a policeman customer who let them know. They hid the still, and the cart. Then waited until the police were finished and headed out for other parts."

He glanced down at Cat, who was purring steadily on his knee. "But they didn't have much, and she wanted us to help pull the cart, and be runners and salesmen and stuff. They were going to set up again farther south. Pa talked about Kingsgate, but I don't know if that was where they was going or not."

Will put a hand on his shoulder. "We heard you went down the South Road, but then you disappeared. Where did you go from there?"

"The South Road? Oh, yeah, the one that leads out of town at the other end, huh?"

Will nodded.

"Yup, we went down there, but Pa didn't want to stay on it. Ma is easy to spot, you know? She's dark like me, and not many dark ladies around. So we went into the bush. Pa knows all the roads and where they go. We followed one, then we needed to go through the bush to get to another one, going east. That's when I got wet, I fell in the creek pulling the cart and I got the cough. Ma was mad at me, said I should have known better. But I didn't."

Tears gathered in his eyes, and trickled down his face, and his hand moved faster in Cat's fur. "Pa let go of the cart just when it hit a stone and it throwed me into the water. It wasn't so deep but I got nothing dry to put on, so I slept wet."

Will put his hand on the boy's nape and held him. "Of course you didn't, Ben. If it had been your Pa instead, he would have gotten a cough, too. Nobody gets sick on purpose. You're a smart boy, and don't you believe it when someone says you're not."

Will pulled him closer and rocked for a bit, stroking Cat.

Then Ben looked up. "Pa was different than I remember. He didn't have no moonshine, and he was different. He'd talk to me sometimes, and I felt like he could actually see me. Like when Mama Julia talks to me, she hears what I say. And Pa could hear me. He made some food too, he never did that before."

He shrugged helplessly. "He didn't look too good. He was kind of skinny and his face was pale. He cooked the cornmeal and Ma had a fit, 'cause she wanted to make moonshine with it. Then she looked for the sugar, but Pa used it for the berries. She was mad, boy." He stroked Cat silently.

Will reached over and scooped the boy into his arms. He dragged him onto his lap and held him protectively. "This is a very tough thing for a child," he said. "When his parents don't look after him with love and care, then that child is at great risk. He can be badly hurt physically, we've seen that, right?"

Ben's face went still, his hands twitched in Cat's fur.

"But," said Will, "He can also be hurt emotionally. Your heart will be sore, or it might be very angry and you won't know why. Then you have to let other adults help you with that. Other adults who care about you, and want to treat you properly, with love and care."

Ben nodded against his shoulder, the tears falling in a steady stream. "You mean like you and Mama Julia," he sobbed.

Will held him tenderly. "That's exactly what I mean. Like me and Mama Julia. Let us care for you, like you deserve to be treated. We see the value in you. We see what you're worth, and you're worth a great deal, Ben. Ollie too. If you look in our eyes, you'll see how much you're worth. We love you."

They sat for a long time, just rocking and hugging.

Will heard the sound of the others approaching and looked up to see Maggie peering around the door frame. Ollie stood uncertainly behind her. They took their shoes off and walked softly over to lean against Will and rub Ben's arm. He gathered them all in.

~~~**~~~

Part Nine – The Wedding

CHAPTER FIFTY TWO

The children talked nonstop about the wedding which was coming up now in less than a week. Julia had stopped panicking. Everything was so far out of her control, she didn't even try. The ladies at the church had stepped in to organize the dinner after the ceremony. The music was already organized for the dance. The cake was coming from the bridge group.

"Dance?" asked Will. "I didn't realize there'd be a dance."

"There's always a dance," Julia said. "You can't get out of it. You do dance, don't you?"

Will shrugged and grinned. "'I guess I do now. I'd better, it's my wedding."

Julia leaned against him. "Yes, you'd better. I'll want to dance with you, Maggie will want to dance with you. You'll have to dance with my mother and your mother. You're going to be a busy fellow." She smiled.

Will rubbed her back and pulled her close. She looked happy, but tired. And he wanted her. It was way too long since they'd made love, he constantly searched for a time in their schedules where they'd have a couple of private hours, and he couldn't come up with anything.

She saw the frown in his eyes. "You don't want to dance?"

He gave her a quick kiss. "I'll dance, don't worry, and I'll like it."

She burst out laughing and he laid his cheek against her temple and held her close, pressing against her. It was all he was likely to get for a while.

Sarah came back ahead of Sam and Annie, to be there for Julia before the event. She brought her wedding dress from her own marriage, and Julia tried it on upstairs with Maggie and Sarah helping. There was a great deal of sighing and admiration, discussion of tucks and stitches.

Will sat downstairs with Ben and Ollie, thinking he should probably cover his ears or go out and milk the goat. He grinned at Ben. "Men aren't supposed to know about these things, wedding gowns and all."

"I'll bet she looks beautiful," smiled Ben.

Will nodded. "I know she does."

He waited until the women came back down and stood at the foot of the stairs. "Julia, I've come to take you out for dinner, just you and me. How does that sound? We can go to Chin's Chinese restaurant."

He'd already told the children and they were hopping up and down in vicarious excitement. "Go, Mummy, go. It would be so much fun."

Julia put her head to one side and studied him. "Have you recruited supporters amongst the crew?" she asked mischievously.

Will nodded. "Absolutely. Whatever it takes. Is that okay with you, Sarah? Can I take her out and leave the rest with you?"

"You know it is, Will. You asked me earlier."

Will's eyes laughed back at Julia. "So it seems to be okay with everyone else."

She chuckled. "I can't really decline now, can I? I'll just brush my hair and get ready."

She walked slowly back up the stairs. Will watched the sway of her hips, thinking she must do that on purpose. It pushed his fever up a notch, and he'd started the day with an elevated temperature to begin with. It had been like that for weeks. This latest plan for dinner out was the last in a string of unsuccessful attempts to get her on her own.

He stared at the wall until he calmed, then turned to the children. "You'll be extra good for Grandma, won't you? You'll eat your dinner, help with the dishes. Go to bed when she says, yes?"

They had lined up in front of him, promising their best behavior when Julia came back down. She had changed into a lovely silk dress covered in flowers in all the fall colours. It matched her hair exquisitely and made her skin look like porcelain against the deep rosy shades.

Will held his breath as his eyes met hers. She paused, then walked toward him to take his hand. Wordlessly, he led her through the door.

~~*~~

Seated in the car, Julia watched him give a wrenching swing at the crank and felt the car rumble into action. He was silent as he backed the vehicle into the yard and turned around, pulling slowly onto North Road.

He glanced across at her for a second but didn't say anything, just reached for her hand and gripped her fingers in his. He had to release them again to change gears. Just before they entered the village, he pulled the car over to the side of the road. He turned to her, his expression grave.

"Julia. I want to take you to my house. It's been more than a month since we made love and I'm wasting away to a shadow."

"A shadow," she said doubtfully.

"You know what I mean. I'm having trouble being patient, I'm not patient. I'm having trouble keeping my temper."

"I haven't seen any temper. But I have seen exasperation," she said.

"See what I mean? I'm exasperated. And I'm horny as hell, and... I didn't mean that the way it sounds. I want you, Julia. I'm longing for you. Can we... Will you come with me to my house?

Please," he breathed.

She leaned forward to kiss his cheek. "I thought you'd never ask."

His breath huffed out in relief.

"But I want dinner first," she said.

He laughed hoarsely and pulled her close against his side in a one-armed hug. "Me, too," he said. "Let's have dinner by all means. How fast can you eat?"

She chuckled. "I eat very slowly and I hate to be rushed."

He snorted but grinned.

They had dinner at Chin's Chinese Restaurant. Kinko Chin ran the place and her husband, Lu, did the cooking. "Fin in bed," she said. "I guess Ben in bed, too?"

"Yes, I think he is by now," Julia replied. "My mother is here, so she's looking after them."

"Oh, that nice, your mother here. That very nice."

"Oh, Kinko. When did you last see your mother? Is she back in China?"

"Yeah, in China, eleven year now, maybe twelve. But I miss her, too."

"I'm sure you do. I'll have to lend you mine for a while, so you can have a mother for a little bit."

"Lend your mother. Haha," Kinko laughed. "I like that. Lend your mother."

She brought them plates of steaming vegetables with soy sauce and ginger, chicken, onion and celeriac with oyster sauce, and a big bowl of rice. "No like in China, much," she said. "We make what we have here, you know. But good."

"Oh, it's lovely," said Julia. "Very nice. Tell Lu he's done a wonderful job."

There were a few other busy tables in the small room. Mr. Postnikoff sat at one with his wife. They waved and Peter came over to have a word with Will about the plans for next year's hockey teams. As they rose to go, Mrs. Postnikoff asked if they were ready for the wedding.

"Almost," said Julia. "My mother's helping and the rest of the family arrives in a few days."

"Well, let me know if there's anything I can do," Mrs. Postnikoff said." I'm making cabbage rolls for the dinner."

"I love your cabbage rolls! And I'll probably be too nervous to eat any."

She laughed. "Don't worry, I'll make you some more another time, so you can eat to your heart's content."

Will paid the bill and hustled her toward the door. "Time to go," he said under his breath.

"Are we late?" she asked anxiously.

"I hope not. But it's time to leave." He held her jacket, the lovely jacket with fur collar and cuffs that he'd given her for Christmas. She pulled it on and looked up into his face. He moved closer, his jaw set, and nudged her slightly with his body. "Come on, let's go."

She nodded and headed for the door, calling her goodbye's to the Chins. Helping her into the car, he cranked it up and was back in his seat in record time. They headed to the edge of town and turned in at the surgery. Julia looked up at the dark windows.

"Should we park out front like this?" she wondered aloud.

"No." Will continued around the side of the house. "I don't want anyone knocking on the door, thinking I'm home. And if I'm home, why I don't come to the door. I need to get you into my house. Come inside, Julia. Let's have some time just for us.

His eyes were intense in the night as he reached for her. He took her hand as she climbed out and tugged till she fell against him. Putting his arms around her, he hustled her to the back step where he'd left the porch light burning.

"Come on." Opening the door, he ushered her in. He took her coat, tossing it on the back of a chair, and tugged her down the hall to his bedroom. He'd prepared for this, tidied everything away and straightened up. The bedspread was pulled up square with the pillows. He ripped it off onto the floor, then had her out of her clothes before she could catch her breath, easing her down onto the sheets as he stripped her panties off.

"There you are," he whispered. "There you are. Oh, baby." And he pressed his face into her breasts and breathed deeply, then put a fierce kiss on her mouth, forcing her lips open to give him access. He groaned, tugging at his shirt buttons, finally popping them off with an impatient tug and struggling to shrug out of the garment. Julia wrestled with his belt as he pushed his suspenders off his shoulders. He spread her legs with the pressure of his knee.

"Julia," he managed. "I'm coming in," and he surged into her as she wrapped her legs around him. He thought his heart had stopped. He lurched to a halt, finding the control to raise his head. She lay there beneath him, her head resting on his forearm. Her eyes were closed and her face pressed into his bicep. She opened her eyes when he stopped and turned slowly to look up at him. Those big gray eyes seemed to look right into him, into his deepest part with a bring light. This is what he wanted, this is what he needed. She completed him in a way he'd never envisaged. He hadn't known this kind of connection existed.

He pulled back, then surged forward again and her eyes took on a different look as the lids slowly lowered. He felt her tightening around him and he thought, *not yet, not yet*. He went slow and then faster. He paused to lick her throat, running his tongue languidly down to her nipple and tugging it slowly into his mouth. She moaned, her fingers biting into his arms.

"Slow, easy now," he murmured. "Take it slow." She bit him on the shoulder with sharp teeth, and he flexed his hips, pressing deeper into her secret place.

"Okay, maybe not slow," he wheezed and started a heavy forceful entry and swift withdrawal that caused her to shudder beneath him. She flexed her hips, forcing closer contact as he moved, pressing and pushing until she seized in mighty contractions that caught him and milked him dry.

He collapsed on top of her but couldn't find the energy to move. *Just another few minutes*, he thought vaguely. *I'll make sure she's okay, just another...* Impatient hands shoved at his chest and he rolled, pulling her against his side. Her head lay on his shoulder, her knees curled against his side. She was so small to his long length.

"Are you okay, did I hurt you?" His chest still bellowed.

She shook her head and sighed deeply. "I'm fine. I don't think I've been better."

He shook with laughter, and hauled her fully onto him, so she was looking down into his face. She braced her arms on his chest.

"I wondered if we'd be able to be alone," she murmured.

"You could have told me," he said. "I've been trying to get us alone for a month. Damn, nearly five weeks. And I've been going crazy. I contemplated telling the kids you'd come down with the flu and had to be quarantined at the surgery. I thought I could probably come up with someone who'd stay with them, maybe Mrs. Shandy."

Julia giggled, and tugged at the hair on his chest.

"Ouch!" He covered her fingers with his to stop the torture. "No fair. You shouldn't torment a man whose only goal is to make your life easier."

"No," she said, placing a slow kiss on his mouth. "I think you're trying to make things hard." She wriggled against his rising erection.

He took in a quick breath. "Julia, you don't know what you do to me. Sweetheart, I want you again, but slow this time. So I can feel every inch of you, kiss every inch, rub my hands all over you. You walk up those stairs at your house. I watch you go and my heart turns over in my chest at the thought that I'm not going up there with you.

"And you come down those same stairs and my insides turn to mush and other parts of me turn very hard. Look at you." His hand cupped her breast and fingered the nipple. "You're perfect."

He slid his palms down her back, grabbing her bottom and pulling her tight against him. "Feel that? That's there all the time. I hardly get anything done, I'm so distracted. I'm probably giving out bad medical advice. It's a good thing we'll be married in a week."

She sighed and laid her head on his chest, that broad chest that she fantasized about. She rubbed her nose in the curly dark brown hair and breathed him in. "Will, love me now. Make love to me."

"Yes, baby. Anything you want," and he pulled her legs up and slowly pushed himself home. Her breath caught in her throat and she rose over him, bracing with her hands and pressing him further in. He dragged her head down for a drugging kiss.

~~~**~~~

CHAPTER FIFTY THREE

The wedding was poignant and Julia even more lovely. Will put his finger in the collar of his shirt and tugged. It was warm in the hall, and the dancing made it even warmer. He looked around the big room.

The stove in the corner hadn't been lit, it was too mild an evening for that. The wedding supper had been a mixture of a great deal of cooking and baking by Julia's family and friends and a potluck ritual that seemed to include the whole community. The heavily laden tables had just been cleared away and the small orchestra composed of a drum, a guitar, the pump organ that resided in the hall and a violin had moved into place. He could hear the instruments being tuned up for the dancing to begin.

Will had asked who was going to play at the reception, and Jerome Hoskiss told him, 'the Folks.' He thought that must refer to some family of Jerome's who played together. But when Mrs. Rasmussen remarked, as he picked up the children from school one afternoon, that the Folks were going to play, it caught his attention. He asked Julia that evening. 'Whose folks are playing at the reception in the hall?'

She looked at him oddly, and said, yes the Folks are playing.

"Well, but whose folks are we talking about?"

Sudden comprehension dawned on her face. "It's the Folks, Will. Their name is Folk, the father and his son and daughter, plus another relative, I think. They play all around the area at dances."

They chuckled together at the unintended joke.

Now, the Master of Ceremonies cleared his throat loudly and tapped a glass with his spoon to get everyone's attention. He waved to the band to begin playing and indicated the bride and groom.

Will stepped forward, grasped Julia around the waist and led the first dance. He loved it. It was a waltz and she fit in his arms perfectly, her head just at his shoulder even with those little heels she wore. He knew he wasn't Prince Charming but she was certainly Snow White and this was his own fairytale.

Then he danced with the mothers, first Sarah, then his own mother, and soon everyone joined in. He spotted his brother Ray in the corner discussing something with Luke Harrison. Danny, the teamster, was dancing with his wife to a two-step that had them both panting and red-faced from exertion at the end. Maggie danced with him, and then dragged Ollie onto the floor while Julia danced with Ben.

Will noticed a fellow dancing with his daughter, where the little girl was standing on the toes of her father's shoes as they moved around the floor. Even the Luchinskis were there, Gerald had been a decent fellow. Will liked him, found he was well educated and someone to talk to about things that normally he didn't encounter in his practice. They might become friends. Their little boy Gerry straggled along with the crowd of small children swooping about the hall.

In the end, all his siblings had come. It was such a blessing and his eyes became suspiciously damps as he looked around. His oldest brother Frank, named after their father, had come by himself and only arrived this morning. His wife Flo stayed home with their children, the youngest just a baby. Luckily the others had arrived earlier and picked Frank up at the train because Will had been too busy. Danny and Kimmy brought their whole family, as had Ray and his wife. Agnes came with her husband, Alex Hubbard, but left the children at home, and Mary, his sister, came with them, glad that medical school was out so she could attend.

Then there was Julia's family. Right now, Sam the Third slept among the wraps on the bunk beds in the back room of the hall, but Jasmine was cavorting with Jims, little Gerry Luchinski and some other children on the dance floor. And he had finally met Susan Butler, her parents James and Sue-Ann were here to see Julia married and wish them both well. Will's heart was grateful for the generosity of spirit that allowed them to move on from Stephen's death without resentment.

It had been a very busy few days. There was a lot of visiting, introducing Julia to each of his siblings as they arrived and she'd begun to look exhausted. So he'd taken everyone off her hands. Keeping the children for the day at his place hadn't been a problem, and his mother had taken over the job anyway, getting them all settled somewhere. In the end, Sam was right. It had been a job for Luke Harrison, after all, to find them accommodations. Luke had organized rooms with his mother in the station boarding house, and they had meals at the little restaurant in town.

Everyone in the community seemed to be here. His hand had been shaken to death by the well-wishers and those warning him to take good care of Julia and her family. There was a flock of young men outside the door in the dusk who he suspected were partaking of something somewhat stronger than the punch being offered in the hall. Every now and then one of them would get his nerve up, wander in and ask a young lady to dance. He could smell the alcohol. For a moment, he almost felt like joining them.

Getting married was a stressful event, he hadn't realized quite how stressful. This was a celebration and the community needed something to celebrate. But he was just waiting for the clock to run down so he could grab his bride and escape. He'd been waiting a long time and it was near, so near, but still he waited.

Frank sidled up to him. "Will, I need to talk to you about something. Could you come with me for a minute? Nothing serious, just a quick chat."

Will glanced over to see Julia dancing with Luke, and what looked like a whole group of men waiting to the side for their turn.

"Sure, Frank. Maybe step outside for a minute, get a breath of cool air."

They made their way through the crowd and out the wide door. Frank pulled Will off to the side into the darkness and reached into his suit jacket. He pulled out a silver mickey and twisted the lid. "Have a drink of this, Will. It'll settle you down a little."

Will stared in astonishment, and Frank threw back his head and roared with laughter. "What, you think I don't know what it feels like? I remember vividly."

"It's not that," Will said. "It's just that I was standing there, thinking I'd love a stiff drink right about now, and here you are. Plus, a mickey? You never struck me as the type."

"No?" Frank grinned in the darkness. "I was a Boy Scout just like you, and the motto is *Be prepared*. And I have vivid memories of my own wedding, although I was a bit younger than you, but the principle is the same. You've waited all this time for the woman to make up her mind, you finally get her to the altar and then you have to go through an interminable celebration before you can haul her away to bed. Right?"

Will took a long tug at the bottle. Whiskey, not his favourite but it sure worked. He shuddered and took another drink, handing it back to his brother. "Thanks, Frank."

Frank nodded, and put it back in his jacket. "I'll save some for later, if you need it." He tipped back his head to look up at the sky, the stars barely visible against the light pouring from the windows of the community hall. "She's pretty nice, Will, and beautiful, too. I can tell what you see in her. A ready-made family, but nothing wrong with that. You can handle it and they need a dad. Congratulations. I'm proud of you, just sorry that you're so far away. We won't see you as often as we'd like."

He shook Will's hand, then gave him a one-armed hug. "You're doing just fine, little brother." They both snorted with laughter at the old family joke. Frank was the eldest brother but the shortest of all of them. He used to say that he was glad he could call them all 'little brother' as once they were fully grown it was his only position of superiority.

When they got back inside, the music was still playing and the women were gathered around Julia, talking intently. Ray walked over to join them. "They're organizing," he said. "Don't know what. Better look out." The men chuckled warily.

Ray turned to Will. "Step over here a minute, Will. I've something to show you." Will dragged his gaze from the group of women and followed his brother, eventually going down the side stairs to the dark of the landing. Ray put a hand on his arm to detain him there in the gloom, and reached inside his jacket. "Here, this is to tide you over till this whole folderol is finished." He drew out a small flask from his pocket and handed it to him. "It's rye, if I recall that was your drink of choice."

Will chuckled as he twisted off the cap. "I hope I'm not going to be fall-down drunk at my own wedding." He took a swig and lowered the bottle. "Frank just gave me a shot from his mickey a minute ago." Both men howled with laughter.

"Let's hope Danny doesn't drag you outside in a minute," Ray gasped. "You'll be too drunk to take the lady home." They broke into gales of laughter again, then Ray slapped him on the back and dragged him back inside the hall.

Frank Sr. walked over and said, "Looks like the women are organizing."

Danny snorted and the others chuckled. "Sure looks that way," he said. Just then, Mary broke free from the group and walked purposely toward them.

"We're about to find out," said Will. The rest of the men nodded.

Mary stopped in front of them. "Will, you and Julia are supposed to get on the stage now, and you give your speech. Then Julia will throw her bouquet of flowers. Then Dad can say something. Luke Harrison wants to say something, then we'll have a toast to you both. Then one final dance and you can leave, but the rest of us will stay for a while."

The men nodded. "What about the kids?" asked Will. "Do

they know that they're going home with Grandma and Uncle Sam, back to the house?"

Mary nodded. "Everyone is organized. And they don't expect you back for a week, this is a real honeymoon. Pretty nice, and with Dad staying to cover your surgery while you're gone, everything is pretty well looked after. What train are you catching tomorrow?"

"Uh…" Will stalled. He couldn't remember what train they were catching. He could barely manage to handle what was happening right now. He looked over and caught Julia's eye. She smiled that luminous smile, and suddenly his hearing seemed to go, the noise dimmed and he just started walking to get to her as fast as he could. "He's hooked," he heard Ray say behind him, but it didn't really register. All he had to do was get there, a few more steps.

~~*~~

They lay in his big bed, the sheets tangled about them, slick skin cooling in the mild evening air. He pulled her head more firmly onto his shoulder and heaved a sigh.

"Yes, I know," Julia said. "It's finally over, it's finally done. Thank God."

He peered down at her in the gloom. "That's for sure, I thought we'd never get here. I thought it would never end."

She began to giggle and soon they were both laughing. Slowly they calmed.

"But we did it," he said. "And the family came and they all had their say, every last one of them. I guess that's what families are for. God, I can remember how opinionated I was when my brothers got married, I suppose they were pretty restrained today under the circumstances."

Julia watched him, her expression guarded. "Were they trying to talk some sense into you? Too many children, and all of that? Or the poor little widow, maybe it's just pity?"

Will glanced down at her. "No, sweetheart, nothing like that.

279

They like to rib me, I've always been so independent, didn't stay on in Winnipeg, didn't toe the same line as the others. And they admire you, with children of your own, raising them alone, then taking in two more that landed on your doorstep. I think Frank said it best. Those little guys need a Dad and I can be that Dad."

He kissed her nose. "They all like you so much, they think you're too good for me."

She laughed.

"Plus," he went on doggedly, "every last male in the good town of Creston warned me to take good care of you. I'll be in big trouble if I so much as step out of line."

"You're joking," she giggled.

"Nope, I'm serious. If I heard it once tonight, I heard it a hundred times. And I promised each one of them that I'd look after you, so I intend to. And I'll start with this." His mouth came down on hers with intent, and she instantly succumbed.

"You'll have to put up more of a fight, or I'll suspect you like me."

She giggled again, and shoved at his chest. "I'm *starting* to like you," she said, "so don't spoil it."

~~*~~

The train ride to Banff was spectacular, the scenery breathtaking. Will had reserved a room at the grand Canadian Pacific Hotel with its distinctive copper roof and they walked around the town and explored the countryside, spent afternoons in bed, talking and loving in turn.

By the time they returned home, Julia was rested, which eased Will's heart mightily. But they were ready to get back. She had never been away from her children that long, and she pined for them.

Everyone was fine, the children ecstatic to see them. Jims jumped up and down and then burst into tears and had to be held. Maggie clung to her mother's skirts, until Julia sat on the couch and hugged them both close. She beckoned to Ollie and he came over and sat beside her so she could put her arms around them all. Ben stood back but leaned into Will as he gave him a hug. It was good to be home.

Not back to the same routine, though. Will was a big man and he took up a lot of space. He had something to say about a lot of things, how to make it better, do it faster, save time. Often he was looking for a way to make it easier on Julia, but she didn't see it that way if it cost more to do it his way. Sometimes she'd get so exasperated, she would give him a look that he had come to recognize, and he'd say, "Oh, all right then, do it that way, that works too." And give her a wink that made her laugh.

Will had organized a baseball team of boys and it had carried on with Jerome Hoskiss, of all people. He'd apparently played as a young man, and had trophies in his house that dated back years. He was a detail man, and got involved in training the older boys, especially the pitchers. Will had tried out everyone who came and chosen two to be trained as pitchers for the team, one being Ben. Baseball practice kept things lively for the rest of the spring.

Sam came with a group of boys from Sparwood for a tournament in Creston, and stayed with them at the house. He was doing well. He didn't have a lot of stamina, but had learned how to take things easy and not push himself. He and Luke, the referee, spent some time chatting over baseball games.

One day, Julia saw another man at her gate and went down to investigate. This man seemed different than some of the others who walked by. He was carrying a cloth bag on his back and didn't ask for food, but for work. He looked cleaner than most, and workmanlike, somehow. His clothes were old but not dirty. Julia had him clean the barn, then fed him supper and asked if he'd like to sleep in the shed. She hauled out the canvas ticking and in the morning went out to find he was stacking wood on the woodpile that Will had started.

"Come for breakfast," she called, and sat him at the table on the verandah.

Will came out to chat with him. "His name is Jerome," he said when he came back into the kitchen.

"Really," said Julia, "that's a coincidence, isn't it? He seems like a decent man."

Will nodded.

"What do you have in your sack," Julia asked him as she went out to clear away the lunch dishes.

"Well," he squinted up at her in the bright sun. "I have a change of clothes and a couple of books. And I have a few photos," he added.

"Oh." She paused. "We're doing laundry today, can we wash your spare clothes for you while we are at it?"

He blinked and then nodded, the colour high in his cheeks. "Yes, Ma'am," he said. "Much obliged." He hauled out a shirt and pants that were well worn but mended.

Julia brought two mugs of tea and sat down. He was from Donegal, and she probed further. Yes, he knew of at least one family up in the low hills that lived off the sale of moonshine. He didn't know the names, well maybe something like Vallady.

Julia just nodded.

"Moonshine," he said, "has a bigger market now that there are no jobs. People want to numb the pain." He sounded like he spoke from personal experience.

His wife had died and then their child within months of each other. He lost his house when he was laid off from the mill, and couldn't find another job. So, he sold the cows and took to the road, hoping to find some work somewhere. Being on the road didn't suit him, he commented. He was a man who liked to put down roots.

Julia suggested he spend the rest of the week with them as they had some work for him. He nodded and thanked her.

Meanwhile she put on her sunhat, grabbed a jar of lemonade and took the children across the road to talk to Jerome. Jerome had gotten more sociable with Will at the house. He came over more often when invited and as a consequence had put on a bit of weight and had more colour in his face.

He welcomed them on his front step where he was lounging in the shade. The children played at their feet and then went to visit the cows, while Julia and Jerome talked.

But when she left, she had a place for the man who was staying in her shed. He would sleep in the loft of Jerome's barn for now, and help look after his herd of purebred Holsteins. It was certainly warm enough till winter.

The man seemed to know quite a bit about cows, and Jerome could use the help. They would talk about whether he moved into the house when the time came.

~~~**~~~

Part Ten – The Picnic

CHAPTER FIFTY FOUR

The picnic was planned for weeks in advance. The children urged Julia to set the date but she was waiting for the pond to be warm enough for swimming.

Finally, the day arrived. It had been an extraordinarily temperate May, and the first weeks of June were downright hot. Julia announced they would not go to Church tomorrow, just this once, but instead they'd have the picnic. Ben and Ollie were excited. Swimming was something they'd never done before, but were definitely game to try.

Saturday, Will spent the day turning over the soil in the garden with Prince pulling the plow. He came in hot and dirty. Julia had just finished the baking in preparation for the picnic lunch. She made egg and bacon pie, a family favourite and had cucumber and beet pickles. She made a cake, a rich chocolate that traveled well. There were raw vegetables to munch on, and lemonade in a crock.

They took Prince to carry the baskets, the blankets and all the rest of the paraphernalia that was involved. The children would each bring a book they could read in the shade when taking a rest from the water, or merely trying to warm up. The water was still pretty cold.

The day dawned clear and warm. There wasn't a cloud in the sky, and Julia could feel the heat building already. Will was up earlier and he and Ben finished the chores in record time. Julia went to milk Daisy Mae only to discover Ben had already done it.

Baskets of food were packed, and bags of books, towels, and blankets added to the mêlée. Prince was loaded with all the items they could stuff in the saddlebags and hang off his saddle. The swimming hole was down the back road bordering the property but the children got sidetracked along the way with discoveries in the long grass.

Will led the horse and persuaded Julia to ride. The road led onto the railway right of way. From there they travelled along the creek. Far at the back, behind the Morris place, were a waterfall and a large pool. The small valley was tipped just right to catch the rays of the midday sun, so was warm and sheltered from the breeze. The pool was sandy at the edge, surrounded by a low meadow filled with wild flowers.

Wagsy was first to bound into the clearing and leaped straight into the water, sitting down on her haunches to soak her belly in the pool. Ollie looked worried, calling to her to come out, but Julia laughed. "She's okay, Ollie. She loves the water and knows how to swim. She's just hot and wants to cool down. She'll be swimming with you when you get in."

Will unpacked Prince and piled their gear at the edge of the field under the shade of the big old pine. He handed the reins to Ben who took the horse to stake him out to graze while Julia spread blankets and towels in the sun.

She began with Jims, stripping him down and putting his swim trunks on him. Maggie was next, although she was more modest and Julia held up a towel for her. "Come on, boys," Julia called. "Might as well get changed. You can lie in the sun till you're warm before you go in the water." Will took the older boys off with him into the brush and they all came back changed.

Then the fun ensued. Will went in first and declared it was so warm, it felt like soup. Ben followed and yelped at the cold. Ollie, right behind him, declared Will was right. Jims just jumped in. Will darted forward to catch him before he took too big a mouthful of water as he went under. Meanwhile Julia went behind a bush and got herself into her bathing suit.

The splashing was tremendous, the noise even louder. Will started a game of tag in the water leading the boys into the deeper end and soon they were jumping and starting to swim. When the game petered out, Will gave a swim lesson, and Maggie turned out to be the best, dogpaddling around and round.

~~*~~

By lunch time, everyone was chilly and they settled down in the sun on the blankets to eat. The pie was a big hit, and Julia watched with satisfaction as the boys hurriedly consumed it. There followed desultory conversation before Ben and Maggie went back in the water to swim with Wagsy, and Ollie settled down to read his book. Jims dozed on the blankets under a big towel, slowly dropping off to sleep. Will pulled Julia back against his chest, and wrapped his arms around her.

"Did you know," she said suddenly, "Mary is coming back to Creston for the summer?"

"Mary, you mean my little sister Mary?"

"Yes, that Mary. Although she's not so little. She's coming to spend a month here so we'll have her with us for a while. It will be nice to get to know her a bit more. Maybe she can help in the surgery."

Will was silent for a minute as he thought that over. "Why didn't I know that? How did you hear, did you get a letter or something?"

"No, Luke told me."

"Luke?" Will was outraged. "Luke Harrington? What's Luke got to do with Mary, how should he know? He must have been reading our mail!"

"Don't be silly," said Julia, laughing. "He got a letter from her, and he told me she was coming."

"Why that's ridiculous! Why would she write to him?" Will's arms tightened reflexively. Damn the man, he meddled with Julia and now he was interfering with his sister.

Julia chuckled. "Because he's sweet on her, and I think she feels the same way about him."

Will sat up in stunned amazement. "Mary, sweet on Luke? That's preposterous." His voice trailed off uncertainly.

"Didn't you notice when she was here, Will? She had her eyes on him the whole time. He must have danced with her five or six times at the wedding. And I gather he took her out to dinner the next evening. They've been writing to each other ever since, and she wants to come out and see him, and you too, of course." She gave him a pointed look, laughter in her eyes.

"Minx," he said. "Well, I guess I've been busy paying attention to other things." His hand reached under her towel and he watched the blush rise up her cheeks.

After a bit, he said, "That would be kind of nice, if she settled out west. It would give the folks more reason to come visit that's for sure. And as the community grows maybe Mary could come in as a partner in the surgery. Who knows what we'll need by then? I think she has a couple more years before she's a doctor. And she could probably do a part of her training here if she wanted to."

Just then Ollie jumped up at a shout from Maggie and raced into the water. Will smiled as his gaze followed. The children played well together, following Ben's lead in caring for each other.

Julia watched the children for a moment, and Will watched her. She turned her head to smile up at him. "They get along pretty well, don't they?"

He nodded.

"I wonder what will be the result of the way they were treated by their parents."

He sighed and leaned his cheek to the side of her head. "I wonder that too. It was such a horrendous experience that it's possible they don't even remember it. Ollie knew Ben was sick and he was worried about him. But when he was knocked into the fire, the burn was so bad I don't think he was aware of what happened after that. He doesn't seem to try to puzzle out why his Pa suddenly changed his mind and brought them out of the woods near the farm. Ben knows that something happened that he didn't understand."

Julia patted his arm. "Ben thinks his Pa was different. There was no moonshine. Normally his Pa was drinking, and if not drinking then he was sleeping off a drunk. But Pa was sober this time. He seems to puzzle over what happened at the end though. Pa hit Ma with the fry pan for burning Ollie. Then he told the boys to let Ma have her nap while he took them off. Ollie thinks they didn't work hard enough, so Pa didn't want them."

Will took in her hurt look, and rubbed his hand up her arm. "What I wonder is what happened to Ma?" he said. "If he really did hit her in the head with the cast iron fry pan, then she's probably dead. He realized she was dead and hustled the boys out of there to prevent them from seeing that. But I think he meant to kill her. He saw how sick Ben was, then she knocked Ollie into the fire, and she peeled the shirt off the wound, for heaven's sake! What kind of maniac was she?"

Will watched Ben splash with Wagsy near the shallow end. "I think Pa was sober for the first time in a long time. And what he saw was pretty awful. So he took things into his own hands. He knew he couldn't look after two hurt boys, so he acted in their best interests. Maybe for the first time."

They both turned their heads at a shout from the water and watched Ben dogpaddle across the pond, while the others yelled. He rose triumphant from the water at the other side and stood with his arms in the air. Will and Julia cheered, and he dove back in to swim the other way.

"How are you feeling?" Will slanted a look at her, as his hand slid lower under the towel to rest on the slight rise of her belly. "Not too tired?"

She shook her head.

"It's hard to get you to slow down," he muttered.

She laughed. "There's a lot to do, with seven people in the house, soon to be eight."

"I know, but not that soon. And Heddie's coming twice a week. This way she and I can do most of the garden and all you have to do is tell the kids to pick it."

"True," she said.

"And I like that fellow you found for Jerome. Jerome Two is a good man. Stop your giggling, we have to call him something, and he's a hard-working fellow. I'm going to get him over to work for us when we need him, and he can earn a bit of cash that way. Hoskiss is fine with that, whatever the little Mrs. Butler needs."

He glowered at her menacingly and she grinned impudently back at him. "In spite of the fact," he gritted, "that you are now Mrs. Stoffard, or Spofford as Ollie says."

They both chuckled.

Julia nestled closer in his arms. "How is the work on the surgery coming? I haven't stopped to see it for a few days."

"It's coming just fine." His fingers caressed her cheek. "You're going to like it. The new wing will give us just enough room for the crew we have and the crew we might have." He chuckled. "We Stoffards have big families, you know. I hope you realize you have your work cut out for you."

"Big talk," she scoffed.

"You doubt it?" he growled, and pushed her over onto the blanket, looming above her. "I'll show you."

"That's what I've been hoping," she simpered.

He snickered, then sobered quickly. "You won't be sad to leave the farm, will you? I know it's a big link with Stephen and it's been your home for a long time."

She shook her head. "No. That is, I'll be sad, but only for a minute. I'm very excited about moving to the surgery. It's got a garden, fully as big as mine, and there's room for Prince plus a cow. You know Prince has to come? He's as much a pet as he is our transportation."

He nodded solemnly, looking out at the kids playing in the shallow water at the edge of the pond. "I know that, and there's lots of room for Prince. He'll give the kids some freedom. They can hitch up the cart and go off to visit or fetch stuff on their own. Ben's certainly old enough, and soon will be experienced enough to do that. And just think of having Sam and your Mum close."

Her eyes glowed, and his heart eased at the sight.

"I can't believe how it's turned out," she sighed. "Luke needed someone part-time for train station attendant, and that's just exactly what Sam can manage. And with their herd of goats and the cheese business, they'll do just fine. And they're going to live at the farm. It means we won't leave the farm behind at all, we'll just be back and forth to visit it like always. It really is wonderful, Will."

"I know, sweetheart."

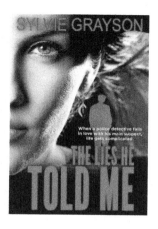

...when a police detective falls for his main suspect, life gets complicated...

When Chloe Bowman wakes to find her husband gone, never does she imagine it will take so long to find him, or that in the midst of the search she'll discover she doesn't really know this man at all. She soon realizes she has been left alone with her young son and a time bomb on her hands. Then the earthquake throws everything into question. Lurking in the shadows is the mysterious Rainman who travels under an unknown name.

Police Detective Ross Cullen was already investigating Chloe's husband when he disappears. Although he's powerfully drawn to Chloe, Ross also knows that when one member of a family disappears, the first place to look for the suspect is among those closest to him. No one is closer than Chloe.

But the deeper Ross digs the less he knows, and the more he's attracted to the young wife as she struggles to put her life back together. Can Ross break through the Rainman's disguises to solve the case so he can be with Chloe?

Sylvie Grayson has found her niche, you'll love this book...

Emily moves to a new town to hide her secret, but it follows her. Can Joe protect her from her past?

When Emily Drury takes a job as legal counsel for an import-export company, she doesn't make the decision lightly. She needs to get away to someplace safe.

Joe Tanner counts himself lucky. He's charmed a successful big city lawyer into heading up the legal department of his rapidly expanding business. But why would a beautiful woman who could easily make partner in the high profile legal firm where she works, give it all up to come to a place like Bonnie?

A mystery surrounds her arrival that wraps them both in ever tightening tentacles. As Joe realizes she has become essential to his happiness, his first reaction is to protect her. But he doesn't know the whole story.

Can Emily trust him enough to divulge her secret? Will he learn what he needs to know in time to stop the avalanche that's gaining speed as it races down the hill toward her?

...romantic suspense at it's best...

Jenny has already made a big mistake. Can she risk her heart again, or will this just be another one?

Jordie was heartbroken when he returned to town to find Jenny had married another man. Now she lives beside him, and he'll either go crazy or do what he should have done before - claim her for his own.

Jenny is back and she's angry, her husband cheated and she can't let it go. But when her boss dies and someone comes after her, who will she turn to? With her cousin living right beside her it's becoming harder to ignore the chemistry they have always shared. Can Jordie help put her life back together?

Find Sylvie Grayson at her website-
www.sylviegrayson.com
on facebook www.facebook.com/sylvie.grayson
or email at sylviegraysonauthor@gmail.com

Sci-fi/ fantasy from Sylvie Grayson

The Last War series is a stunning portrayal of a new world created from fire and consumed at the edges …- sci fi and fantasy at its best…

The Emperor has been defeated. New countries have arisen from the ashes of the old Empire. The citizens swear they will never need to fight again after that long and painful war.

Bethlehem Farmer is helping her brother Abram run Farmer Holdings in south Khandarken after their father died in the final battles. She is looking after the dispossessed, keeping the farm productive and the talc mine working in the hills behind their land. But when Abram takes a trip with Uncle Jade into the northern territory and disappears without a trace, she's left on her own. Suddenly things are not what they seem and no one can be trusted.

Major Dante Regiment is sent by his father, the General of Khandarken, to find out what the situation is at Farmer Holdings. What he sees shakes him to the core and fuels his grim determination to protect Bethlehem at all cost, even with his life.

Ms Grayson has created a fascinating new world with a lot of the same old problems. Sci fi and fantasy rolled into one with a sure hand and enormous imagination

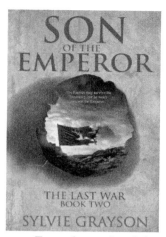

From the mud and danger of the open road to the welcoming arms of the Sanctuary, from attacks by the dispossessed army to the storms of the open sea, Son of the Emperor takes us on a wild ride into danger and on to the dream of freedom.

The Emperor is defeated yet already unrest is growing in the north of Khandarken. After Julianne Adjudicator's father disappears, she seeks to escape the clutches of her vicious stepmother Zanata, and flees to the Sanctuary. This is the safest place for a woman in a hostile world of unrest and roving dispossessed. But when Julianne seeks asylum, it soon becomes clear all is not as it first appeared.

Then Abe Farmer arrives at the Sanctuary seeking medical help. Abe isn't interested in taking a young woman with them, as he and his injured bodyguard struggle to return to the Southern Territory. Yet when he discovers her fate if she stays, he finds he has no choice.

But the journey becomes more dangerous as they encounter the army of the New Emperor and are caught in the middle of a firefight as they flee toward the Catastrophic Ocean. Can Abe keep her safe till they reach home?

...a whole new world with the same old problems - fantasy at its best...

TRUTH AND TREACHERY

THE LAST WAR
BOOK THREE
SYLVIE GRAYSON

When Emperor Carlton makes an offer to Cownden Lanser, can he refuse? Lanser has his own ambitions and Carlton may be offering everything he's dreamed of.

The Young Emperor has been backed into a corner. He holds a bit of land in Legitamia, but the skirmishes they've launched to expand his empire have had limited success. Now his ambitions are aimed at overthrowing everything Khandarken has cobbled together since the Last War.

Cownden Lanser, Chief Constable of Khandarken, is a private man with a close connection to the Old Empire that he doesn't divulge to anyone. Although he's dedicated to his position, things are not what they seem in the rank and file of the police.

Selanna Nettles is a sookie, healing the mine workers and the dispossessed in the Western Territory. But her life takes a startling turn when Chief Cownden Lanser hires her to attend a set of high-level meetings in Gilsigg.

When these three meet up in Legitamia, the result is explosive. Not just for them but for the future of Khandarken. The Emperor makes Cownden an offer that might be everything he's secretly dreamed of. How can he refuse?

The Last War series is a stunning portrayal of a new world created from fire and consumed at the edges... sci fi/fantasy at its best...

ABOUT THE AUTHOR

Sylvie Grayson has published romantic suspense novels, *Suspended Animation, Legal Obstruction, The Lies He Told Me* and *My Best Mistake*, all about strong women who meet with dangerous odds, stories of tension and attraction.

She has also written *The Last War* series, a romantic sci fi / fantasy set in a new world she has created. Although it's a series, each book stands alone.

She has been an English language instructor, a nightclub manager, an auto shop bookkeeper and a lawyer. She is a wife and mother, and lives in southern British Columbia with her husband on a small piece of land near the Pacific Ocean, when she's not travelling the world looking for adventure.

Made in the USA
Middletown, DE
01 June 2021